CHALLENGING DESTINY

To Imogene!

(signature) 9/16/14

Other Titles by Suzanne Purewal

Embracing Destiny
From 14 to 41

CHALLENGING DESTINY

SUZANNE PUREWAL

PUREWAL PUBLISHING, LLC

Published by

Purewal Publishing, LLC
176 West Logan Street
Suite #105
Noblesville, Indiana 46060-1437
www.suzannepurewal.com

This book is a work of fiction. Names, characters, places, and incidents either are products of the author's imagination or are used fictitiously. Any resemblance to actual persons, living or dead, events, or locales is entirely coincidental.

Copyright © 2015 by Suzanne Purewal

Cover Art and Design by Joseph S. Anderson—TheForgottenArtist.com

ISBN: 978-0-9829048-3-1

Library of Congress Card Catalog Number: 2014915704

Printed in the United States of America

To My Best Friend, Dawn

CHAPTER 1

SARA Taylor stared at the barren walls of her steel gray cubicle. She had removed all of her personal items from the dingy fabric partitions. Although she had occupied this cube for over a year, it felt foreign to her.

Being an industrial engineer for DAGS Engineering had not been satisfying. Every day she felt frustrated and marginalized. She hated corporate politics and refused to get sucked into the game.

The idea of playing golf with a manager to secure a promotion disgusted her. Sara wanted to be recognized for her talents and abilities, not playing games. There would be no love lost departing this corporate world.

Her attention turned to the towering pile of paperwork on her desk. Smiling, she picked up the unwieldy pile. With deliberation, she ceremoniously dumped the hefty stack in a recycle bin. As she did so, the oppressive force that had weighed heavily upon her lifted. She felt genuine relief.

As she bent over to collect a few paper stragglers, her long brown hair fell forward. She stood and discarded the sheets in the bin. Sara's blue eyes sparkled. She swept back her hair and brushed off her red blouse and jeans before sitting in her chair.

She had imagined this day in her mind numerous times. Each time, she pictured herself telling off the people that had made things difficult for her. The ironic thing about all that rehearsing—she no longer felt the need to follow through with it anymore.

Her coworkers held her going away party over the lunch hour. The administrative assistant presented a funny card the entire group had signed. Many colleagues stopped by to wish her well. Others just wanted free cake.

Although apprehensive about leaving a good paying job with benefits, she knew it was for the best. She was meant to accomplish greater things. It also meant veering off her plan—having a lucrative career, getting married, and having a family. She still longed for the ideals of the plan. But she was throwing away an enormous piece—financial security. She always thought that piece would allow all of the other elements to fall neatly into place. That was no longer the case.

Returning to the task at hand, the checklist in her mind was almost complete. She trained her replacement, transferred her files, wiped out her hard drive, and established "Out of Office" messages for her e-mail and voice mail accounts.

On her last day of work, all that remained was to empty out the overhead cabinets and top desk drawer, pack up her personal belongings, and go through the mandatory exit interview.

All recyclable materials were tossed into the recycle bin. The majority of the other items were relegated to the trash can. Personal items, such as her favorite purple pen, were placed in a cardboard box. After confirming all of the drawers and cabinets were empty, she leaned back and relaxed in her chair.

Content, she reached for the largest framed picture on the desk. The silver-plated engraved frame held her engagement picture.

The engraving read: *Joe and Sara—Always*.

Sara and her high school sweetheart, Joe Lazaro, were finally getting married, after over a decade of an on-again, off-again relationship. With great care, she positioned the picture upright in the box.

Next, she plucked the Taylor family picture from the desk. It was the last picture taken of her entire family before her oldest brother, Robert, died in a tragic accident.

Her desk phone rang. It startled her. The display identified the caller—her boss, Ben Roberts.

Sara answered the phone, "Hello?"

"Taylor, are you ready for your exit interview?" he asked.

"Almost. I need another ten minutes."

"Fine. Come to my office when you're ready," he instructed.

"Okay." Sara hung up the phone and resumed packing. She smiled as she handled the next picture.

The high school graduation snapshot was of Sara with her look-alike best friend, Laura. They had dreamed of making a difference in the world. Today, Sara was taking the first step to fulfill that dream.

She deposited the remaining personal items in the sturdy cardboard box and tucked the flaps inward. She did not tape the box, in case a security guard needed to check it on her way out.

The wall clock, which always read two minutes slow, indicated she had a few minutes to gather her remaining possessions and get to her boss' office.

As she was about to depart for her exit interview, her cube mate, George Russell, appeared.

The fifty-four-year-old inquired, "Do you have time for a last cup of coffee before you go?"

"Sorry, George. I'm due for my exit interview. Don't want to be late for that," she responded.

"I guess not," he chuckled. "Do you need any help carrying out your stuff?"

"No, the box isn't that heavy. I'll just grab it after my exit interview is over."

George approached and extended his hand. "Good luck to you then."

She shook his hand. "Thank you. Same to you."

"Thanks," George replied, settling into his chair.

Sara walked down the aisle, head held high. She smirked at the inspirational posters lining the walls, most of which were hanging askew. She wanted to shout, "Look at me! I am reaching for the stars!" But she did not. There would be time for that later.

When she arrived at Ben's office, he was squinting at his computer screen.

Sara knocked.

Ben motioned for her to enter. "Taylor, take a seat."

Sara sat in one of the worn blue guest chairs and crossed her legs. She glanced at the company calendar on the opposite wall, each expired day crossed out in black permanent marker. His retirement day was circled and highlighted in yellow. It was not for another two months.

"I've got a checklist here to go over," he explained.

"Okay," she replied.

He began, "I need your user IDs and passwords."

Always prepared, Sara slid a piece of paper across his desk that contained the pertinent information. Ben nodded as he checked off boxes on the form. "And your procurement card, work cell phone, and desk keys."

Sara placed the items on the desk as well.

Ben checked off more boxes. "And lastly, your badge."

Sara unclipped the badge from her blouse and tossed it to him like a Frisbee. It flew farther than she anticipated, hitting him squarely in the chest and dropping into his lap.

He flinched.

Embarrassed, she apologized, "Sorry."

Ben extracted the badge from his lap and placed it on his desk. Annoyed, he grumbled, "You need to read and sign these." He pushed the papers toward her.

She carefully read the legal paperwork. It included a traditional non-compete clause. Finding nothing objectionable, she signed and dated the forms and returned them to Ben.

Ben gathered the papers and stapled them. "Well, I guess that's it. You are free to go."

She thought, *Not much of an interview.*

Outwardly controlling her glee, her mind celebrated, *Free to go. Wow! I'm free! Free! Free! Free!*

Sara stood. "Okay. I just have to grab my box of stuff. Then I'll be leaving."

Ben rose and joined Sara on the other side of his desk. "Best of luck to you, Taylor." He shook her hand and slapped her on the back.

Wincing, she said, "Thank you." *One last back slap for the road. I definitely won't miss that.*

The cube that Sara worked in was empty when she returned. She felt nothing for this place. She would miss a few of her colleagues, the ones she considered friends. But she would never give another thought to the rest of these people.

She lifted the box off the table. It was not as heavy as she imagined. She walked down the aisle for the last time.

The security guard nodded and waved to Sara as she crossed the lobby. She smiled and nodded back. As she reached the set of double doors, she turned around and backed into the first door. The double set created a type of odd airlock, complete with a whooshing sound, making it difficult to push. As she approached the next set of doors, two men she did not recognize held them wide open for her.

Sara thought, *Probably suppliers.*

"You have quite an armful there," the one man observed.

"Yes. Thank you," she replied.

The second man winked. "No problem."

Stepping outside of DAGS Engineering for the last time, on a beautiful Wednesday afternoon in autumn, Sara grinned from ear to ear. The warmth of the sun felt glorious on her skin. Tilting her head back, she lifted her face toward the clear blue sky. She inhaled deeply.

Today is the first day of the rest of my life!

She allowed herself a moment for that sentiment to sink in before proceeding to her blue Impala in the company lot. Once she reached it, she popped the trunk, dropped the box inside, closed the trunk, and unlocked the doors. She flung her black purse onto the passenger seat as she settled into the driver's seat. She did not start the car right away. Instead, she looked back at the building.

Shouldn't I feel nervous or anxious? Sad? Regret, maybe?

She reflected. *I don't. I honestly don't. I feel happy, really happy!*

She glanced around the parking lot.

For the first time ever, I am doing something totally unexpected. This is the most irresponsible thing I have ever done. I have quit a perfectly acceptable, high-paying job.

She paused. *And it feels good. I should have scrapped my plan years ago. Why was I such a slave to that damn plan?*

Before she could answer, her cell phone rang. She fumbled for her purse and pulled out the phone. The display indicated it was her fiancé, Joe Lazaro.

Joe and Sara had started dating in high school. The handsome six-foot, two-inch tall sophomore had been immediately drawn to the ravishing freshman beauty.

Sara had been enamored by Joe's twinkling blue eyes, black wavy hair, deep dimples, and most of all—his charm.

The chemistry between them was undeniable. Everyone assumed

they would marry, buy a house with a white picket fence, raise a few kids, and live happily ever after. That was the case until an education opportunity presented itself.

Joe accepted a full college scholarship to study abroad in Italy. The distance proved to be too much of a strain on the relationship, and after two years, he broke up with Sara, and they parted ways. She was devastated.

Then midway through his senior year, Joe unexpectedly returned home to Clear Brook, New York to finish his degree at St. Peter's University. He realized that Italy lacked the one thing he could not live without—Sara.

Of course, by that time, Sara had moved on. Upon graduation, Joe accepted a teaching position at St. Peter's University to remain close to Sara.

Over the next three years, mixed signals between the two had prevented a reunion. The timing never seemed right. However, a recent near-fatal accident was the wake-up call they needed to admit their love for each other and rekindle their romance.

Sara answered the phone, "Hi!"

"Hey, baby," Joe purred. "Did you get your 'Get Out of Jail Free' card yet?"

Cheerfully, Sara answered, "Yes! I'm sitting in my car, getting ready to leave."

"Fantastic! We're still doing wedding stuff tonight, right?"

She started her Impala. "Yes. Everybody said they could come."

"Great. I'll see you at your place in about a half an hour. I'll pick up pizza on the way."

"Okay. See you soon. Love you."

"Love you. *Ciao!*"

"*Ciao!*"

Sara shoved the phone into the cup holder in the center console. She drove out of the lot for the last time. And she never looked back.

Sara pulled up to her childhood home on Springhill Drive. She shared her parents' brick ranch with her friends, Anna Cristo and Laura Delaney. Sara's parents, Nick and Chris Taylor, were down south helping disaster victims recover from the latest storm devastation that had befallen them. They had been living as nomads for the past few years, roaming the country, helping those in need.

When Anna needed a place to live after graduation, Sara offered her a room in the house. And when Laura's parents moved to Florida a year ago, Sara invited her to stay as well. The girls had been best friends since kindergarten.

Sara parked in the garage, slung her black purse over her shoulder, and released the trunk. After retrieving the box of what was left of her engineering career, she entered the house. Her purse landed on the desk in the corner of the mudroom.

She lugged the box to the kitchen table, separated the flaps, and extracted the pictures from the box while trying to determine where they should be placed. The family picture found its home on the fireplace mantle, after she nudged another picture over to make room for it.

The graduation picture joined others on an end table. Her engagement picture was relocated to her cluttered bedroom dresser.

She placed the partially full box in the back of her closet. She would deal with the remainder of its contents another day.

After changing into a navy blue short-sleeved sweater, she freshened up and waited for everyone to arrive.

Anna arrived home first in her yellow VW Beetle. Entering the house, the blonde, green-eyed roommate said, "Hi!"

Sara sat on the mauve couch, tucking her right leg underneath her. "Hi! Did you have a good day?"

"Yes. But more importantly, how was your *last* day?"

"Weird. The lunch was okay. The cake was really good. They got it from Roselli's. So, there were a lot of moochers hanging around."

Anna selected a drinking glass from the cupboard and pressed the water button on the refrigerator. "You can't blame them. It is awesome cake."

As the girls chatted, the doorbell rang. Sara jumped up to answer the door.

Joe's brother, Tony, their cousin, Vinnie Varone, and Joe's best friend, John Lombardi, stood on the porch. All three men were tall, dark, and handsome.

Tony, the self-proclaimed entrepreneur, had a killer smile, a devilish gleam in his eye, and was a slightly overweight version of his younger brother, Joe.

Vinnie, a police officer, was the tallest, measuring six feet, three inches. In top physical shape, he turned women's heads when he walked into a room. His biceps, triceps, and pectoral muscles always tested the stretching integrity of his polo shirts.

John, a lieutenant in the fire department, was ruggedly handsome. He did not work out as often as Vinnie, but his six-pack abs and overall physique were quite impressive. And his innate sexiness was beyond compare.

Sara welcomed them, "Hi, guys! Come on in."

As they entered, each hugged and kissed Sara on the cheek.

Anna waited in the family room.

Vinnie greeted Anna with a kiss as he joined her on the couch.

John teased, "Get a room."

Anna thought, *I'd love to.*

Anna and Vinnie had been dating for a few weeks. She was ready to escalate their relationship to the next level. He, on the other hand, was not.

Sara addressed John, "Laura should be here soon." To the group, she said, "Joe's picking up pizza on his way."

Tony's stomach growled. "Great. I'm starving."

Vinnie joked, "With a gut like yours, you could survive in the wilderness at least a month or two before you would die of starvation."

As Tony went to the kitchen, he replied, "Screw you." He grabbed three bottles of beer out of the refrigerator and removed the caps. He handed the first one to John.

"Thanks, Tony."

Tony nodded. Then he offered one to Vinnie.

Vinnie questioned, "You didn't spit in it, did you?"

"Not this time."

Vinnie accepted the bottle. "Thanks. Truce?"

"For now."

Changing the subject, Anna asked Vinnie, "Any exciting cases today?"

"No. Just the usual."

Sara asked Tony, "Any new business opportunities?"

"I'm still looking into a franchise deal. Just ironing out the financial details. I'll be out of town for a few days this week."

Attempting to be supportive, Sara said, "I'm sure whatever you do, it will be successful."

"Thanks."

Their conversation was interrupted by Laura shouting, "I'm home!"

John sprang from his chair and made his way through the family room and kitchen. He met Laura in the mudroom.

She had bought a few bottles of wine on the way home. Her arms were full.

John offered, "Here, let me take those from you." He placed the bottles on the desk in the corner.

"Thanks," Laura replied.

He brought up his right hand and caressed her left cheek.

She smiled and tilted her head slightly, enjoying his gentle touch.

His blue eyes had a smile of their own as he traced her bottom lip with his thumb.

Laura purred, "Mmmm …"

John slipped his hand behind her head and pulled her close.

Laura yielded to him. His kisses possessed a magical quality. There was plenty of heat and fire, but it was the sensuality and the spirituality of each kiss that left her breathless, always wanting more. Her entire body responded to his kiss.

John's reaction mirrored Laura's. Each time they touched, he was overwhelmed with the need to protect her, care for her, and most of all—love her.

The need he felt at this moment was not the animalistic ripping off clothes type of desire, although he enjoyed that as much as would any red-blooded male. His love for Laura came from a deeper place. No other woman had ever evoked this type of longing in him. He ached for her.

From the other room, Tony shouted, "You guys get lost over there or what?"

Laura pulled back from John.

He whispered, "Ignore him."

"I would love to, but we can't."

"Shhh …" John kissed her again, slowly, tenderly.

As the couple reluctantly finished their kiss, John laced his fingers behind Laura's back.

She attested, "That was a wonderful welcome. I could get used to that, you know."

John professed, "There's a lot more where that came from."

"I think I will have to take a rain check. The house is full of people."

Gazing at her longingly, he proclaimed, "You can have as many rain checks as your heart desires."

Laura lightly caressed John's cheek. "Why did it take us so long to get together? We hung around each other for years."

He brushed a wisp of her hair back. "Honestly, I was intimidated by you. You were so smart. You always dated smart, nerdy guys. I wasn't in the honors classes. I didn't think you would want to date a guy like me."

With a quizzical expression on her face, she asked, "A guy like you? What is *that* supposed to mean?"

"You know," he paused. "Average."

Surprised, Laura replied, "John, you are *anything* but average."

"Go on," he joked.

"Really, aside from your obvious attributes." She giggled as she pressed her pelvis against his.

He warned, "You better watch it, baby. I'll take you right here."

Laura batted her eyelashes. "Okay. I'll be good. Seriously though, you risk your life every day as a fireman for strangers. Most people are not willing to do that. You're brave. You're special."

John minimized it, "I don't see it that way."

"Well, I do. And my opinion is the only one that matters."

"You're right about that."

Tony yelled from the family room, "Are you guys going to join us or what?"

Laura shouted back, "We're coming!"

Shortly thereafter, Joe arrived in his red Pontiac Grand Prix. He smoothed his pale blue polo shirt with his right hand as he walked up the sidewalk. Balancing the pizza boxes in his left hand, he rang the bell.

Tony answered the door and relieved his brother, Joe, of the four pizza boxes. Tony announced, "Food's here!" And he carried the pizza to the kitchen.

Joe yelled, "Hey, I'm here too!"

Sara welcomed him, "Hi, handsome!"

Joe kissed her and wrapped his arms around her waist. "Hi, beautiful! Congrats on being sprung from corporate jail."

"Thank you."

Joe pulled Sara close and whispered, "I guess we missed our opportunity to have a conjugal visit before you busted out."

Sara rolled her eyes. "Sorry to disappoint you."

"That's okay. You can make it up to me," he replied, patting her rear end.

After eating dinner at the kitchen table, the group relocated to the family room.

John and Laura commandeered the love seat, so they could cuddle. Vinnie and Anna sat in separate chairs. Tony, Joe, and Sara occupied the couch.

Sara distributed copies of the wedding program. "Okay. Here is a rough draft of the program. I want your input before sending them to the printer."

Anna complimented, "I love the picture of the rose and the wedding bands on the front. It's really pretty."

Laura agreed, "Yes. I love this one the best. The other ones weren't as nice."

While the women discussed the intricate details of the program and the music, the men feigned interest. They did not care one iota. However, the attentive women reassured Sara that she had made perfect choices.

Sara said, "Okay. I'm glad that's settled. Vinnie, you said you would do the readings, right?"

"Yes, ma'am," Vinnie confirmed.

Sara proposed, "Why don't we run through everything?"

Joe took a swig of beer.

Vinnie opened the program and cleared his voice. "The first reading is from the *Book of Genesis*. It is not good for the man to live alone. I will make a suitable companion to help him …"

Everyone listened respectfully while Vinnie read the entire passage.

Sara said, "Good job. You might as well read the next one too."

Vinnie nodded. "The second reading is from the *First Book of Corinthians*. Love is patient and kind; it is not jealous or conceited or proud; love is not ill-mannered or selfish or irritable ..."

Sara reached for Joe's hand and squeezed. He squeezed back and kissed her nose.

Vinnie read the verse at a constant pace and paused in the proper places.

A single tear from Sara's right eye trickled down her face. This verse always made her emotional.

"Love never gives up; and its faith, hope, and patience never fail. Love is eternal." Vinnie closed the program. "The Word of the Lord."

In unison, the group responded, "Thanks be to God."

CHAPTER 2

MITA Scotto walked barefoot down a narrow, deserted street in Italy. The sun had set hours ago. Window air conditioning units and fans hummed. The week's heat wave soldiered on.

Mita loved the heat. It caused men to do things they might not do in cooler weather. She avoided cool, level heads. She sought hot, impulsive targets.

Tonight's ensemble consisted of a white tank top, sans bra, and short-shorts. Her knockoff Gucci purse hung from one shoulder. Its contents were minimal—lipstick, driver's license, an apartment key, a pack of cigarettes, a lighter, and six hundred euros.

It would have been an even better night if she had not punched a potential john in the jaw. He had the audacity to say, "Don't get your nose out of joint. Oh, I see you already have!"

Mita had always been self-conscious about the bump in the middle of her nose. She swung out of habit. And her reaction shortened her evening at that particular establishment.

A battle-scarred rat scurried on the sidewalk. Its presence did not faze her. Her buzz wore off quickly. She was not pleased. She picked up the pace, swinging her stilettos in her left hand. In her right, she held a cigarette. She exhaled a plume of smoke as she passed the neighborhood bakery.

Mita's long black hair was completely disheveled. Her bangs hung into her brown, vacant eyes. Her mascara and lipstick were smudged. Too many hours in the sun had given her skin a leathery appearance. She looked much older than her thirty years.

She reached her apartment building. The paint flaked off the aging stucco façade. She opened the security door and climbed the three narrow flights of stairs to her third floor apartment. The stairwell smelled faintly of urine. She let herself in and shut the door behind her.

She extracted the wad of cash from her purse before dropping the purse and her shoes on the floor, not caring where they landed.

From the couch, the babysitter, Joanne, asked, "How was your evening?"

"Fine. Any problems?" Mita asked in her raspy voice.

Joanne replied, "No. Perfect as always."

Mita grunted and peeled off several bills. "Here's your money," she said, ushering the girl out.

Accepting the cash, Joanne responded, "*Grazie. Buona sera.*"

"*Buona sera,*" she parroted, locking the door behind the girl.

Mita's bare feet slapped the tile floor in the kitchen. She opened the cupboard door on her right, extracted the bottle of vodka, unscrewed the cap, and took a drink.

As Mita studied the bottle and its last inch of liquid, she contemplated taking the bottle to bed with her but thought better of it. Instead, she downed the remaining alcohol in three large gulps.

Mita awoke the next morning to the sound of her daughter's voice.

"Mama! Mama!" Flora shouted, shaking her mother awake. The darling five-year-old's black curly hair bounced as she moved.

Holding her pounding head, Mita growled, "I'm up. What time is it?"

"Breakfast time," the blue-eyed child cheerily announced.

Mita groaned, "I'm not feeling well today. Get yourself some cereal."

Flora sprang off the bed. As she skipped to the kitchen, she thought, *You don't feel well every day, Mama.*

By lunchtime, Mita had showered. Her wet hair was pulled back in a ponytail.

Flora colored at the kitchen table. A typical sight.

What surprised Mita, however, was the presence of her mother, Helen.

A natural beauty, Helen Scotto had flaming red hair and green eyes. Originally from New York, she had met her Italian husband while working as a tour guide one summer.

Heavy with sarcasm, Helen commented, "Well, look what the cat dragged in!"

Pissed off, Mita warned, "Do not start with me. Why are you here?"

Smiling, Helen answered, "I decided to visit my granddaughter.

We're having a nice time. Aren't we, Flora?"

"Yes, Nana. Mama, look at my pictures." Flora sorted through the pile, showing off the best.

"Nice," Mita said dismissively. "I need to talk to your grandmother. Go play in your room."

Flora knew what would come next. She hung her head, retreated to her room, and shut the door.

Mita accosted her mother, "What the hell? You just show up unannounced?"

Helen crossed her arms. "I have been calling you for days. You won't return my calls."

Rummaging through the cupboard, Mita grabbed a mug. "Get the hint. I don't want to talk to you or see you."

"You have a problem."

Mita poured herself a cup of coffee. "Yeah—you!"

"You know what I mean," Helen stated flatly.

Mita leaned against the counter. "I don't give a shit what you think."

Helen threatened, "Well, you should. If you don't get yourself sober and stop living this trashy life you're living, I am going to take you to court over Flora."

"Go ahead," Mita called her bluff.

Wagging her index finger, she warned, "Watch me, Mita. You are a horrible mother. You only think about yourself. You don't think about Flora at all. You're a terrible role model. Sleeping with God knows how many men. Drunk all the time. Smoking up a storm. This place stinks. This is no way to live."

Mita glared at her mother. "Fuck you and the broom you rode in on."

Ignoring the blatant show of disrespect, Helen announced, "You know that I am moving back to New York in a few days. Now that your father's gone, I don't feel the same about Italy."

"Good. The sooner, the better. I don't give a shit. Go already."

Helen continued, "We have family there, and I miss them. I want to take Flora with me. You should come too."

"Why the hell would I want to do that?"

"You don't have a job that is keeping you here. And I will get Flora into a good school in New York. There are more opportunities for her there." She paused and added, "And for you."

Mita gulped more coffee. Her headache was not improving.

"It would be wonderful for Flora to get to know the family better. She would have cousins to play with."

Mita found the bottle of aspirin and popped two pills. She chased them with more coffee. "Big deal."

Exasperated, Helen interrogated her daughter, "So, you like it here then? Living hand to mouth? Having meaningless sex with all of these men? Having no security? No love? *This* is the perfect life you have always dreamed of?"

Sarcastically, she snapped back, "Well, since you put it that way, sure! You're such a bitch!"

Helen stood and slapped her daughter across the face.

Shell-shocked, Mita slowly brought her hand up to her face. Her cheek stung from where her mother slapped her.

Curtly, Helen said, "I should have done that a long time ago. Maybe you would have turned out differently."

Although the slap infuriated Mita, it upset her more to think her mother might be right.

Flora cowered in the corner of her room with her pillow wrapped around her head. No matter how hard she pressed the pillow to her ears, she could hear them yelling. Sometimes she thought it would be nice to live with her grandmother.

Nana always smells of happy things, like chocolate chip cookies. Mama never smells like that. Nana never swears or yells at me. She likes to color and play games. She even takes me shopping with her. And we have tea parties. Maybe if I pray really hard, I'll get to live with Nana.

She pulled the pillow away from her head. She turned toward the bed and knelt, hands clasped together.

God, please make Mama better. And if you can't, please can I live with Nana? She's really nice. I promise to be good. Amen.

As Flora finished, her door swung open. She froze.

Mita commanded, "Flora, say good-bye. She's leaving."

Flora deflated. She hoped to spend the day with her grandmother. Gingerly, she ran past her mother and leapt into her grandmother's open arms.

Helen promised, "I will be back tomorrow."

"No, you won't," Mita argued.

"Yes, I will. And I'll be taking Flora to the park to give you some time alone to think about what I have said."

Mita thought, *Time without Flora would be good*.

A better plan developed in her mind. Mita reconsidered, "Take Flora with you now. That way I won't have to get up early."

Flora's blue eyes sparkled in anticipation. She looked eagerly at her grandmother, praying she would agree.

"I would love to," Helen replied.

Flora hugged her grandmother. "Thank you! Thank you!"

Helen instructed, "Run along now and pack. I will check on you in a few minutes."

Flora scampered away, smiling from ear to ear.

Mita asked, "Happy?"

Helen answered, "I would be happier if you shaped up. I'm glad you're letting me take Flora today. I know you didn't do it for her. There's something in it for you. There always is. But that doesn't matter. I am happy to spend time with her."

Mita muttered, "Whatever."

"Get your act together. I am serious about taking Flora. And if you're not going to take me up on my offer to go to New York, then you need to find a real job and a husband, for Christ's sake. You're getting old. You need to settle down and act like an adult."

"Thanks for the lecture." Her mind added, *Bitch*.

"Apparently, you need more of them. Think about what I said. You need a change."

Since Mita did not have to get back to relieve the babysitter, she prepared for a long night. She squeezed herself into her best lacy push-up bra, a low-cut pink shirt, and white short-shorts. She replaced the partially full cigarette pack in her purse with a new one. She tucked fifty euros in the zippered pocket for incidentals or cab fare, just in case. She hid the rest of the money in her panty drawer. But before she closed the drawer, she saw the baggie in the corner. It contained a few white pills. She decided to bring those with her as insurance.

Not one to normally reminisce, Mita thought about a time when she did not need to rely on pills to get what she wanted. She had only had two relationships in her adult life, neither of which involved love. One was a business arrangement. The other was just an opportune arrangement.

Ten years earlier, Mita had entered the Luna Bar and spied Lorenzo Cossi, sitting at his usual place at the bar—third stool from the end. She had spent every afternoon with Lorenzo for a month. He had been telling her how his wife did not understand or appreciate him.

A good listener, Mita made sure Lorenzo knew she was on his side. She had spent time honing her skills, figuring out how to manipulate men to her best advantage. She had received a lot of jewelry from attentive men, most of whom were married. Some even took her on fictitious business trips.

However, Lorenzo Cossi was special. He had more money than he knew how to spend. He flashed it everywhere and bought rounds of drinks for everyone at least three times a week. He talked about his sports car, his boat, his vacations, and his summer home in the country.

He also wanted an escape from his overbearing, frigid wife. Mita was more than happy to oblige. He proposed an arrangement to Mita. He would keep her comfortable in a luxury hotel suite. All expenses paid in exchange for being his mistress. Mita swiftly accepted the lucrative deal.

To Mita's surprise, Lorenzo performed like a man half his age. She underestimated his persistence and resilience.

Solidly cruising on the road of infidelity at full throttle, Lorenzo could not stop. He was insatiable, demanding some type of sex or sexual activity two or three times every day. He did little to satisfy Mita. Now she knew why his wife tired of him.

However, Lorenzo showered Mita with lavish gifts. That made up for his selfish lovemaking. He bought her designer clothes and expensive jewelry. They even took several weekend trips together to different cities. It was a stellar arrangement.

She could have gone on that way forever. As it was, the arrangement lasted for years. Then the most unimaginable thing happened—Lorenzo suffered a heart attack and died.

Mita was shocked and depressed by the news. Granted, she never loved Lorenzo Cossi. She loved the lifestyle. Since she was his mistress, he had not provided for her in the event of his death. Mita had nothing except for the clothes, jewelry, and thirty-two thousand euros in the hotel safe. That did not last long.

After Lorenzo's death, Mita found other men, some who were around for a weekend or two, others who stayed for longer periods. They were all just looking for a good time. Nothing more. What she had not counted on was getting pregnant.

There were numerous candidates for the baby's father. She informed the only man she could physically locate that she was pregnant with his child. He was less than pleased.

Although they lived together for some time, he refused to marry her. One day, they had a particularly ugly argument. He packed his bags and handed her a sizeable check. Mita never saw him again.

Ever since that incident, Mita had been looking for a new man, one with the kind of money Lorenzo threw around. She longed to establish an arrangement like that again. Unfortunately, there had been no real contenders. Tonight, she hoped her luck would change.

CHAPTER 3

A T the crack of dawn, in a windowless war room, on the outskirts of Clear Brook, New York, an elite team assembled. Five clean-cut men and two women sat around a long, rectangular table. They flipped open the identical file folders in front of them. They each scanned the dossier.

Four team members were former military, Spaulding and Sully, and the two females, Georgopoulos and White. The remaining team members, Lee, Ashby, and TJ, were civilians.

Lee, a former hacker, typed quickly on the computer in front of him.

The oldest member and natural leader of the group, Sully, liked to hit the ground running. "TJ, bring everyone up to speed."

The resourceful, smooth-talking team member, TJ, replied, "Three females. Sixteen years old. Sabrina Fuentes, Tina Robb, and Amber Vaughn. Their abductions were highly publicized when the friends went missing seven months ago."

Lee asked, "Seven months? And we're just being brought in now?"

Sully confirmed, "Yes. No evidence of a break-in. No evidence of a struggle. No unidentified fingerprints, trace evidence, or DNA found."

TJ continued, "We believe the girls knew their abductors. Although all three families vehemently deny that's a possibility."

Doubtful, Sully insisted, "Never say never."

TJ resumed, "Sabrina's step-father, Al Fuentes, a high-profile lawyer, offered a sizable reward. The families' pleas were all over the news and social media. Sabrina surfaced yesterday. The other two girls are still missing. No suspects. No leads. Sabrina was returned, reportedly unharmed."

Spaulding, the member who preferred to shoot first and ask questions later, asked incredulously, "Unharmed?"

TJ responded, "The family refused to let anyone except their family doctor examine and treat her."

Jack-of-all-trades, Ashby, cocked his head. "Says here she was found near a creek behind a bait and tackle shop."

TJ confirmed, "Yes, she was."

Expert markswoman, Georgopoulos, asked, "Witnesses?"

TJ replied, "Not to the dump. The fisherman who called it in said he heard the Fuentes girl screaming for help."

Georgopoulos followed up, "The fisherman checked out?"

TJ nodded. "Affirmative."

Georgopoulos inquired, "Surveillance footage?"

Still processing the data populating his screen, Lee answered, "No cameras at the shop."

Swiveling his chair around to face Lee, Ashby asked, "Traffic cams?"

Shaking his head, Lee said, "No. Too remote."

Human behavior expert, White, questioned, "Anyone talk to the Fuentes girl yet?"

TJ replied, "No. They say she's too traumatized to talk."

White inquired, "What do we know about the other missing girls?"

"They were some of her closest friends. All abducted at a sleepover at Fuentes' house."

Georgopoulos pondered, "Fuentes offered a huge reward for the safe return of his step-daughter and her friends. But only his step-daughter was returned after seven months. It doesn't make sense."

Scratching his head, Spaulding inquired, "Do the parents of the other girls have money?"

Sully responded, "No. Fuentes is the only one with deep pockets."

Reading from his monitor, Lee offered, "The parents of Tina Robb are both middle school teachers. No debts other than their mortgage and car payments. Modest savings. No criminal histories. The parents of Amber Vaughn are very similar. The girls are squeaky clean. Good students. No disciplinary issues. Nothing stands out on either family."

Ashby asked, "Think Al Fuentes paid a ransom instead?"

White questioned the logic, "A ransom would have made sense if we were talking days or a couple of weeks. But seven months? The timing really bothers me. Why wait so long if it was about money?"

Leaning back in his chair, Spaulding thought out loud, "I agree. Doesn't make any sense. They could have released the other two girls first and held out for more money for the step-daughter. Strategically, that's the best move."

Sully suggested, "Maybe money wasn't the motive."

Throwing up her hands, Georgopoulos asked, "What then? The other families don't appear to have anything to leverage."

On a hunch, TJ said, "The only one with money or access to people with influence is Fuentes. Something's not right about this. I say we stick with him."

Sully concurred, "Agreed."

Lee interjected, "Al Fuentes' bank records show a major transfer of funds to his mother's hotel, The Grand View Hotel."

Sully asked, "And?"

Scanning and scrolling, Lee added, "It occurred shortly after the girls went missing."

Georgopoulos noted, "People give family members gifts from time to time. Maybe his mother was having money problems."

Suspicious, TJ replied, "It's possible. But is it probable, considering the timing?"

Not knowing the answer, she shrugged. "Guess that's something we need to find out."

Sully asked, "Any repetitive smaller withdrawal amounts?"

"Several. Sorting through those now."

"Good. Stay on it."

Sending the data from his computer to one of the wall monitors, Lee announced, "Check this out. Got an update. Doctor's report was filed for Sabrina Fuentes. Ligature marks on her wrists and ankles. Otherwise unremarkable."

They all turned their attention to the monitor. They read the report.

White questioned, "Unremarkable?"

Lee commented, "That's what the good doctor said."

Skeptical, White asserted, "There's got to be more to it than that."

Georgopoulos asked, "Does anyone else find it odd that although there are two pages listing the condition of every part of this girl's body as unremarkable, other than the ligature marks, there isn't any mention of an exam to rule out sexual assault?"

Sully scratched his chin. "That is odd. There's no mention either way."

TJ stated, "That's highly unusual to omit that completely, especially considering how detailed he was with everything else."

Ashby deduced, "More evidence of a cover-up."

Crossing his arms, Sully remarked, "It's sure looking that way, isn't it?"

Lee continued typing and scrolling. "I've got something on the financials. A lot of withdrawals and transfers, leading back to his mother, Esmeralda, her hotel, and his brother's construction company. Lots of expenses."

Sully instructed, "Keep following the money."

"On it. He contracted his brother, Carlo, to renovate the hotel and a house on the hotel grounds."

Sully responded, "Keeping it all in the family."

Lee replied, "Normally, the brother just does commercial properties."

TJ interjected, "But it's not far-fetched he would fix up the house. It's for family."

Sully suggested, "Cross-check to see what Esmeralda and Carlo are doing with the money."

"Doing that as we speak."

After a minute or so, Sully inquired, "And?"

Lee read the information in front of him and swiped it to a monitor so they all could see it. "The mother doesn't have any large expenditures. Nickel and dime stuff. The brother is buying building materials. Nothing out of the ordinary."

As they read the report, Lee threw a second document to another monitor. "However, there's actually more money being spent on renovating the house than on the hotel."

TJ asked, "Does the mother own the house too?"

"No, Al owns the house."

Sully observed, "All roads lead back to him."

TJ offered, "The police looked into Fuentes and his family and didn't find anything."

Sully stated, "That's why we're on the case now. If there's something to find, we'll find it. Ashby and White, go to Fuentes' home, interview the girl."

They nodded.

He continued, "Lee, dive deep into the Fuentes family."

"Will do."

"Spaulding and Georgopoulos, check out the brother and his

construction business."

Spaulding said, "Sure thing."

Looking at TJ, Sully instructed, "Drop in on Al Fuentes at his office."

Turning to Lee, Sully added, "Make sure TJ has an appointment before he gets there."

Lee confirmed, "Consider it done."

TJ donned a crisp blue shirt and black dress pants as he approached the young, blonde receptionist.

She looked up. "May I help you?"

TJ flashed a winning smile. "Dom Perno to see Al Fuentes."

In a slightly condescending tone, she asked, "And may I ask what this is concerning, Mr. Perno?"

Sensing a challenge, he responded, "No, you may not. Confidentiality, you know. He should be expecting me."

Confident, she replied, "I'm sorry, but you are not on his schedule, sir."

Smiling, Dom urged her, "Check again. I am positive you'll find me."

To humor him, she pulled up the schedule. To her surprise, his name appeared. This confused her. Only she and her boss had access to the schedule. Since Al scheduled this man himself, she deduced that he must be an important client.

Her demeanor changed immediately. She stood and apologized, "I'm sorry, Mr. Perno. Let me show you into his office. He should be back from lunch any minute."

Once he was alone, TJ scanned the room. Family pictures littered the lawyer's desk. The pictures that hung on the wall were of Fuentes with various local and state politicians. There were commendations from the mayor and governor. Plaques and awards fought for space with law books on the book shelves. No papers were left on Fuentes' desk or tables.

Smart guy.

Al Fuentes entered his office. He wore a charcoal gray, single-breasted Armani suit with a royal blue silk tie. His black Ferragamo Oxfords were impeccably shined. "How may I help you?"

"Dom Perno. Nice to meet you." He extended his hand.

Al accepted and shook his hand. "Likewise."

Al motioned for TJ to sit in a guest chair as he sat in his black, high-back leather chair.

TJ sank into the comfortable guest chair. "My wife and I are starting a business, so I want to retain you as our business lawyer."

"What type of business are you considering?"

"She loves antiques. So, we are thinking of opening a store to buy and sell. Of course, I want more of an import/export business."

Fuentes smiled, "I would be glad to help you with that. It's a perfect business to last generation after generation, for your children and grandchildren."

Creating a plausible cover story, TJ replied, "My wife and I don't have any kids. We have been trying for years. She can't get pregnant."

"I am sorry to hear that."

"Thanks. It has been really tough on her. She always wanted to be a mother."

Al sat back, tented his fingers, and studied his potential client for a moment. "I don't advertise publicly, but I also handle private adoptions for couples in your situation."

TJ's mind raced. This was not part of the original game plan, but he rolled with it. "Really? You can find us a baby?"

Confidently, he answered, "Yes. I know I can. We'll set up a time to discuss it with your wife."

Curious where this lead would take him, TJ replied, "That's fantastic. You have no idea how happy you've just made me."

"That's why I do it. But let's talk about your import business first."

Ashby and White arrived at the Fuentes' estate. They flashed FBI badges as they introduced themselves.

Rita Fuentes was reluctant to allow the agents into her house. She complained, "We made it clear that we would notify the police when Sabrina was ready to answer questions."

Ashby explained, "Ma'am, this has been escalated higher than your local police. This is an active federal investigation. There are two girls still missing. We need to know what Sabrina can tell us. She might be the only person who can help us bring them home safely."

She picked up her cell phone and pressed her husband's number. "My husband is not going to like this. I'm calling him."

The call went straight to voice mail. She paced as she left a message.

Ashby and White took the opportunity to enter the house. They closed the door behind them.

After Rita disconnected the call, she turned to see the agents standing in her foyer. She sighed.

Ashby pleaded, "Ma'am, children's lives are at stake."

Rita motioned to them to follow her to the kitchen. They sat at the kitchen table. Rita served them iced tea.

Ashby and White observed pictures on the wall of Sabrina playing softball and singing in a choir. One photo collage featured a young man proudly wearing a Marine uniform. The adjacent pictures were of Sabrina, posing with different types of weapons and firearms. All showed a trim, healthy girl.

Rita noticed them staring at the collage. "That's Sabrina's father, my late husband, Aaron. He served in Iraq. He taught Sabrina how to shoot. She's won several competitions over the years. And she's usually the only girl."

Uncomfortable, Rita tried her husband again. It yielded the same result.

White attempted to persuade her, "Ma'am, those girls, your daughter's friends, are running out of time. You've been in those girls' mothers' shoes. You know the torment they are going through. Your daughter might know something that can help us find them. Please."

She explained, "My husband left explicit instructions."

White countered, "Ma'am, your late husband, Sabrina's father, was a Marine. He would never think of leaving a man behind. And I'm afraid that's what might happen if we don't talk to Sabrina now."

Rita looked down, conflicted.

White badgered, "Don't let Sabrina leave her friends behind. Aaron would want her to live by his code of ethics—the Marine code of ethics. Don't leave those girls behind."

After contemplating it, she left the room to retrieve Sabrina. Rita returned alone. She stated, "She doesn't want to come down. But you can go up to her room. Second door on the right."

Being the human behavior expert, White offered, "I'll go up alone. Since I'm female, I'm less of a threat than if we go together. I think she'll feel more comfortable one-on-one."

Ashby concurred, "Agreed."

White knocked on Sabrina's open door. "Can I come in?"

Sitting cross-legged on the bed, Sabrina nodded. She clutched a well-worn teddy bear against her chest.

In a soothing tone, White introduced herself, "I'm Agent White. I just want to ask you a few questions."

Visibly nervous, Sabrina fidgeted. She wore loose clothing and appeared quite a bit heavier than she did in her pictures.

White entered the room. "Your mom and another agent are in the kitchen. I thought it might be easier for just the two of us to talk."

Sabrina said, "Okay."

Agent White sat in the desk chair opposite the bed. "I know you're scared, and you have been through a horrible ordeal. But we need your help finding your friends. I'm just asking you to try. Do you think you can do that?"

Sabrina replied, "Yes."

"Good."

Sabrina avoided eye contact and chewed on a fingernail.

White maintained an open and friendly posture. "Did you recognize the place they were holding you?"

Quickly, Sabrina responded, "No."

"Did you hear anything like train whistles or church bells?"

The girl shook her head. "No."

"Was it quiet or a place with lots of traffic?"

"Quiet, I guess."

"Can you tell me anything about the people who held you?"

She shifted uncomfortably on the bed. "No. They wore masks."

"Men or women?"

She looked up. Her demeanor changed. "A bunch of stupid guys and the mean old bitch."

White noted the way Sabrina emphasized her hostility toward the woman. The woman elicited a visceral emotional response.

White decided to focus on the woman. "Did you deal with the woman primarily?"

Sabrina came alive. "Every damn day, she would personally check on me. I never want to see that bitch's face ever again."

In a soothing tone, White assured her, "We'll make sure of it."

Sabrina rolled her eyes and muttered softly, "Yeah, right."

White found that odd. "So you saw her face then? She didn't wear a mask?"

Biting her lip, she answered, "Um, yeah, I saw her face."

"Just the men wore masks?"

Unconvincingly, she replied, "Yeah."

White's hunch about Sabrina knowing at least one of her captors seemed right.

"Were you all together?"

"I was in a room by myself."

"So you never saw or interacted with your friends?"

The girl shook her head. "We could hear each other crying. But if we tried to talk, the bitch threatened to hit us."

"Did she hit you?"

"No. Just threats."

Moving on, White asked, "Your captors fed you?"

"Yeah. Three times a day. And snacks."

Astonished, White questioned, "They gave you snacks?"

"Yeah. Fruit and veggies. Healthy crap. I begged her for Doritos, Cheetos, or any kind of chips. She never brought me any. Just more stupid fruit."

"Huh."

"A few times she gave me ice cream. But everything else was healthy."

White thought, *What kind of captors provide ice cream and healthy snacks?* She asked the girl, "Did anyone drug you?"

"No." Sabrina rubbed her wrists.

"They kept you tied up?"

"Most of the time I was chained to the bed. It was just one arm or one leg."

"They didn't have you fully restrained?"

"No. I could walk around the room and to the bathroom that was attached."

"And then this week they just let you go?"

Sabrina sighed heavily, "Yeah."

White thought, *You would think she'd be happier about being let go.*

White did not want to draw attention to the girl's remark, so she followed up, "Did they ever say why they were holding you?"

Before Sabrina could answer, Al stormed in. "What the hell do you think you're doing?"

Sabrina scrambled to the head of the bed and sat against the wall.

On instinct, White stood. "Talking to your daughter. She's doing a great job."

Al grabbed for Sabrina.

White blocked him.

He yelled, "Get out of my way! You have no right to question her without me being present. Sabrina, go downstairs. Now!"

As Sabrina held the stuffed bear tighter to her chest, hate blazed in her eyes.

White stood her ground, countering, "Mr. Fuentes, why don't *we* go downstairs and leave Sabrina alone?"

Puffing his chest out, he bellowed, "You have the gall to question my authority in my own house? Who do you think you are?"

Maintaining an even, calm tone, White replied, "Sir, I think she's been through enough. She should rest. There's no better place for her to do that than her bedroom. You can escort me out."

Fuentes fumed, "I'm going to *throw* you out."

White exited the room with Fuentes on her heels.

As they descended the stairs, White explained matter-of-factly, "I was questioning her as a material witness and victim. She's not being accused of anything. She's helping in the investigation to bring her friends home. She doesn't need representation."

Al seethed with anger. "You have gotten all you are going to get. You're done here."

White coolly stated, "I apologize if I upset Sabrina in any way. We're just trying to get justice for her, and we're trying to find her missing friends."

The team reconvened in the war room.

Sully demanded, "Lee, report."

"Fuentes' mother, Esmeralda, has had several complaints by former employees about unfair treatment and unpaid wages. Not unusual for the hotel business. Born in Colombia. Became a U.S. citizen in 1981. No rap sheet. Current on taxes."

Sully asked, "Husband?"

"Dead. Heart attack in 1979. She never remarried."

Sully pressed, "Other son?"

"Carlo. Married. Two kids—toddlers. He owns the construction business outright. Currently, he's doing two other projects in addition to the hotel and house. Juvenile records show assault, petty theft, drug possession, vandalism. No adult record. Current on his taxes."

Finding none of that information relevant, Sully ordered, "Continue."

"Al Fuentes and his wife, Rita, are lauded as upstanding citizens. Lots of volunteering in the community. Generous patrons of local artists. Lots of commendations. Current on taxes. No criminal record for either as adults. However, Al had a juvie record. It's sealed."

Sully ordered, "Get it unsealed."

"Trying to get access."

"Good. What about the girl, Sabrina?"

Lee reported, "From the wife's first marriage. The girl's father was a Marine and died in Iraq. Fuentes changed her last name to his, but I find no record that he officially adopted her. Good student, athletic, on the honor roll. Got her driver's license before she went missing."

Sully commented, "Okay. Anything else?"

"Not on the girl."

"Okay. Next."

Spaulding volunteered, "The brother's construction business plays by the rules. All permits and licenses are current. No obvious red flags."

Disappointed, Sully turned to White. "White, tell me something I don't know."

"The mother let us interview the girl. A few men and one woman held her. She despised the woman, called her a 'mean old bitch.' She was more nervous than traumatized, until the father came in. Couldn't get away from him fast enough. But if looks could kill, he would have been dead on the spot. She despises him. There is definitely something wrong there. And I'm positive she knew the people who were holding her, or at least the woman. She said they gave her ice cream and healthy snacks."

Sully could not believe his ears. "Ice cream and healthy snacks?"

"Yes. That was in addition to three meals a day. And she's heavier now than she was in any of the pictures in the house. Most kidnapping victims lose weight, not gain it. I'm thinking this could be a tough love detox or something."

TJ questioned the rationale, "Involuntary drug or alcohol rehab is possible. But why the need for the elaborate abduction ruse? Why draw more attention to something that you're trying to hide?"

Sully stated, "Distraction tactic. The government does it all the time."

Lee disagreed, "Reviewing the footage of the parents' pleas to the abductors, it doesn't look like they're acting. They were hysterical and beside themselves. Al comes off somewhat cool. But the rest of them are basket cases."

Sully demanded, "Show me."

Lee threw the video to one of the monitors.

The group watched and agreed with Lee's assessment.

Spaulding suggested, "Maybe Fuentes took everything in his own hands. He decided to play God with all of them. Assuming Sabrina was an addict; wouldn't it make sense that two of her best friends were also addicts?"

White said, "Probable."

Georgopoulos surmised, "So, he had to make sure they were all clean. Otherwise, as soon as Sabrina got out, she'd fall back into old habits with her friends."

The scenario gnawed at TJ. "It's possible. But something still doesn't sit right with me."

Sully moved them on. "It's something to think about though. Anything else from the girl or her mother?"

Ashby added, "The mother didn't seem to be hiding anything. Just kept deferring to her husband."

Sully turned to TJ. "How'd it go with Fuentes?"

Proudly, he answered, "I'm in with him. I have a follow-up meeting scheduled for Monday."

"So we've got to sit on this until Monday?"

TJ replied, "On the contrary, I plan to see him before that. The only catch is that I need a wife." He glanced in Georgopoulos' direction.

Georgopoulos put up her hands. "Don't look at me."

TJ insisted, "You fit the bill, Georgie. And he's already seen White."

She sank into her chair. "One of you, shoot me now."

Chapter 4

BRIGHT and early Friday morning, Laura read the paper while Sara ate breakfast. They were still in their pajamas. Anna breezed past them, dressed in a tight yellow T-shirt and jean shorts. She poured herself a cup of coffee before joining them.

Sara addressed Anna, "You're wearing that to go shopping?"

Anna replied, "I know we all took today off from work to shop and hang out, but Vinnie has today off too. You know that he rarely gets time off. So, when he asked me to go on a picnic, I couldn't turn him down. I'm sorry."

Sara reassured her, "No need to be sorry. Go and have fun."

Relieved, Anna said, "I knew you'd understand."

"Of course."

"So, things are going well?" Laura pried.

"Not well enough. We still haven't slept together."

Surprised, Sara asked, "Really?"

Laura inquired, "Are you sending the wrong signals?"

Anna threw her arms up. "No. Look at how I'm dressed! This push-up bra has the girls on full display."

Sara agreed, "They sure are."

Laura added, "He would have to be blind not to see them."

Anna continued, "I fawn over him constantly. I compliment him. It doesn't seem to matter what I do."

"What does he say?" Sara questioned.

"He says he doesn't want to rush into anything. Says he's had some really bad relationships and doesn't want to screw this up."

Laura commented, "Sounds reasonable."

"Short of attacking him, I don't think it's going to happen for a long time," Anna complained.

Jokingly, Laura warned, "Be careful about attacking a police officer."

Sara snickered.

Anna attested, "Don't get me wrong. He's nice. He treats me well. He's a *great* kisser. I just want more. A lot more! I'm the only one in this house not having sex!"

Laura patted Anna's shoulder. "Give him time. The wedding is coming up. A lot of people hook up at wedding receptions. Maybe it will put him in the mood."

Resigned, Anna muttered, "I'm not holding my breath."

Sara asked, "Laura, are you eating breakfast before we go?"

Laura shook her head. "No, I'm good."

Sara suggested, "Let's get dressed and get started then. We've got a lot to do."

Sara and Laura exited the party supply store after an hour. Fortunately, they were able to check off the bridal shower favors and wedding reception favors.

The next task on Sara's list was her wedding gown fitting. She drove to Theresa's Bridal and parked in the small lot. She and Laura had bought all of their semi-formal dresses and prom dresses at Theresa's. So they knew the staff well.

Kay, the daughter of the owner, a woman in her sixties, greeted them at the door. "Welcome! Welcome! So wonderful to see you."

"Hi. Nice to see you too."

"Come back to the fitting room. We're ready for you."

Sara and Laura followed the woman to the fitting area.

Kay pulled back the curtain to the first room on the left and announced, "Here you are!"

The gown was as beautiful as Sara remembered.

Kay helped Sara into her gown. When Sara stepped out of the room, a sturdy, middle-aged Italian seamstress waited with Laura. This was Sara's third fitting.

Sara twirled around in her strapless, fit and flare gown with a sweetheart neckline. The bodice was hand-beaded. She glowed. "I feel like a princess in this gown."

Kay corrected, "A sexy princess."

Laura embellished, "A hot, sexy princess."

"Thank you. I just *love* this dress!" Sara admired herself in the three-way mirror.

"You look gorgeous," Laura gushed.

Sara admitted, "I feel beautiful."

Pressed for time, the seamstress directed, "Okay, Miss Hot Sexy Princess, time to get to work. Up on the pedestal."

Sara mounted the pedestal. It seemed like a dream. She was finally getting married.

The woman pinned several areas. "Every time you have an appointment, I take it in a little more. If you keep losing weight, there is not going to be any of you left by your wedding day."

"I'm not trying to lose weight."

Holding straight pins between her teeth, the seamstress suggested, "Then eat more. I am going to sew in the cups after today. It will make you bigger up top."

Sara protested, "Not too big."

The woman reassured her, "No, no, not too big. No need to worry. It is just so you don't have to wear a bra."

Right on time, Vinnie picked up Anna. Armed with a picnic lunch from Carmine's Deli, the best delicatessen in town, they headed to the park. He parked in the lower lot. They found a picnic table under a large sugar maple tree. The combination of the shade and the light breeze made it cool.

Anna was glad she brought along a hooded jacket. Although she wanted to show off her assets, she did not want to freeze.

The leaves had started to change. It was a beautiful day.

Anna was not focused on the leaves or the weather. Her eyes were glued on Vinnie's bulging muscles. She had dreamt of those muscles many times. She began to daydream about them as he sat next to her.

She was jolted back to reality when Vinnie handed her her favorite sandwich. "I got you ham and Swiss cheese on rye."

She made sure her hand brushed his as she accepted the sandwich. "Thank you. You remembered."

"Of course!"

Guessing she already knew the answer, she asked anyway, "What did you get?"

Predictably, he replied, "Capicola and provolone with oil and hot peppers. There's also fresh fruit and chocolate chip cookies."

She unwrapped her lunch. "Perfect."

"And I got you a Coke." He handed her the bottle of pop.

She smiled as she took it from him. "Thanks. You know, it was so sweet of you to offer to do the readings at Joe and Sara's wedding."

"It's nothing. I give public speeches all the time. I made them a promise. And I keep my promises." He took a bite of his sandwich.

"Good to know."

When they finished eating, Vinnie asked, "Would you like to go for a walk?"

Anna replied, "I'd love to."

They cleaned up and tossed their garbage in the nearby trash can. Then, they strolled along the leaf-littered path. When they reached the top of the hill, the breeze whipped Anna's blonde hair around. She did not mind.

Birds squawked as they flew overhead.

Vinnie pointed as he suggested, "Let's go off the path and walk down the hill. I love the color of those red maples. They're just starting to turn. I want to see them up close."

Enthusiastically, Anna agreed, "Sure. Why not?"

As they descended the hill, leaves crunched under their feet.

Vinnie led the way.

Navigating around the ruts in the uneven ground, Anna asked, "Vinnie, do you find me attractive?"

Stunned, he turned to face her. "You're beautiful, Anna. Why would you ask me that?"

"Don't get me wrong. I like that you are a gentleman, but sometimes I wish you weren't."

"Oh." Vinnie looked away.

Anna proposed, "I was thinking after the wedding, we could go to the Adirondacks for the weekend to look at the leaves."

Vinnie kicked a stone out of his way. "Um, I'm not sure I can get any time off."

They reached the cluster of maple trees.

Sensing evading tactics, she confessed, "I want you, Vinnie. I just want to make that clear. I *really* want you. I know you're not ready for sex. I respect that. But sometimes I feel like you don't even want to kiss me."

A heaviness filled his heart. "It's not you. It's definitely me."

Anna thought, *Oh, here it comes.*

"You're beautiful, funny, and intelligent. I really want to make this relationship work. I do. More than you can imagine. And I understand how you feel. I'm just not ready yet. I'm sorry."

Feeling slightly more hopeful, Anna probed, "When will you be ready?"

He did not answer immediately. Instead, he looked up into the boughs of changing leaves.

She wondered if her question was too forward. Then she reconsidered, *I can't get what I want if I don't ask.*

Vinnie met her gaze. Answering truthfully, he replied, "I honestly don't know. But I swear to you, I'm working on it."

Counting his comments as progress, she accepted them. "Well, as long as you're working on it."

Sara and Laura left the bridal shop and went to Kleinman Fine Jewelers. Joe's mother, Rose, went to high school with the owners. So, she arranged a good deal for the gifts Joe and Sara were giving to the bridal party members.

As Sara and Laura entered the shop, Gladys exclaimed, "Look who it is, Marvin!"

Marvin yelled, "I'm in the back! Who is it?"

"It's Sara, Rose's daughter-in-law-to-be."

"Who?"

"Rose's and Sal's son's fiancé."

"Who?"

"Never mind!"

To the girls, she said, "Don't mind him. He never remembers anybody. So good to see you and your friend."

"It's nice to see you too, Mrs. Kleinman."

Placing the pendant and watch boxes on the counter, she beamed. "I have everything ready for you. Marvin did a fantastic job. You'll be very pleased."

Sara examined the delicate teardrop sapphire pendants and the custom engraved wristwatches. "They're beautifully done."

Gladys smiled widely. "Let me gift wrap them for you. It won't take long."

"That would be great. Thank you."

Laura perused the diamond rings in the cases.

Sara inquired, "See anything you like?"

"Several."

"Have you gone ring shopping with John?"

"No. We've talked about it though."

"Was he receptive?"

"Yes. He even had his own ideas."

"Really? That's impressive."

"I thought so."

Gladys reappeared, bags in hand. She handed them to Sara and hugged her. "*Mazel tov*!"

"Thank you, Mrs. Kleinman."

"Come back soon."

After that errand was complete, Sara reviewed her checklist. Satisfied, she stuffed the list in her big black purse. "I guess that's it for today."

Hesitantly, Laura asked, "Would you mind if we ran one more errand?"

Sara started the car. "Nope. Where to?"

"I need to stop at the drug store."

"Does it matter which one?"

"No. The nearest one is fine."

Sara drove two blocks to the nearest store and pulled into a parking spot.

Laura noted, "I will only be a second. You don't need to go in with me."

"Okay. I'll check my messages."

Laura made a beeline for the family planning aisle. She grabbed the first pregnancy test she saw and purchased it.

When Laura returned to the car, Sara asked, "All set?"

Laura confirmed, "All set."

CHAPTER 5

MITA Scotto entered the Luna Bar. It usually had a reserved, intimate vibe. But tonight, the music blared and pulsated. The bar teemed with loud, rowdy college kids. Curious, she cozied up to the bartender.

She yelled over the music, "What's going on?"

He shouted back, "The American kids from the University asked to have a party here. Business has been slow. So, I agreed. If they keep ordering like they have been, this will be my best night of the year."

The bartender poured her usual vodka, straight up. She downed it as she watched the happy, partying kids. This was not the crowd that would contain an ultra-wealthy businessman looking for something extra on the side.

After a short while, one of the boys approached. He shouted over the music, "Come join us! Have some fun. We're buying!" He tugged at her arm.

She allowed herself to be led into the sea of college kids.

They welcomed her jovially. A boy handed her the first of many shots. She threw the drink back quickly.

For the first time in her life, she felt old and out-of-place. She was thirty years old and partying with teenagers.

They played the usual drinking games. Mita was confident she could drink all of them under the table. So, she challenged them readily. If she was not going to score big, she might as well drink for free and have a good time.

When Mita awoke the next morning, her head pounded like a jack hammer. She opened her eyes. The room spun furiously. As she struggled to achieve a sitting position, her stomach lurched.

When her eyes finally acclimated to daylight, she looked around. Mita did not recognize her surroundings. She was on a couch next to another girl who was passed out cold.

Unconscious kids covered the floor and furniture. Miraculously, her purse was wedged in between the couch cushions next to her. She tugged it free. When she opened it, cash spilled out. She struggled to collect the wads of crumpled up bills. She stopped counting at two thousand euro.

As she shoved the cash back into her purse, she wondered, *What the hell happened last night?*

She closed her purse. *Whatever happened, I made a shitload of money. Couldn't have been all bad.*

A barefoot boy, wearing a gray T-shirt and shorts, walked in with a mug of coffee. He was surprised to find her awake. "Morning, ma'am."

Mita grunted. She hated being called that.

He rushed over to her. "You were the life of the party last night! I've never seen anyone like you."

With cotton mouth, she grumbled, "What's that supposed to mean?"

He sat down in front of her, cross-legged. "Don't you remember?"

She stared at him with bloodshot eyes. "Refresh my memory."

Smiling and shaking his head, he said, "You went down on every guy here *and* a couple of the girls. You were incredible to watch. You were a machine, ma'am."

Mita remembered none of it. She demanded, "Stop calling me that!"

"Huh?"

Mita growled, "I hate being called that."

Apologetic, he tried to think of something else to call her, "Sorry, um, lady?"

She held her head and muttered, "Fuck."

Excitedly, he proclaimed, "It's all on video. It's going to go down in history as the best party ever! Do you want to see the video?"

Mita had made sex videos before, so the concept did not faze her. "Let it roll."

The teenager pulled his cell phone out of his pocket. He swiped a few screens and held the phone up for her to view the recording.

She took the phone and placed it on her leg. Her head throbbed. *This ought to be good.*

The boy offered her his mug of coffee, "Looks like you need this more than I do."

No shit, Sherlock. If I look half as bad as I feel, I'll need the whole damn pot. Mita accepted the mug and drank deeply.

The student instructed, "You just have to press the arrow for it to play." She followed his direction and waited.

The video began with a sea of naked college boys standing in a straight line, eagerly awaiting their turns. She was on her knees. She watched as she expertly took care of them, one by one.

She agreed with the boy's assessment. *I did function like a machine. With that much money being thrown my way, I would have even done that sober.*

From what she could gather from the chanting, the two girls had been a dare. And Mita was not the type who would ever walk away from a dare. She had experimented with girls before and did not mind when the opportunity arose. Money was money.

When the video ended, she handed back the phone. She had noticed that this eager-to-please teen appeared in the video more than once. She drained the mug of coffee.

He offered, "If you need a ride home, I can give you one."

She looked at him sideways.

He rambled, "I didn't get drunk last night. I don't drink for personal reasons. My mom was an alcoholic. So I don't touch the stuff."

She thought, *I don't care about you or your bitch of a mother, kid. I just want this pounding headache to go away.*

She decided to take him up on his offer. "Get me out of here."

Promptly, he jumped up. "Okay."

As soon as Mita stood, the room started spinning again. She lost her balance and grabbed at the air.

The student caught and steadied her. "Let me help you."

In no position to refuse, she said, "Thanks."

As the teenager pulled into the alley next to Mita's apartment, he said, "I don't want to assume or insult you, lady. But I was wondering something."

Not in the mood for banter, she snapped, "What?"

He turned to face her. "If you have the next few hours free, I'd be willing to give you three hundred."

This is Mr. Moneybags, college-style. Wasting no time, she confirmed, "Three hundred?"

"Yeah."

Mita needed the money. "Money upfront."

"Of course." The boy quickly pulled out his wallet, peeled off the bills, and handed her the cash.

Head still pounding, she agreed, "Okay, kid. Let's go."

Thrilled, he replied, "Awesome!"

He held all of the doors for her and helped her navigate the stairs. Mita did not know whether to laugh or cry. She was not a crier. But watching this boy fall all over himself, being polite, and treating her nicely messed with her hungover head.

In her apartment, she slugged back two shots of vodka before indulging in his sexual fantasies. It was easy money. He was not into S&M or anything that would be considered kinky or a fetish. He was just a horny kid. And he made sure that she was satisfied, twice. That had never happened with any other man, ever. Mita had to admit the orgasms helped alleviate some of the searing pain in her head.

As he slipped his underwear and shorts back on, she stared at him. She wished he was older and established.

He proposed, "I'm going to see what you have in the kitchen. I'm sure I could whip up something."

Reality hit her like a ton of bricks. "What?"

He brushed her hair back. "Breakfast. I can make you something."

Her mind overloaded, and she freaked out, "No! Get out!"

"Huh?"

She pushed him off of the bed. "You have to leave."

Confused, he stammered, "I just thought ..."

Scrambling off the bed, she picked up his shirt and threw it at him. She yelled, "Don't think! I'm not your girlfriend. You're not making me breakfast. Just get your clothes on and go!"

Stumbling backward, pulling his shirt on, he apologized, "I'm sorry."

She chased him to the door, opened it, and shouted, "Just get out!"

He tried to say something else, but she slammed the door on him.

Alone in her apartment, she downed three aspirin tablets with a swig of vodka and a water chaser.

Then she crawled into bed to sleep off the hangover. When she awoke, it was dark. She had slept all day and still felt lousy.

Her mother's words crept into her thoughts. She hated when her mother was right, which was most of the time. It aggravated her and caused most of their arguments.

Mita had to admit that this was not the life she envisioned for herself. The blackout was overboard even for her. And freaking out over a kid treating her nicely gnawed at her.

Moving back to New York could not be worse than here. And it might be the solution to all of her problems.

CHAPTER 6

THE Grand View Hotel was an oasis at the end of a winding road, near Canandaigua Lake, in the Finger Lakes region of New York. Standing eight stories high, it commanded attention.

The groundskeeper maintained meticulous landscaping. The trees and shrubs were beautifully sculpted.

It appeared business was booming as construction vehicles peppered the east side of the property.

A handsome couple pulled up to the front of the building. The slightly overweight gentleman was dressed in a dark blue polo shirt and khakis. His blue eyes were bright and his black hair was slicked back.

The brown-eyed woman wore a teal maxi dress and a long gold necklace. Her reddish brown hair hung loosely. It rested just below her shoulders. The diamond on her left ring finger weighed in excess of two carats. Their matching wedding bands were encrusted with diamonds.

TJ turned to his passenger. "Are you ready, Mrs. Violet Perno?"

Georgopoulos smiled painfully. "Yes. Are *you* ready, Mr. Dominic Perno?"

"Yeah. Let's do this."

TJ allowed Dee to enter the hotel's revolving door first. He followed her into the lobby.

The desk clerk greeted them, "Hello! Welcome to Grand View. How may I help you?"

TJ replied, "Reservation for Perno."

The desk clerk typed on her keyboard. "Yes, here it is. Dominic Perno. Two guests, two nights. I will need a credit card to put on file."

TJ handed over his card. The clerk ran it and handed it back.

"We have a lovely room ready for you. It's Room 408."

Dee inquired, "Is that on the east side?"

"No, ma'am, it is on the west side."

"I have to have an east view."

"There is construction on the east side of the property. I'm sure you will find it more comfortable on the west side."

Dee insisted, "No. I have to have the east side."

TJ leaned toward the clerk. "It's some hocus pocus, mumbo jumbo. She was told by some psychic guy that she should always sleep in a room with the windows facing east."

The clerk's eyebrows rose. "I see."

He continued, "I will never hear the end of it if she doesn't get a room on the east side."

Dee prattled on, "And I prefer the fourth floor. I could do the fifth or the seventh floor, but never the sixth floor."

TJ rolled his eyes as he beseeched the clerk, "Please, whatever you can do, I'd appreciate it."

"Since that side of the hotel is essentially empty, I will have no trouble accommodating your request."

Dee remarked, "Thank God! Now I know I'll get a good night's sleep."

TJ concurred, "You and me both, sweetheart."

A bell boy commandeered their bags and escorted them to their room. He unloaded their luggage. "Is there anything else I can do for you?"

TJ pulled back the curtain and gestured. "What are they doing over there?"

The bell boy walked over to the window and looked out. "The owner is renovating that house. They replaced all of the windows months ago. But they found asbestos and black mold. So everything's on hold."

"Really?"

He stepped back. "Yeah. But then they planted the new trees and stuff."

"Huh. That's odd."

The bell boy shrugged his shoulders. "Anything else?"

"No. Thank you." TJ tipped him generously.

Pleased with his tip, he replied, "Thank you, sir. Enjoy your stay."

After the door closed, TJ asked, "So, Vi, how do you like the view?"

"I love it. It's picture perfect, Dom. Come see for yourself."

TJ joined Dee at the window. They assessed the house.

Two stocky men monitored the perimeter of the yard.

TJ questioned, "So, what do you think?"

"Old siding. Brand new windows. New roof. New landscaping. Basically, what the kid said."

"He failed to mention the guys on patrol. Those two don't look like construction workers to me."

"No, they don't."

TJ squeezed in closer to improve his view. His body pressed against hers. "Doesn't look like they're the hazmat suit kind of guys either."

Uncomfortable with TJ's proximity, Dee shuffled a few inches to her right. "Nope."

He pretended not to notice she moved away from him. "From the ground, the trees obstruct the view. But we can see over the trees from up here."

Dee deduced, "Which is probably why they aren't booking this side of the hotel."

He backed away from the window. "Must be eating into their profits though."

"And draw suspicion."

TJ rationalized, "Maybe not. Most people would want to be away from the noise of a construction project. So, they wouldn't complain. They would be relieved to be on the other side. People on a real vacation aren't going to notice. We noticed because we're looking for something out of the ordinary."

Listening to his argument, Dee agreed, "I'd say we definitely found something out of the ordinary. But being on the property isn't smart. It's too risky."

"A lot of things don't make sense. It might be temporary, for convenience."

"That's what we need to find out. Time for a walk on the beach."

"That's a good place to start."

Together, they set out for the beach.

TJ joked, "Remember to channel your inner girly side."

Dee plastered on a fake smile. "I'll do my best."

He patted her rear end. "Attagirl!"

Dee threatened, "Do that again, and you'll lose that hand."

"It was just a love pat."

"Love pat, my ass."

He kidded, "Technically, it *was* a love pat to your ass."

Gritting her teeth, she muttered, "Shut up. Just shut up."

A pile of discarded shoes sat near the edge of the patio. They slipped off their shoes and added them to the mix. Barefoot, they padded out toward the water.

TJ reached for Dee's hand.

She accepted it. "Nice touch."

TJ winked at her. "Let's look out at the water for a few minutes. Isn't it peaceful?"

Flatly, Dee answered, "Yeah, it's great."

Cajoling her, TJ encouraged, "Come on now. You need to relax. Get into character." Closing his eyes, he breathed in deeply.

She stared at him. "What are you doing?"

Calmly, he urged, "Listening to the waves. Try it. You might like it."

Impatiently, she answered, "I just want to get this part of the job done."

His Zen-like moment interrupted, he opened his eyes. "Part of this job is being my wife. So, relax. We're on vacation. You do know how to relax don't you?"

Indignant, Dee replied, "Of course I do!"

"Good. Then do it already. That's an order."

Sarcastically, she responded, "Yes, sir. Anything else, sir?"

He grinned. "I'll let you know."

As they gazed into the incoming waves, he slipped his arm around her.

Dee cocked her head in his direction. "Are you going to be this touchy-feely all weekend?"

"Sorry, doll. Italians are touchy-feely all of the time. It's virtually impossible to turn off."

Dee rolled her eyes. "Wonderful."

After a few minutes of silent meditation, TJ said, "Let's move out. Time to get a closer look."

Relieved, Dee turned to lead the charge. "It's about time."

As TJ and Dee neared the house, they caught the attention of one of the men patrolling the perimeter.

The man advanced toward them.

TJ whispered, "Hostile. Two o'clock."

Dee observed the short muscular man. "You're not kidding." After sizing him up, she declared confidently, "I can take him."

TJ snorted, "I'm sure you could. But we're not here to actively engage. Remember, we're tourists."

They strolled until they were behind the house.

The unknown man quickened his pace.

TJ whirled Dee around and swept her up in a kiss.

The kiss caught Dee off-guard.

The man halted his advancement.

"He's maintaining position," TJ reported, tugging Dee's earlobe with his teeth. "Act like you're enjoying yourself."

Dee struggled to maintain focus while TJ's warm breath and kisses sent shivers down her spine. She allowed her hands to wander through TJ's hair before tracing the outline of his torso. She had not been close to any man in quite some time. In her line of work, relationships were a luxury she could not readily afford.

She asked, "What do you see?"

While placing kisses down the length of her neck, TJ whispered, "Same thing we saw from the room. The windows are new, but the house hasn't been touched. They're high-tech windows. Can't see in. There's fresh landscaping on this side facing the hotel. No trees or bushes in back though. There is a table and some chairs on the patio."

TJ's lips found Dee's again. This time, she kissed him back. After a few moments, she opened her eyes, and the kiss ended.

She had never noticed how crystal blue his eyes were until now.

TJ's eyes twinkled as if they knew they were being critiqued.

He leaned in and kissed her again. TJ ran his fingers through Dee's hair. "You have the softest hair."

Determined to focus on the task at hand, she asked quietly, "Is he still holding position?"

He kissed her nose. "No. He lost interest and kept going."

"Are you kidding me?" She twisted around.

The stout man was no longer in view.

Dee punched TJ in the arm.

"Ouch! What?" He rubbed his arm.

Her eyes narrowed. "You know what!"

Justifying his actions, he declared, "I was just staying in character."

"Well, my character is pissed off at yours right now."

"Oh, honey. Don't be that way."

Dee turned and stomped off in a huff. She was not sure if she was more upset that he kept kissing her, or with the fact that she liked it.

TJ followed her up the beach, smirking.

CHAPTER 7

TJ had arranged for a candlelight dinner for two on the beach. Despite Dee's mood, they kept their reservation. A string quartet provided soothing background music and created the perfect ambiance for a romantic evening.

Dee wore a cocktail dress with a light shawl. She glanced across the table at her dining companion.

TJ wore a crisp white shirt and a dark blazer. Smiling, he complimented her, "You look beautiful."

"Thank you. You look nice too."

"Thanks."

TJ made small talk while the waiter placed the bread on the table and poured the wine.

Dee's mind fought with itself. *He needs to learn to respect professional boundaries. But he looks handsome when he's dressed up. But this is a job, remember that. But that smile of his!*

As if on cue, TJ smiled.

She fussed with her silverware. *Okay, Dee, time to focus. You have a job to do. You can't allow yourself to get distracted. Laser focus!*

TJ could tell she was not paying attention. "What's wrong?"

Dee sulked as the appetizer was served. "Nothing."

"It's something. What?"

Avoiding eye contact, she claimed, "I'm still mad at you."

TJ begged, "Honey, please let me make it up to you."

Aloof, she replied, "I can't imagine how you could."

He reached for her hand and held it. "Come on, Vi. Let me try."

The waiter interrupted, "Is everything to your satisfaction?"

TJ acknowledged, "Yes. Thank you."

The waiter departed to allow the couple to enjoy their jumbo shrimp cocktails.

She withdrew her hand.

TJ pleaded, "Baby, don't be that way."

She ripped the shell off the first shrimp with her bare hands. "Don't call me that."

"Geez. No wonder you're still single."

Dee dunked the shrimp in the cocktail sauce. "Says the single guy."

He declared, "I just haven't found the right woman yet."

"Huh! Imagine that."

He peeled the tail off his first shrimp. "It's one of the hazards of the job."

"Tell me about it."

Famished, Dee consumed the remainder of the shrimp while TJ was only on his second shrimp.

TJ snickered.

She retorted, "Doing recon makes me hungry. And being married to you is hard work."

In a mocking tone, he said, "Right! Because I make you hold my hand and kiss me."

She furrowed her brow as she tore off the heel of the bread.

"And let's not forget how I plan romantic dinners on the beach. I'm just a horrible husband."

Frustrated, she muttered, "The things I have to put up with to serve my country."

TJ and Dee finished the bottle of wine after dessert as they listened to the music. The breeze off the water turned much cooler. A chill ran through Dee's body.

TJ noticed and offered, "Why don't we call it a night?"

"Whatever you say. You're the man."

TJ shook his head. As they strolled, he draped his arm around her.

She leaned against him. *He's so warm, and he smells amazing.*

TJ was surprised when Dee slipped her arm around his waist.

They could still hear the music when they reached their room. With his free hand, he took the keycard out of his pocket and inserted it into the lock. They entered the room together.

The door closed behind them. They found themselves face-to-face, embracing each other.

Damn, she's beautiful. He found himself brushing back her hair.

She wanted to close her eyes and enjoy his touch, but instead, she pulled back and moved away.

Concealing his disappointment, he locked the door and threw the bolt.

She grabbed one of her bags and went into the bathroom. She needed to clear her head. "I'm going to change."

"Okay. I'm going to get set up then." He rummaged through his black duffel bag for his binoculars. Once he found them, he extinguished all of the lights.

When he did, he noticed a shadow pass by their entry door. He watched intently. The person walked by a second time. Then the shadow returned and remained.

Thinking quickly, he started to shout, "Oh, Violet! Oh, baby!"

Dee opened the bathroom door wide. "What?"

TJ put his hand over her mouth immediately and pointed to the room's entry door. She saw the shadow outside their room and nodded her head.

She had just spent the last several minutes pushing this idea out of her head. Now, she was going to have to role-play it. The irony was not lost on her. In a throaty voice, she urged, "Oh, Dom! That's it!"

TJ scrambled on the bed to make it squeak. Dee joined him. But separately, their rhythm was off, so TJ grabbed her and held her to him, so the squeaking would be in unison.

The position was uncomfortable for Dee. So, she rolled on top of him, yelling, "Oh, baby! Yes!"

TJ's eyes adjusted to the darkness. She was wearing a tank top and shorts as she rode him. He fought his initial instinct of grabbing her hips.

She desperately fought the urge to rip off his clothes. She had not expected to develop feelings for him, let alone these types of feelings. *It must be the wine.*

He looked up into her eyes.

She refused to hold his gaze. It was too tempting to get swept up in the heat of the moment. She had a job to do. So, she closed her eyes and moaned loudly.

He was not sure if she was doing her best impression of Meg Ryan's pretend orgasm in that dating movie or if she was actually enjoying herself. As his brain tried to process the situation, she rolled off of him.

From her vantage point, she saw the shadow outside the door had disappeared. "Shadow's gone. Show's over."

TJ swallowed hard. Highly aroused, he sat up and swung his legs over the edge of the bed, not believing what had just happened. After a moment, he trudged to the bathroom and threw cold water on his face. Leaning on the vanity, he contemplated taking a cold shower. He inhaled deeply several times as he attempted to clear his mind. Then he splashed more cold water on his face.

After composing himself, TJ reentered the main room.

Dee avoided eye contact and pretended to be engrossed in her computer screen. As if nothing happened, she stated, "Nothing new to report." Then she closed her laptop.

He acknowledged, "Okay. I'll take first watch." Then he dragged the desk chair over to the window, picked up his binoculars, and peered into the darkness. The night had just begun.

TJ observed a white panel van drive down the gravel road to the house. Less than thirty minutes later, it travelled back the way it came. An hour later, the van repeated its journey. But it did not come back out before sunrise.

His disciplined mind struggled with balancing the need to know what was in that house at the end of that road and the physical desire of taking Dee to bed.

CHAPTER 8

MITA opened her bedroom window. She lit a cigarette with a cheap disposable lighter. She exhaled into the Italian countryside air. The scent of freshly baked bread wafted from the bakery down the street. To a passerby, the smell would be heavenly. However, Mita's senses were deadened from years of smoking. She hardly noticed it at all.

The sun rose to her right. The hilltop obscured the actual sunrise, casting a shadow over the village.

She took another drag from the cigarette as she pushed her hair back. It immediately fell back into her eyes. She let the cigarette dangle from her bottom lip as she used both hands to twist up her hair and fasten it with a clip. She walked to the dresser with the mirror hanging above it. Almost without looking, she plucked a few bobby pins off the top of the dresser and strategically placed them to keep the wispy hairs in place. Satisfied, she returned to the window and finished her cigarette.

Mita was not a nostalgic creature. She did not consider this apartment home. She would not miss it. There were no trinkets or sentimental personal items to pack. She had her clothes, shoes, and purses. All of the jewelry she had received as gifts had been pawned.

When Flora found the drawings and art projects she had made for her mother in the trash, she cried.

Mita told her there was no room to pack them, and she could make new ones.

Clearly, Mita Scotto was not mother material. She often resented Flora. But she resented the man who had gotten her pregnant even more. And lately, she resented the entire world.

Mita finished packing her last suitcase and secured the locks. She dragged it off the edge of the bed and wheeled it to the front door.

Flora bounded out of the second bedroom. "Mama, are we leaving for America now?"

In an annoyed tone, she replied, "Soon."

Bursting with energy, Flora twirled around in a circle. "I can't wait! Are we going to Disney World? Maria from next door went last summer, and she had *so* much fun. She met all of the princesses."

Mita demanded, "Stop spinning. You're making me dizzy."

Flora stopped and fell on the floor. She laughed at herself.

"Disney World is in Florida. We're going to New York."

Curious, Flora asked, "Are they far from each other?"

"Yes. So, forget about it."

Flora deflated, "Okay."

As they entered the airport, Flora was on sensory overload. All of the sights and sounds amazed her.

Every few minutes, she urged, "Look, Mama!"

It grated on Mita's nerves.

Mita did not book the same flight as her mother. She did not want to be stuck on a plane with her, enduring lecture after lecture. Now she thought being stuck on a plane with a five-year-old might be worse.

After passing through security, Mita and Flora boarded their flight.

Once the plane was airborne, Flora provided non-stop commentary.

"Mama! That man over there has a funny hat."

Mita did not answer, although her mind screamed, *Shut up!*

She craved a cigarette and a strong drink.

"Mama! Look at that lady. Ewww! She's picking her nose," Flora grimaced.

"Don't look at her," Mita admonished.

"Ewww, she's doing it again." Flora shivered in disgust.

Grinding her teeth, Mita scolded, "What did I say?"

"Sorry." Flora sank meekly into the seat.

A few scant minutes passed. Pointing and pulling on Mita's arm, Flora exclaimed, "Mama! Mama! Clouds! We're above the clouds!"

"Uh huh. Take a nap," Mita growled.

Flora giggled. "You are so funny sometimes. I don't take naps." Her attention returned to the view. "Everything is so small. I can't see our village anymore."

"Hopefully, we won't see it ever again."

Wide-eyed, Flora asked, "Ever?"

Reclining her seat, Mita said, "New York is better. We'll be staying with your grandmother. You should like that."

Flora exuberantly agreed, "I can't wait! It's going to be *so* fun living with Nana."

Irritated, she jumped down Flora's throat, "Will you shut up? It's going to be a long flight. Why don't you color or something?"

Flora pouted and crossed her arms. After a few minutes, she unzipped her backpack and pulled out one of her coloring books and crayons. She colored quietly.

Mita's craving for a cigarette increased by the moment. A short time later, the opportunity to satisfy her other craving presented itself when the flight attendant arrived with the beverage cart.

"Give me a double shot of vodka, straight up. She'll have ginger ale," she stated, pointing at Flora.

The plane made an uneventful landing at the Rochester International Airport. Mita and Flora stood at the luggage carousel waiting for their luggage to appear.

Flora marveled at all of the different things on the luggage belt—suitcases, duffel bags, cylinders, and odd-shaped things wrapped in brown paper and secured with silver duct tape. When they finally retrieved all of their luggage, they headed toward the taxi stand.

Mita lit up a cigarette as soon as they cleared the airport doors.

Flora tugged on her. "All the taxis are leaving."

Mita inhaled deeply and exhaled a large plume of smoke. "Chill out, Flora. I need to finish my cigarette."

Flora wheeled her pink suitcase to the other side of her mother. Now she was positioned upwind from the smoke.

Flora hated that her mother smoked. She begged her to quit smoking a few months earlier as a birthday gift and was yelled at for her trouble.

Mita smoked the cigarette down to the filter and flicked the butt. It landed on the sidewalk in front of Flora.

Flora furrowed her brow and stomped on the butt as if it was a spider.

Mita slung her large bag over her shoulder and wheeled the other pieces of luggage toward the curb.

The nearest taxi driver inquired, "Where to?"

"Clear Brook."

Flora asked, "Is it far?"

The taxi driver replied, "No. About forty-five minutes or so."

"Yay!" Flora clapped her hands.

Attempting small talk, the driver asked, "Are you in town for business or pleasure?"

"Just moved back," Mita responded.

Flora piped up, "This is the first time I have been to America."

He asked, "Really? How do you like it so far?"

Flora giggled. "I don't know. I just got here."

The driver laughed. "Right. Good point."

After safely stowing their luggage, the driver joined them. "Address?"

"Seventy-six Park View Terrace. It's an apartment complex."

"Okay, I'll look it up." The driver's fingers glided over his GPS screen. He found the address. "Got it."

"Good."

Flora ogled passing cars and the scenery. Her excitement amused the driver, but it continued to grate on her mother's nerves.

After riding for forty minutes in light traffic, the taxi pulled into the Park View Apartment complex. After finding the right building, they stopped.

The driver announced, "Here you are. Number seventy-six."

Flora opened her door and ran from the taxi as Mita settled the bill with the driver.

Helen had been looking out the window. She met Flora in the hall. "Look who's here!"

Flora rushed into Helen's open arms. "Nana!"

Helen enveloped Flora in a warm, loving embrace. "It's so wonderful to see you!"

Flora agreed, "You too, Nana!"

They met Mita in the doorway as the driver finished unloading the luggage.

Greeting her daughter, Helen said, "I trust you had a good trip."

"It was long," Mita complained, pulling the suitcases behind her.

Helen asked, "Do you need help?"

"No. I got it."

"Okay."

Mita looked around. It was a nice, clean apartment. It was twice as big as the one she had been living in the past three years with Flora.

However, on the downside, she was living with her mother. That was a fate worse than death in Mita's mind.

Mita asked, "How'd you get all of this set up so fast?"

"It was fully furnished. My cousin arranged everything. I still need to unpack some boxes. But for the most part, it's already feeling like home."

"Huh."

"Let me show you the guest room. That is where you will be sleeping," Helen said.

Flora skipped after her grandmother.

Mita stayed behind.

Within seconds, Flora zoomed out of the bedroom and down the narrow hall. "Mama! Mama!"

Jet-lagged and peeved, she barked, "What?"

"Our room has two beds. It's so pretty. Come see! Come see!" Flora grabbed her mother's hand and dragged her toward the room.

Mita could not believe she agreed to live with her mother. She told herself the arrangement would be temporary.

"I trust you will be comfortable here," Helen said.

Flora jumped on her bed. "I love it!"

"Looks fine," Mita stated.

"Coming from you, that is a huge compliment. Let's get you settled. Then we'll get something to eat."

"Where do you keep the vodka?"

"I don't have any alcohol."

Surprised, Mita questioned, "None?"

"No. I've decided to give it up. So should you."

"I'm living with you again. I don't think now is the time to give it up."

"This is a fresh start. Clean living. That means no alcohol, no drugs, and no men. We'll work on the cigarettes later."

"So, this is a convent? And you're Sister Mary Screw-Me-Over?"

Quick-witted, Helen responded, "Call me, 'Mother Superior.'"

Melodramatically, she said, "Ha, ha, ha. I suppose I have a curfew too?"

"I hadn't thought of it. But now you mention it, that is a good idea."

"Jesus Christ! Am I fourteen all of a sudden?"

"No. But you're going to have to follow my rules. This is your opportunity for a fresh start, a clean start. Make the most of it, Mita."

In her new room, Flora unzipped her suitcase. She carried the small step stool over to the closet and cheerfully hung up her clothes. She hummed a happy, made-up song as she worked.

Helen said, "I went to the cell phone store this morning. The nice boy there showed me how to use my new phone. He also told me it was cheaper to add your phone to my plan than for you to get your own." She handed Mita a phone. "So, I got this one for you."

Mita accepted it. "Thanks."

"You're welcome. He also put my phone number in there for you."

Sarcastically, she replied, "Great."

"Mita, I will cut you some slack today because you're suffering from jet lag. But starting tomorrow, you need to adjust your attitude. And you need to start looking for a job and a car."

She griped, "Already with the lectures."

"I am your mother. I will always lecture you when you need it. Now why don't you go in your room and unpack with Flora? Maybe some of her enthusiasm will rub off on you."

"Doubt it."

"Try to be happy, Mita. Please, just give it a try."

CHAPTER 9

WHEN Laura awoke Saturday morning, she tiptoed to the bathroom and locked herself in. She positioned her cell phone on the vanity, so she would have a timer. She ripped open the pregnancy test box. She read the directions twice. She unwrapped the stick, threw the wrapper in the wastebasket, and sat on the toilet.

As Laura urinated on the stick, her cell phone rang. It startled her. She jumped and dropped the stick into the toilet.

"Damn!"

She got dressed, plunged her hand into the toilet, and pulled out the stick. She threw it into the trash can and crumpled up some tissues to serve as camouflage. Then she washed her hand and arm twice.

The phone rang again. It was not a number she recognized. She ignored it and shuffled to the kitchen. She slumped into one of the kitchen chairs.

Sara sensed something was amiss. "What's wrong?"

"I'm late."

Glancing up at the wall clock, Sara pointed out, "You have plenty of time to get ready."

"No. I'm *late*, late."

"Oh, God! Aren't you on something or using something?"

Laura propped her elbows on the table and covered her face with both hands. "Yes. But I guess there was a malfunction of sorts."

"How late *are* you?"

Speaking through her hands, she replied, "Late enough. I am *never* late. Never! Ever!"

"We have to get you a pregnancy test."

Laura lowered her hands. "Bought one already and just tried, but I dropped it into the toilet."

Sara pictured it and laughed.

Laura shot her a look.

Realizing the insensitivity of her reaction, Sara apologized, "Sorry. Go get ready. I'll get my keys. Let's go get you another test."

In the family planning section of the neighborhood drug store, Sara suggested, "Buy a multi-pack. That way you'll have extras in case you drop one again."

"Yeah, thanks," Laura concurred in an annoyed tone.

Sara read the directions on one of the boxes. "Have you said anything to John?"

"No! Of course not."

"Well, if you are pregnant, you're going to have to tell him." Sara returned the box to the shelf.

Laura selected a different brand. "I will cross that bridge when I come to it."

"Get your hiking boots ready," Sara muttered.

"What?"

Sara motioned toward the door. "Speak of the devil. John just walked in."

A sense of panic welled in Laura's stomach. "No!"

"Yes. Just chill out."

Laura pleaded, "Hide me."

"Hide you?" Sara asked incredulously. "Where am I going to hide you?"

Laura looked around frantically. "He's coming this way. Do something!"

"Like what?"

"Here," Laura said, shoving the box into Sara's hands. "You take it."

"Like it's a hot potato? Sheesh."

Before Sara could put the box back on the shelf, John approached. "Hi!"

Laura remarked, "Fancy, running into you here." *God, that sounds like something my mother would say. Way to go trying not to act suspicious.*

John kissed Laura quickly. "Yeah, it is."

Sara greeted him, "Hi, John."

"Hi, Sara."

John slipped his hands into his front pockets. "I figured I better stock up for the weekend. Did you have the same idea?"

Laura nervously shifted her weight from one foot to the other. She lied, "No. Sara needed a few things."

Sara plastered on a really big smile. She looked and felt goofy.

John glanced down and saw the pregnancy test. "Whoa! Good thing the wedding isn't too far off. You know, just in case."

Sara pretended to be embarrassed. "Just don't tell Joe."

John pulled his hands out of his pockets and held them up, palms facing out. He reassured her, "Don't worry. I will leave that up to you."

"Thanks," Sara said.

John whispered to Laura, "Any particular style you want me to buy?"

Laura thought, *Save your money.* Instead she said, "Surprise me."

Barely able to contain his excitement, he acknowledged, "Okay. I've got a great night planned."

"I can't wait," Laura replied truthfully.

He grabbed an economy pack of condoms. "See you later, honey. Pick you up at six o'clock."

"I'll be ready."

He kissed her before walking to the counter to check out.

Sara observed, "The economy pack. Nice! Looks like you two are going to have a really fun time." She giggled.

Laura gave Sara a back-handed smack to the arm.

"What? It's true."

The girls approached the cashier.

Sara shoved the box at Laura. "You can take it back now."

Laura accepted it and placed it on the counter. As she pulled out her wallet, she said, "Thanks for covering."

"Any time. You would do the same for me."

CHAPTER 10

TJ and Dee disembarked from the elevator. There was a palpable awkwardness between them. They had not spoken a word to each other all morning.

TJ nodded at the clerk as they passed the front desk. His blue eyes sparkled as he winked at the clerk.

The clerk smiled. "Good morning."

"Good morning to you. Beautiful day," he replied.

"Yes, it is, sir."

"We're going to walk around."

"Very good, sir. Just take care to avoid the area under construction."

"Will do." The couple smiled and exited the lobby.

TJ inquired, "Where to, my dear?"

Curtly, she replied, "The flower gardens."

Jovially, he tormented, "Obviously, since you're named Violet."

Annoyed, she answered, "I didn't pick my name. You did."

"I picked it because I always liked that name. But you're definitely not the shrinking type."

"Huh?"

"You know—shrinking violet? Wallflower?"

She kicked a rock in her path. "Whatever."

They strolled arm-in-arm to the flower gardens.

Feeling self-conscious, Dee said, "I want to apologize for my behavior last night. Sorry if I made you uncomfortable."

TJ tried not to smile. *It was the best kind of uncomfortable.*

"I got carried away. You know, caught up in the role playing."

He played dumb. "I have no idea what you are talking about." He bent over and pointed. "This is a pretty rose, don't you think?"

Relieved, she said, "Thanks."

Smelling the rose, he replied, "Don't mention it."

Satisfied with the resolution of her awkward indiscretion, Dee leaned over to smell the rose. "How's your back?"

He stretched backward. "It would be better if I hadn't spent the entire night in that damn chair."

She chuckled. "I'm sure it would."

Pretending to be interested in the flowers, he said, "We've done all we can from a distance."

"Roger that."

TJ reviewed, "We've got a construction site with no construction going on. Two guys guarding the mystery house. A white Chevy panel van that comes and goes. We need to find out what's in that house. They considered us harmless yesterday. Let's hope for the same today."

Dee suggested, "Let's take a walk toward the orange cones."

Taking the lead role, he said, "Just let me do all the talking."

She shot him a look. "Don't count on it."

TJ sighed.

When the couple reached the end of the sidewalk, they walked toward the house. They passed pallets laden with lumber and other building materials. They appeared to not have been touched since they were delivered.

A black Chevy Suburban pulled up. Immediately, the two men patrolling the property met the vehicle.

Hugging the new landscaping, the couple reached a window.

TJ said, "That distraction helps."

"Sure does."

Tapping on the glass, TJ commented, "I'm impressed. Very high end."

"Bet it's sound proof."

"Mirrored too. Can't see in."

"Private."

"Seems they thought of everything."

A deep voice, with a hint of a Hispanic accent, boomed behind them, "Hey! What do you think you're doing?"

TJ and Dee spun around.

The five-foot, eight-inch tall man was built like a tank. His head was shaved clean. Tattoos peeked out from his shirt collar.

Assuming an overbearing tourist persona, Dee began, "I've been dying to peek into this house. The windows are so unusual. They look

New Age or something. Are they like solar panels? I told my husband that they look like solar panels to me. Didn't I, hon?"

Playing along, TJ replied, "Yes, dear."

The man scowled, "You need to go. This here's a construction zone. It's off-limits."

"I make Dom take me to all of the houses under construction back home. Don't I?"

"Yes, dear."

"And I love watching all of those home improvement shows on cable, especially when they gut the houses and flip them. Those are my favorite. This looks like one of them. I love walking into houses under construction to snoop around. It's so exciting. The possibilities are endless!"

TJ stood back and let Dee roll with it. He was impressed with her acting abilities.

The angry man demanded, "Snoop somewhere else, lady. There's asbestos that needs to be removed. This here is off-limits."

She pleaded, "Oh, can't I take a quick look inside? The asbestos isn't flying around. I won't tell anyone. It would be our little secret."

He pointed for emphasis. "No! You need to go. Now!"

Dee glanced down at the man's feet. "Oh my! I love your shoes." She touched TJ's arm. "Those are the kind of shoes I wanted to get you for your birthday. Aren't they fabulous?"

TJ replied, "Yes, dear."

She turned back to the unhappy man. "They're Ferragamo, aren't they? Where did you get those shoes? I just have to know!"

TJ thought, *Interesting coincidence this guy and Fuentes have the same taste in designer shoes.*

Approaching Dee, he sternly said, "Lady, I'm trying to be nice. I'm not going to tell you again. Go! Leave!"

The other man, possibly the first man's brother, rounded the corner. His head was also clean-shaven, but he had a scar on his chin. "Is there a problem?"

The first man's expression turned dark. "No. They were just leaving."

The second man stood with his arms crossed.

Maintaining their tourist cover, TJ said, "We'll just continue our walk down the gravel road. We didn't mean to bother you."

The first man growled, "No, it's private property. That's off-limits too. Go back to the hotel. Don't come this way again."

TJ grabbed Dee's arm. "You heard what the man said, honey. We need to go."

Dee complained, "Party poopers!"

TJ apologized, "Sorry, guys. We're leaving."

The man warned, "Don't come back."

When they were a good distance away, TJ remarked, "Wow! You're good."

Smugly, she responded, "Thanks. That's why they pay me the big money."

"You're worth every penny. I didn't know you had that in you."

"I have a sister. She's a cheerleader-type. I decided to be her."

"The two of you growing up must have been a kick."

"Let's just say that G.I. Joe invaded Barbie's peaceful cul-de-sac a few times."

"Oh wow."

Disappointed they did not make more headway in the investigation, Dee changed the subject. "Guess we'll have to wait until tonight to see where that road goes."

TJ agreed, "Looks like it. And we can safely say those guys are sentinels, not construction workers."

"Highly-paid sentinels. Those shoes cost seven hundred dollars."

CHAPTER 11

SARA leaned against the hallway wall next to the bathroom door. "Take two at the same time."

Laura yelled through the door, "Really?"

"Two test results are better than one."

Laura urinated on two pregnancy test sticks. After cleaning up, she opened the door.

Sara accompanied Laura to the kitchen. She ripped off a wad of paper towels and handed them to Laura.

Laura rested the applicators on the paper towels.

The friends waited in silence, watching the clock. After the correct amount of time had passed, Sara announced, "Okay, it's time."

Laura's hands trembled. She picked up the sticks. "I don't believe this!"

"What?"

Laura held them up. "One is positive. One is negative."

Sara shook her head. "Geez! Only you."

Exasperated, Laura said, "I can't believe this!"

"Maybe it's a good sign."

"A good sign? Are you kidding? It's still fifty/fifty."

Sara pointed out, "Better than both of them being positive."

"Uh huh." Laura threw both tests in the trash.

Sara hugged her friend. "There is nothing you can do about it now. You really need to have a blood test done to be sure anyway. So, don't think about it for now. Just go and have a wonderful weekend with John. Worry about it next week. Just have a good time."

"Easy for you to say."

"Hey, I have had my share of pregnancy scares, you know."

Laura rolled her eyes. "Yes, I remember them well. Each time, the world was coming to an end."

Justifying her previous actions, she declared, "You know it would have!"

"I know."

"Hey, sometimes our bodies get screwed up. I am sure that's all it is."

Laura was silent.

Sara spoke slowly, "Unless you *want* the test to be positive."

Laura pondered the thought as she sat on a kitchen chair.

Sara sat next to her. "Wait, do you? Do you want to be pregnant?"

"I don't know."

Sara read the expression on Laura's face. It contradicted her words. "Oh, wow."

"What?"

Flabbergasted, Sara said, "You do know. You want to be pregnant."

Laura crossed her arms. "I'm not married."

"So?"

"*So?* This coming from the woman who had a conniption fit every time she was a few days late. The same woman who called a justice of the peace, not once, but *twice*, asking how quickly she could get a marriage license and how quickly a wedding ceremony could be performed."

Defending herself, Sara explained, "Well, I was in panic mode. I had to know what my options were."

"I know. I was there." Laura rested her hands on her stomach.

"But you're not me."

Laura stared at her stomach. She imagined it getting larger with each passing month. "No, I'm not. I love John more than I have ever loved anyone."

Sara sat back in her chair. "I can see that clearly now."

"I guess I wouldn't mind if I was pregnant with his baby."

"Well, one thing is for sure."

Laura looked up. "What?"

"The two of you will make an absolutely beautiful baby."

CHAPTER 12

JOE was driving south on a rural country road when his cell phone rang. The ringtone alerted him that it was Sara calling. "Hey," he answered.

"What are you doing?"

Glancing out the side window, he replied, "Driving."

"To where?"

"I'm running errands."

The colors of the rolling hills reflected the beginning of autumn. The mixture of red, orange, and yellow painted a perfect landscape.

"What do you want to do tonight?"

Despite already having made plans for the evening, he said, "Let me think about it."

Sara offered, "I can see what movies are playing."

"Sounds good."

"What time are you going to be done, so I can narrow down the show times?"

Joe scratched his right cheek. He thought, *I should have shaved.* The stubble itched. "I'm not sure. I'll call you when I'm done."

"Okay. *Ciao.*"

"*Ciao.*"

Joe Lazaro's errand list contained only one errand—reserving the honeymoon suite at The Grand View Hotel for their wedding night. He had heard about the upscale hotel about an hour's drive from Clear Brook. He did not want to book the room sight unseen. His GPS indicated he would arrive at his destination in approximately five miles.

TJ and Dee sat in large, overstuffed chairs in The Grand View Hotel's lobby. He glanced at his Rolex watch.

Dee asked, "How much longer?"

"Shouldn't be long now. According to Lee, his schedule showed a meeting with his mother, Esmeralda, in twenty minutes."

A few moments later, a middle-aged man, wearing a deep purple polo shirt and dark gray slacks, entered the lobby. He recognized TJ and approached him.

"Dom Perno!"

TJ exclaimed, "Al Fuentes! What a surprise seeing you here!"

TJ and Dee stood. The men shook hands.

TJ introduced Dee, "This is my wife, Vi. Vi, this is Al Fuentes, the man I was telling you about."

Al shook Dee's hand. "It is a pleasure to meet you."

Exuberantly, Dee replied, "The pleasure is mine."

Al questioned, "Are you vacationing?"

TJ answered, "Yes. Just enjoying a little R&R. How about you?"

Al checked his watch. "I'm here to see my mother. She owns the hotel."

Dee touched Al's arm. "You're kidding!"

TJ shook his head. "Small world."

Al agreed, "Yes, small world."

"Vi has been talking babies nonstop since I came home from our meeting."

Feigning enthusiasm, Dee said, "I'm so excited!"

Al glanced at his watch again. "I have a few minutes. Why don't we step into the lounge?"

Al held out a chair for Dee. "Do you have any specific requirements? Like sex or ethnicity?"

Dee replied, "No. I just want a healthy baby. That's all I've ever wanted. How quickly could this happen?"

"It depends. It could take a few weeks or it might be a few days."

Astonished with his reply, she questioned, "Weeks or days? Oh my goodness! I can have everything ready in no time. I can paint the nursery and order the furniture. Dom's mother will throw me a shower. She'll make sure we have everything."

TJ laughed, "You say the word and our house will be wall-to-wall baby stuff."

Al acknowledged, "That's the way it is with children."

"If I had known we would be running into you, I could have brought our first payment."

"I don't come up here too much. I'm usually tied up with legal briefs and court cases. But my mother is having a bit of trouble."

Dee fished, "Nothing serious, I hope."

"No. Just a human resources type of issue. I should be able to clear it up in no time."

TJ said, "Good to hear."

Dee stated, "I'm sure private adoption clients take up a lot of your time."

"I only handle a small number. This year, I'm only doing three. There's nothing else that brings satisfaction like helping create families. But I might have to step back from it for a time. I can't devote the proper resources or time needed right now."

Dee said, "Then our timing is perfect! We just can't thank you enough, Al. We have been trying for so many years. This is just a blessing. You are a Godsend."

"For me, it's all about fulfilling a need. So, I do what I can." Al leaned back in his chair.

Looking out the window, TJ gestured and changed the subject, "I noticed that old house is getting renovated."

Al responded coolly, "Yes. But renovations are on hold for now. My brother found asbestos and some mold issues."

TJ played dumb. "It's your brother's house?"

Al corrected him, "No. He owns the construction company doing the renovations. The house is mine."

Dee begged, "Oh! Will you give me a tour of the house? I've been dying to see the inside."

Al said, "You'll have to wait, Vi. You know there are OSHA rules. We can't have non-approved personnel in the area when they're clearing asbestos and black mold."

"I was telling Dom that I have never seen windows like that before. They look New Age or something."

"They are part of a green initiative. The distributor guarantees they have the best insulative properties that money can buy. We are hoping it will reduce the energy footprint."

Dee complimented, "That is so environmentally responsible."

"We do what we can." He paused to check the time. "I hate to rush off, but I do have to see my mother. She's a busy one. And she does not like to be kept waiting."

Identifying with him, TJ said, "Sounds like my mother."

"Then you know how it is."

"Yes, I do. Thanks for your time."

"No problem. It was a pleasure meeting you, Vi."

"It was wonderful meeting you, Al. I'm so excited!" She turned to TJ. "We're finally going to have a baby!"

"Yes, we are, honey. Let's go celebrate with drinks by the pool."

Al stood. "Excellent. I hope you enjoy the rest of your stay. I'll see you at my law office next week."

After admiring the architecture of the building, Joe proceeded to the revolving front door.

As he entered the lobby, he noticed the rose-colored marble on the floor. An enormous round table with an equally large flower arrangement on it was centered over a swirling tile mosaic. Classical music filled the air.

Joe soaked in his surroundings. *Definitely gives off a nice vibe.*

The female clerk addressed him, "Can I help you, sir?"

"Yes, I'm interesting in booking your honeymoon suite."

"Excellent, sir. Congratulations! What days shall I reserve it for?"

"I'd like to see the room before I book it. Is that possible?"

The clerk typed on the keyboard and scrolled through several screens. "It looks like it is being cleaned. If you'd like to take a seat, I'll let you know as soon as housekeeping is done."

Joe sat in one of the lobby chairs. He checked his cell phone as he waited. Twenty minutes later, the desk clerk approached Joe. "The room is ready now."

He stood. "Great."

She directed, "Follow me."

They went up in the elevator to the eighth floor. The hallway carpet was dark maroon with a gold scroll pattern. It looked practically new. They passed several rooms until the clerk stopped. "Here we are." She opened the door and motioned for him to enter.

The room was spacious to say the least. He had never seen a hotel room this size.

"There's special lighting. You can control it with this remote," she said, handing him the controller.

Joe pressed one of the buttons. The sconces lit and threw warm, indirect light. *Definitely a mood-setter.*

"And there's a king-sized bed, an electric fireplace, and a sitting area," she continued.

Joe pressed a few more buttons to see the different light settings.

The hotel employee waited patiently, hands clasped in front of her. *The men always have to play with every single button.*

Joe handed the remote back to her.

She accepted it and returned it to the nightstand. Opening the armoire, she said, "Here we have a flat screen television."

He did not think they would be watching much television on their wedding night.

The clerk led Joe to the bathroom. "The bathroom has a whirlpool tub and a large, walk-in shower.

Joe nodded. "Nice."

"We also provide a lovely champagne and rose petal service for an additional charge."

Joe imagined Sara's reaction. "What about chocolate and strawberries?"

"We can do that as well, for an additional charge."

Satisfied, Joe crossed his arms. *It's perfect.*

"Any questions?" she asked.

"Just the big one—is it available the days I need it?"

"Let's go find out."

Chapter 13

I<small>N</small> the privacy of their hotel room, Dee asked TJ, "How can someone guarantee a baby in days or weeks? It takes people years to get a baby." She took her bag into the bathroom to change.

TJ changed into his bathing suit in the main part of the room. "You have to have a supply somewhere."

Dee slipped on her suit and looked at herself in the mirror. Through the door, she responded, "Uh huh. Did you hear him say he's only doing a few this year, and then he's out?"

TJ ruminated, "Yes. We were thinking this racket was about drugs or alcohol. I think it's about selling babies. The human resources issue that his mother is dealing with could be a girl ready to give birth, or who's having complications, or who's just given birth."

"Agreed. And it's possible they're all in on it."

Admiring himself in the mirror, he said, "We have to accelerate our timetable. We need to move on this now."

Luck was on Joe Lazaro's side. The honeymoon suite was available on their wedding weekend.

Al caught the clerk's eye as he returned from his meeting with his mother. He addressed the clerk, "I'm leaving the property. Have a good day."

"Thank you, Mr. Fuentes. Same to you."

Al crossed the lobby as the elevator doors opened.

As the clerk collected Joe's information, Joe glanced toward the elevator and saw the Pernos emerge from the elevator in their bathing suits. They, in turn, saw Joe. TJ turned away.

Joe watched the man grab and kiss his companion. He did a double take.

TJ kissed Dee passionately. She felt almost naked in her bathing suit and semi-sheer cover-up. One of his hands supported her head while the other found the small of her back.

He only wore swimming trunks and had a towel thrown over his shoulder. As she embraced him, she touched his bare skin for the first time.

This kiss had electricity flowing through both of their bodies. It was the kiss he longed to give her when she rode him the night before. When he finally felt her body yield, he ended the kiss.

Breathless and secretly wanting more, Dee asked, "What was that for?"

TJ responded, "Because I felt like it, sweetheart. Seeing you in that bathing suit makes me want to take you back upstairs."

Crossing in front of them, Al joked, "Perhaps you're not so ready for that swim after all."

Dee recovered and adjusted the top of her suit. "He just does that sometimes."

TJ slipped his arm around her waist. He explained, "When you're married to a beautiful woman, you gotta do what you gotta do."

Dee jokingly slapped TJ's arm.

TJ said, "Great seeing you, Al."

"Thank you so much for making our dreams come true," Dee gushed.

"Happy to help," Al declared.

Joe approached the group. "Hey, Tony!"

Neither man turned to acknowledge the greeting.

Joe put his hand on TJ's shoulder. "Tony, what are you doing here?"

TJ turned to face Joe. "Buddy, you have me confused with someone else."

Joe replied, "Come on."

In a menacing tone, TJ said, "Buddy, take a hike. My name's not Tony."

"But ..."

"We're having a private conversation here," TJ warned.

Joe laughed. "That pizza franchise thing again?"

"Buddy, this is the last time I'm going to ask you nicely." TJ's stance was threatening. Fire burned in his eyes.

"Okay, okay." Joe backed away. "Sorry. I thought you were someone else."

Turning away, TJ said, "Honest mistake."

Al looked at his watch. "I've got to get going. I have another meeting. Take care, Vi. Dom."

"You too, Al."

They all shook hands.

As Al left the building, he removed his phone from his pocket.

Dee laced her arm in TJ's. She whispered, "Houston, we have a problem."

"That's why I kissed you. He was looking over here."

She snapped back with sarcasm, "And I thought it was because you find me irresistible."

TJ put his hand behind her head and kissed her again.

When they parted, Dee looked up at him. In an unconvincing tone, she demanded, "Stop that."

He saw that her words did not match her body language. "You don't mean it."

She lied, "Yes, I do. Stop all of this kissing."

Curious of her answer, he asked, "Why?"

She stammered, "Because."

"Because? That's a good one."

"I'm still mad at you."

He knew she liked it and refused to admit it. That pleased him. "For what? Kissing you too long on the beach?"

"Yes."

Coyly, he inquired, "And maybe for kissing you again just now?"

Vehemently, she replied, "Yes."

"Interesting. Especially in light of what you did to me last night."

"Ugh!" She sulked.

It was the first time he had ever seen her blush.

"You said you wouldn't say anything about that!"

Feigning innocence, he shrugged, "Did I?"

She grunted.

TJ joked, "Granted, you weren't *kissing* me. You were doing something entirely different. Although in my book, those two things are related. I refuse to do one without the other."

Dee glared at him. "I hate you."

TJ contradicted her, "You don't. You wish you could. But you don't."

Dee walked toward Joe in a huff.

TJ thought, *The lady doth protest too much, methinks.*

As Al reached his car, he made a phone call. When the call connected, he asked the hotel clerk, "What's the name of the guy who was just at the desk?"

"Joe Lazaro, sir."

He demanded, "Spell the last name."

She complied.

He disconnected and made another call.

The voice on the other end answered, "Yes?"

"I've got a job for you."

Joe returned to the front desk as he glanced over his shoulder at the couple.

The clerk hung up the phone. "I couldn't help but overhear. That's the Pernos. They're here for the weekend. Nice people."

"Huh." Joe leaned on the counter.

The hotel employee typed away on her keyboard, going from screen to screen. Finally, some papers printed. She presented them to Joe, "Here is your reservation. You're all set. Have a good day, sir."

"Thank you. You too."

As Joe turned to leave, Dee bumped into him. She dropped her purse. Its contents scattered on the floor.

Joe apologized as he helped gather her belongings. "I'm sorry. I didn't see you."

Dee discreetly palmed him a slip of paper and whispered, "Go to this address. Go straight there. Do not stop for anything. Talk to no one. We will meet you there in an hour." Then audibly, she said, "That's okay. These things happen."

They stood. Avoiding eye contact with Joe, TJ joined Dee, and they walked away.

Perplexed, Joe watched the couple continue to the swimming pool. Then, he left the hotel as directed.

Sitting in his car, Joe stared at the piece of paper. Curiosity piqued, he programmed his GPS for the address that was scribbled on it.

That specific address was not found. However, it directed him to a building on the same block. Joe figured his GPS needed an update.

The building was a single-story, low-profile office building with mirrored glass. There were no "For Lease" signs; despite that the building directory sign was completely blank. The grounds lacked visual markings of any kind, other than the lines delineating the parking spaces. The few vehicles parked in the lot were dark, late model Crown Victorias, Chevy Suburbans, and Cadillac Escalades.

Joe reached the revolving door. It was locked. He looked up at the security camera wondering what to do. Then he heard a buzzing noise. A voice instructed him to go through the now unlocked door.

He obeyed.

The lobby was barren. It had no desk, chairs, or sofa. There was a single elevator and an unmarked door.

A giant hulk of a man emerged from the elevator. He was dressed in a black T-shirt, black cargo pants, and black military-style boots.

Joe greeted him, "Hey."

Spaulding approached with a security wand in his hand. "Weapons?"

Surprised, Joe answered, "No."

"Spread your legs. Hands up and out."

Joe assumed the position. He felt as if he was going through airport security.

When satisfied, Spaulding pressed his right thumb on a keypad which opened the elevator doors. He motioned for Joe to enter the elevator. Spaulding followed and pressed the button. The only direction to go was down.

Joe attempted small talk. "Pretty cool building."

Spaulding gave him a look and said nothing in return.

"So, what do you do here?"

Staring straight ahead, Spaulding answered, "It's classified."

"Classified? You're kidding."

Turning his head slightly, Spaulding queried, "Do I look like a comedian?"

Joe thought not. He asked, "Do you have a name?"

"It's need-to-know."

Joe joked, "I guess I'll call you 'Horse' then."

Spaulding rolled his eyes.

Joe explained, "You know, I've been through the desert on a horse with no name."

Spaulding grunted. "You're lucky I was given orders to protect you. Otherwise, I would have killed you by now."

Joe smiled uneasily. "Good to know."

The doors opened. Joe followed Spaulding down the hallway. They stopped at the second door on the right. He used his thumb to unlock the door and ushered Joe inside.

"Wait here. Don't touch anything." He closed the door as he exited the room.

Curiosity got the best of Joe. He looked around.

Furnishings were sparse. In the center of the room, there was a long rectangular table and eight chairs. There were six LED screens on the longest wall. There was one door with an odd peep hole on the opposite wall. He tried to look through it. As he did, a light came on, and it scanned his eye.

A computer voice barked, "Identity unconfirmed. Access denied."

"Whoa!" Joe jumped back.

The door crashed open. Spaulding admonished Joe, "What did I say?"

Joe opened his mouth to defend himself but reconsidered.

Spaulding grabbed Joe's arm and planted him in the nearest chair. He yelled, "Sit! If you touch or do anything, protection order or not, I swear I will kill you. Got it?"

Grasping the peril of his situation, he replied, "Got it."

Approximately an hour later, the door opened. The couple from the hotel entered the room.

Feeling confrontational, Joe stood. "Tony, what the hell is going on? Why am I being guarded by The Incredible Hulk sitting in wherever the hell we are? Who's she? And why do people think your name is Dom Perno?"

The woman answered his third question, "I'm Dee Georgopoulos."

Sarcastically, he replied, "Great! Now I know you're Greek. That clears up everything."

Dee said, "I've heard a lot about you."

Joe retorted, "Well, I would like to say the same, but I can't." Turning toward his brother, he threw up his hands and yelled, "What the hell?"

Tony rested his hand on Joe's shoulder. "Calm down."

Joe shrugged him off. "I'm not going to calm down. What's going on here?"

Dee approached the door with the odd peephole.

The light scanned her eye.

The computer voice stated, "Identity confirmed. Access granted."

The lock mechanism released. She pushed the door inward. There was a cavernous vault behind the door.

Dee disappeared into the room and deposited her jewelry on the shelf with all of the other pieces of jewelry. Then she rejoined the men and made herself comfortable on a nearby chair.

Tony interrogated Joe, "This is very important. Why did you go to Grand View today?"

"To check out the honeymoon suite."

Dee asked, "Did anybody know you were going there?"

"No. And you are answering my questions with questions. What's going on?" Joe pressed.

Tony removed the Rolex watch from his arm. The light reflected off it.

Awed, Joe asked, "Is that real?"

"Yes."

"Can I see it?"

He handed the watch to his brother.

Admiring the fluid movement of the hands, Joe exclaimed, "Holy shit! Do you know how much one of these costs?"

"Yes." Tony took back the watch and disappeared into the secret room.

Joe followed. The room's contents astonished him.

Two additional Rolex watches sat neatly in front. Women's jewelry was displayed on pedestals next to them. Stacks of cash, a large cache of guns, ammunition, body armor, night vision cameras, and military-type gear filled the room. Badges and vests were emblazoned with FBI, Homeland Security, ATF, DEA, and Police logos.

Dee's phone chirped. "The mission is a go for tonight."

Tony emerged from the room. "Good."

Wide-eyed, Joe accused Tony, "Oh my God! You're selling drugs, aren't you?"

"Will you shut up for one damn minute? You're worse than Ma."

Frantic, Joe gestured wildly. "You're not denying it. It's drugs! Oh my God! My brother is a drug dealer!"

Exasperated, Tony declared, "It's not drugs."

"Then what? I can't think of anything else that would need this kind of stuff and bring in that kind of money."

Tony interrupted, "Shut up, and I'll tell you. Swear on Ma's life you won't tell anyone."

Distraught, Joe promised, "Okay. I swear. Do I need a Bible?"

"No. That's good enough." He paused. "We're working undercover."

Joe crossed his arms. "I'm not buying it. You're not a cop. You dropped out. You never graduated from the Academy. And she sure doesn't look like a cop."

Tony confessed, "You're right. I'm not a cop. Neither is she. However, Dee is former military. While I was in the Academy, I was approached. I was asked if I would be interested in undercover work."

"Yeah, right." Joe rolled his eyes.

Tony pushed his brother in the chest.

Surprised, Joe stepped back. "Hey, there's no reason to get physical," he complained.

Tony reined in his anger. "I'm giving it to you straight. Are you going to listen or what?"

Joe sat down in the chair behind him. "Yes."

Tony continued, "Anyway, a few of us were selected for this program. Some of the team members are former military. Some, like me, aren't. We work together to carry out special assignments."

"Dangerous ones?"

Honestly, he admitted, "Most of the time, yes."

"Jesus, Tony."

"The majority of the operations have been in different cities. Which is why I have to come up with those cockamamie schemes to explain my whereabouts to the family. For the past year, I have been working on assignments closer to home."

"Like what?"

"I can't tell you."

"For who?"

"I can't tell you that either."

Joe whined, "Come on."

Tony deadpanned, "If I told you, I'd have to kill you."

Skeptical, he quipped, "Right, like in the movies."

"Exactly."

"Come on. Seriously?"

Gesturing widely, Tony said, "Look around, Joe. Does this look like fun and games to you?"

Joe scratched his head. "No."

Tony waited for the next question.

"So, you work for the government?"

"I can neither confirm nor deny that."

Joe laughed nervously. "I'll take that as a 'yes.' So, which three letter agency is it?"

Tony shook his head. "Knowing we are undercover is bad enough. You're not getting any more information than what I have told you."

Frustrated, Joe threw his hands up. "You haven't told me anything."

"Exactly."

"Geez! And you're still living with Mom and Dad. Wow!"

Tony ran his fingers through his hair. "I have to maintain that part of my life for this to work. I can't have you, or anyone else for that matter, poking around."

Awed, Joe complimented, "You're doing a damn good job. I don't know how you do it."

"Failure is not an option. It's tricky, but I manage. I have to."

"Obviously! Because Ma hasn't figured it out yet. Wait until she does. She's going to be so proud of you. Her son, Anthony, saving the world!"

Tony put both hands on his brother's shoulders. Sternly, he emphasized, "She can't find out, Joe. You need to understand that. It would compromise the whole operation. Not to mention, it would put us and all of you in serious danger."

"Okay."

Not completely satisfied with his brother's answer, Tony instructed, "Joe, you need to forget about all of this. You need to just go on with your daily business. Get ready for your wedding."

"That's what I was trying to do when I got caught up in this mess!"

"Remember, you can't breathe a word of this to anyone. Not Ma. Not Dad. Not Sara. Not John. Not Vinnie. Nobody. You can get us all killed. *Capisce?*"

"Yes, I understand."

Chapter 14

OVERWHELMED by the shocking revelation, Joe's mind had difficulty processing his discovery. The news about his brother's clandestine life was beyond mystifying. And the worst part was that he could not tell a living soul.

Joe had a huge surprise planned for Sara. He attempted to focus on that as he drove toward home and dialed her number.

Sara answered her cell phone, "Hi, handsome!"

In a deep sexy voice, he replied, "Hi, beautiful!"

She loved when he deepened his voice. It brought a smile to her face every time. "What's up?"

Joe desperately wanted to share what he had learned about Tony. It was incredible news. Instead, he declared, "I've got a surprise for you."

She shook her head. "You *always* have a surprise for me. But it's not much of a surprise when it happens every day."

Joe laughed. "Not that. Well, okay, you'll get that too. It's a *bigger* surprise."

"I don't know if I can handle anything bigger," she joked. "I love you just the way you are. We're a perfect fit."

Fighting the mental picture that materialized in his mind, he professed, "You're killing me."

In a sultry voice, Sara said, "Just wait until later."

Joe struggled to stay on topic, "Honestly, Sara, I'm being serious."

"So am I."

He rounded the corner on her street. "I'll pick you up in a minute."

"Is that real time or football time?'

"Real time. I'm already on your street."

She flipped on the bathroom light to check her hair. "Sheesh! Thanks for the notice."

"Well, are you doing something else?"

"No."

"See? So you're available."

Her face was shiny. So she applied some powder. "Uh huh. So are you going to give me a hint on what's so urgent that you can't wait to show me?"

"No."

"You're no fun!" she protested.

Confidently, Joe said, "Just wait until tonight. I'll give you all the fun you can handle."

She teased, "Promises, promises."

"I guarantee it."

She applied a thin coat of lip gloss. "We'll see." She turned off the light and walked to the foyer.

"I'm pulling in the driveway now."

Looking out the window, she remarked, "You weren't kidding about a minute. Since you're here, I'm hanging up."

"Okay." Joe exited his Grand Prix and walked up the sidewalk.

Opening the door, Sara observed, "You look nice."

"Thanks. You always look great." Joe entered the house. "Ready to go?"

She leaned forward for a kiss. After receiving a quick peck, she replied, "Yup. Where are we going?"

He winked. "You'll find out soon enough."

Sara shouted to Laura, "I'm leaving. Have fun tonight with John!"

As Laura shimmied into her dress, she replied, "Thanks. You too!"

Once situated in the vehicle, Joe reached into the center console and pulled out a black satin blindfold.

Shock shone in Sara's eyes. "It's broad daylight! And we're in the driveway."

"It's not for that." He paused. "Well, not yet, anyway."

Sara leaned in and nibbled on his ear. "Are you sure? We could go back inside."

Despite enjoying her advances, he confirmed, "Yes, I'm sure. I don't want you to see where I'm taking you."

"Hmmm …" She ran her hand across his chest.

He attested, "I promise it will be worth it."

She whispered in his ear as she moved her right hand up his thigh, "If not, you will owe me big time."

Joe placed his left hand behind Sara's head and drew her to him. He kissed her deeply, longingly.

Sara melted at his touch. The kiss felt marvelous.

Joe pulled back. "I promise that is only the beginning."

Wanting more, Sara leaned into him. With bedroom eyes, she pleaded, "Take me."

Aroused, Joe wanted nothing more than to do just that. However, the surprise he had planned took priority. "I want to. God knows I want to. But I can't," he stammered. "Not now."

Surprised, she sat upright. "Well, that's a first!"

Tilting his head back against the headrest, he stared at the headliner. "I can't explain. It will ruin the surprise."

She held out her hand. "Okay, okay." Reluctantly, she accepted the blindfold from him and tied it behind her head. "Happy?"

"Yes. Thank you."

They travelled fifteen minutes before Joe parked. He announced, "We're here."

Reaching for the blindfold, Sara asked, "Can I take it off now?"

Grabbing her hand, he replied, "No. Not quite yet."

Pulling her hand back, she crossed her arms. "If you say so."

"I say so."

Joe assisted her out of the car. Leading her by the hand, he directed, "Step up."

She followed his order.

After walking a short distance, they stopped.

Sara heard seagulls overhead. The familiar smell of a charcoal grill hung in the air. Her mouth started to water. *He's taken me to the beach for a picnic. Not the biggest surprise in the world, but I'll take it. I'm hungry.*

Joe interrupted her train of thought, "I'm going to take the blindfold off now." He untied it and stuffed it in his pocket.

Sara squinted in the bright sunlight. She held up her right hand to shield her eyes. They were not on the edge of the beach.

"Ta da!" Joe exclaimed, arms extended, imitating a model showing off a prize.

Sara's eyes adjusted to the light. They were standing in front of the Devonshire's house. She had only been to the Dean of the University's house once for a party, but she would recognize it anywhere. It was a quaint white cottage. She remembered it had a large kitchen and great room, two bathrooms, and a library. The bedrooms were a little small. But it was right on the lake.

Anxiously, he asked, "Well? What do you think? Do you like it?"

"This house? The Dean's house?"

"Yes, the house."

She looked at him puzzled. "It's nice. I told you that when we came for that party. I love the water view out back and the gazebos."

Joe pulled a key out of his pocket and held it up. "Sara, it's ours."

"For the week? That's great! What a wonderful surprise!" She hugged him. "Thank you."

He pulled back. "Well, not exactly."

"What then? Wait! You got it for the whole month?"

Playing coy, he claimed, "Better than that."

Tilting her head to the side, she asked, "How much better?"

"When I said 'it's ours,' I meant it. I bought the house. It's ours."

Her expression changed. "You're kidding."

Joe shook his head vehemently. "No, I'm not."

Sara was stunned.

Not able to read the look on Sara's face, Joe worried. "Sara? You aren't disappointed, are you?"

"Disappointed? No. Shocked? Yes."

"Good shocked or bad shocked?"

"Confused shocked." She stood bewildered.

Joe reassured her. "It's going to be wonderful. I promise." He took her hand in his and squeezed. "Let's walk around."

Astonished, she attempted to soak in the news. "I just can't believe it. We never discussed it."

He squeezed her hand again. "Believe it. We have to live somewhere."

"Somewhere is a big step from a house on the lake."

"Eventually, your parents will return and will want their house back. And you hate my condo. So, this is perfect."

As she looked around, still a bit shell-shocked, Joe guided her through the side yard between their house and their neighbor's house toward the rear of the property.

Lake Ontario glistened in the sunlight. He led her into the sand to the water's edge. She breathed in deeply.

From behind, he wrapped his arms around her. They watched the waves lap up on the beach.

Sara relaxed as she leaned into him.

Joe felt the tension leave her body. He whispered in her ear, "So I take it you like your present now?"

She admitted, "I do love it. It's the second best present you have ever given me."

"Second best?"

"My engagement ring was the best, silly."

"I love you, Sara." He held her tightly.

"I know." She separated from him and glanced down. "And I can feel it too."

He placed his hands on her hips and pulled her against his body.

Sara leaned back. "Joe, not in the yard. The neighbors are watching."

"I don't care. They better get used to it." He pinched her rear end.

She smacked him playfully. "Joe! We want them to like us."

"I couldn't care less." Joe turned and waved to the older couple next door.

The aged couple frowned as they shook their heads in a disapproving fashion.

Joe lifted Sara's hand to his lips and kissed it.

Sara giggled. "Take me inside."

"That's my line," he said, sucking on the inside of her wrist.

Sara pretend-slapped him. "You know that drives me crazy. Oh, you are incorrigible!"

Joe squeezed her rear end with his free hand. "Guilty as charged."

Sara challenged, "Race you!" She ran ahead.

Joe thought, *I did good. She's really happy.*

She glanced over her shoulder. Motioning to him, she yelled, "Come on! What are you waiting for?"

He thought, *The waiting is over. We're getting married. This is our house. The only thing left is to say, "I do."*

Happy and content knowing all of that, he ran to her.

Sara taunted Joe about beating him to the door.

Joe did not care. *I'm so happy. Everything is finally falling into place.*

When he reached the front door, he unlocked it.

Sara attempted to push past him.

"Wait!" Joe insisted.

"What now?" she asked, throwing up her hands.

"I'm carrying you over the threshold."

Surprised, Sara stated, "We aren't married yet."

"I don't care. I am carrying you over the threshold. We only enter this house together for the first time as a couple once. This is it."

His eyes told her this meant a great deal to him. Sara gave in. "Okay." She held up her arms.

Swiftly, he swept her up and smiled.

Sara smiled back as she interlocked her fingers and rested them on his shoulder.

Joe turned sideways and stepped across the threshold. "I love you, baby."

"I love you, honey."

They kissed.

Sara kicked her legs. "Are you going to put me down, or are you carrying me through the whole house?"

He answered by twirling around once and putting her down. "The house isn't perfect. It is a bit of a fixer-upper. But we have got a little time before the wedding. That should be plenty of time to fix everything and paint."

Concerned, she asked, "What's the 'everything' part?"

"The inspector said it was okay. There are just some minor repairs. I got Frederick to bring down the price, because I said we would do everything ourselves."

Wary, she followed up, "I'm assuming that means you, your friends, and your family?"

"Yup. You won't have to dirty your hands or break a nail fixing this place up. I will make it perfect for you."

"Are you guaranteeing that?"

"Count on it."

"Okay. If you say so."

"I figure we could put my tan leather couch there," he pointed to the far wall.

"No!" She held up her right hand like a police officer stopping traffic. "Stop right there. None of your condo furniture is coming into this house."

"Why?"

"Are you serious? It all looks like it's been through a war. I am not starting out with crappy stained furniture. We are buying new."

Realizing there was no point in arguing; he grasped her hand and pulled her along. "Okay. Let's look at the kitchen next."

"There's a musty odor in here," Sara noted.

"I'm sure once we air out the place, it will dissipate. I want you to see the master bedroom."

"Of course you do."

Joe led her to the master bedroom.

Sara gravitated to the window. The room had an unobstructed view of the lake. "Gorgeous view." Turning her focus back to the room, she pondered, "I just have to figure out what color it should be. This putrid beige has got to go."

He thought, *I should have known she would want to repaint everything.* "That will have to wait for another day. I made dinner reservations at Mama Lena's. If we don't leave soon, we will be late."

As she surveyed the space, she noted, "There's one thing you haven't mentioned."

"What's that?"

"How much did it cost?"

Sidestepping the question, he responded, "You're not supposed to ask how much a gift costs."

Hands on her hips, she said, "Try again. Can we afford this?"

Evading the question, he replied, "You know that Ma convinced the condo guy to let me out of my lease early."

Sensing his avoidance tactics, she uttered, "Uh huh."

"And I had money saved up."

Sara pressed, "And?"

Acquiescing, he admitted, "And Mom and Dad loaned us the money for the down payment."

Less than thrilled, Sara responded, "So we owe the bank *and* your parents? Great! And you still haven't told me how much."

Joe put his arm around her waist and kissed her nose. "Don't worry about that now. We are going to be happy here. That's all that matters."

Pushing away from him, she declared, "I'm not letting this drop."

Drawing her back in, he acknowledged, "I know you won't. For right now, can't we just go to dinner?" He kissed her forehead.

Sara agreed, "Okay."

CHAPTER 15

J OHN picked up Laura at six o'clock sharp. She wore a slinky black dress, pearls, and high heels. She was ready and waiting.

Dressed in a dark blue suit and a light blue shirt, he escorted her to his Mustang.

As he held the door for her, she complimented, "You look so handsome."

He smiled. "Thank you. You look gorgeous, as usual."

"Thank you."

After a few minutes, she realized they were driving toward John's house. "Did you forget something?"

"No. I hope you don't mind. I planned an intimate romantic evening. Just you and me. No one else. No distractions."

Thrilled with the idea of an intimate evening, she admitted, "That sounds wonderful."

He breathed a sigh of relief. "I was hoping you would agree."

"Honey, as long as I'm spending time with you, I don't care where we are or what we're doing."

He reached for her hand and squeezed. She squeezed back.

As they entered the house, John insisted, "Just make yourself comfortable."

"Okay." Laura kicked off her shoes and sat on the couch.

He busied himself lighting some candles. Then he produced a bouquet of red roses and presented them to her.

Her eyes lit up. She inhaled deeply. "They're beautiful! I love them! Thank you."

He sat next to her. "They're nothing compared to you."

A wave of exhilaration rushed through her body. "Oh, John." She wrapped her arms around his neck and kissed him.

He pushed back her hair and gazed into her eyes. "Do you know how exquisite you are?"

Laura felt the blood rush to her face.

John caressed Laura's cheek. "That's how I feel about you. I just don't know how to say it any other way. You are exquisite. You are radiant."

"Thank you." She continued to blush.

The feelings Laura felt for John were stronger than she had ever felt for any other man. And in that one moment, she prayed she was carrying his child. "I love you."

"I love you, sweetheart," he replied. "I've got such a special evening planned."

"Any time we spend together is special." She leaned toward him, looked into his eyes, and whispered, "Kiss me."

They kissed sweetly, tenderly. When they parted, she sighed happily.

Excited to unfold the evening's plans, John announced, "I should start cooking."

"Uh huh." She smiled at him. "Let me help you with dinner."

"No, Laura. You stay here and relax. I am going to take care of everything."

She leaned back into the comfort of a couch pillow. "All right. If you insist."

John went into the kitchen and pulled out the ingredients to make dinner. He placed a bottle of wine on the counter.

Thinking quickly, she asked, "Do you have any more of that sparkling cider we had the other night?"

Puzzled, he answered, "Yeah, but wine will go better with the food. And it will set the mood."

"Honey, the mood is already set. And I really would like that cider instead."

He acquiesced, "Okay." He exchanged the wine for the sparkling cider.

"Thank you."

"No problem. Whatever you want. I just want you to be happy."

She walked over to him. "I am, whenever I'm with you."

They embraced and kissed warmly.

Laura confessed, "I just want to kiss and hold you all night."

Pulling back, he agreed, "That sounds wonderful. But I have to feed you first."

Playfully, she grabbed his lapels and pulled him close. She gazed at him with bedroom eyes.

He fingered her pearls. "Baby, you drive me wild when you give me that look *and* wear pearls."

Batting her eyelashes, she flirted, "Sorry."

"No, you're not."

With an impish grin, she admitted, "You're right, I'm not." She leaned into him and sucked on his bottom lip.

He responded with a slow, sensual kiss that left Laura in a state of bliss.

"Are you sure we have to eat first?"

Kissing her hand, he said, "Yes."

Laura sighed. "Okay."

John exclaimed, "Music! That's what's missing. Music! How about some music?"

She laughed at his awkward transition. "I'd love some."

John pulled up a music app on his cell phone. Within moments, soft music played in the background.

The candle flames flickered.

Laura sat on a kitchen chair, sipped her cider, and watched him make dinner—pasta primavera and freshly baked bread.

Happy and content, Laura complimented, "Everything was wonderful. You are a fantastic cook."

John held her hand. "I learned a thing or two from my parents. Both of them cook."

Laura declared, "I'm stuffed."

"You haven't had dessert yet."

She leaned back in the chair. "Dessert? I don't know if I could eat another bite."

John tempted, "It's your favorite, crème brûlée."

Wishing she had eaten less pasta, she answered, "No way! You made me crème brûlée?"

He made light of it, "Of course. It was nothing."

"Nothing? I've tried to make it. I always screw it up."

He smirked. "Really, it was nothing."

"I can't believe you went to all that trouble. But I'm serious about being full. Can we eat it later?"

"Sure. Why don't we dance for a little while then?"

"You know I love dancing in your arms. The way you move drives me crazy."

Smugly, he replied, "I know." He got up from the table and extended his hand to her.

She accepted it as she joined him.

He led her through many slow, romantic songs. His hands held her close to him.

John felt her every breath and heartbeat. They moved as one, in perfect unison. No words were spoken. He caressed her face lovingly as he tenderly kissed her lips. They connected on every level.

Laura did not know if it was the cologne John wore, the dinner he had made, the flowers he had presented, or the possibility that she might be pregnant with his child, but she knew John was the man who would fulfill all of her dreams. She gazed longingly into his eyes.

John returned the loving look. He professed, "You complete me."

She felt her heart skip a beat. "You're such a romantic. Every time you say something like that, you turn me into complete mush."

They swayed in time with the music.

He took a deep breath. "I was going to do this later, but I can't wait." He paused. "Laura, the first time that we kissed, I was stunned. The second time we kissed, you captured my heart and my soul. I knew you were special—different. I love you more with each day that passes. You are my first thought when I wake up and my last thought before I go to bed. And I think about you all day and dream about you all night."

Laura smiled and thought, *Me too!*

"Laura, will you marry me?"

Jubilant, she threw her arms around him as she answered, "Yes! Of course I will marry you! Yes!"

As his lips touched hers, their electricity fused them together. The music flowed through them, transcending them to a higher, deeper level of passion. There was no frenzy, no frantic shedding of clothing. Instead, dancing in each other's arms, they glided right into the bedroom. They were as fluid as water as they kissed and caressed each other.

Candlelight bathed the room in a warm glow. They slowly undressed each other, in time with the music—an unchoreographed movement of souls.

As they transitioned to the bed, blanketed with rose petals, John plucked a long-stemmed rose from the bud vase on the nightstand.

Lying down next to her, he offered her the rose. The flickering light reflected off of the beautiful marquise cut engagement ring that was nestled in the center of its petals.

Gently, she removed the ring from its soft petal bed. "Oh my God, John! It's gorgeous! Please put it on me."

John slipped the ring on her finger. "Now, it's official."

She glanced down at the sparkling diamond and then back up into his eyes. "I can't wait to marry you, John."

They sealed their engagement with a passionate kiss that seamlessly eased into the intertwining of bodies.

John sucked on Laura's bottom lip. She moaned and tilted her head back. Unable to resist her exposed neck, he ravished it. Her vocal expressions became deeper and more throaty. The evocative sounds fueled John's erotic desires.

He gently brushed the discarded rose against her alabaster skin, pulling back slightly, admiring her. She was absolutely angelic.

Laura flushed in anticipation. She loved John so completely that she could not imagine her life without him. As her mind flooded with loving thoughts, she closed her eyes.

John's sweet, succulent lips found hers. In that moment, they shared a soulful, spiritual kiss.

Moved to his core, he brushed the rose against her cheek, down her neck, then around each breast and nipple like a feather. He brought the rose down the center of her torso, playfully circled her navel, and then brushed her lightly between her legs.

Feeling his warm breath between her legs, Laura moaned softly. She was in heaven. She spread her legs wider.

The sight of her wetness thrilled him. Despite wanting to drive deeply into her, instead, he bathed the rose in her wetness. Pushing the bloom against her, he drenched it in her juices. As she clutched the bedsheets, he spun the bloom in his fingers. The sensation caused her hips to leave the bed.

Laura exclaimed, "Oh, dear God!"

Delighted with her reaction, he dabbed the bloom again and again, as if trying to soak up every glistening drop of moisture.

Her rising and falling pelvis was too much for him to ignore any longer. He grabbed her hips and pulled her legs up onto his shoulders. His lips and tongue took over for the overworked rose.

Laura groaned loudly. It emanated from so deep within, it sounded animalistic. She grabbed John's head and held it in place.

John's every movement was so sensual, deliberate, and erotic. He desired this moment for her. He wanted her to lose control utterly and completely.

His tongue felt the spasms that would push her over into the state of ecstasy.

Laura bucked wildly. John brought his arm over and across her hips to hold her in place. Her back arched as she succumbed to the most ultimate of pleasures.

John buried his face in her, using his talented tongue to coax wave after wave of pure bliss. He reveled in doing this to her—for her. And he basked in the knowledge that she would always be his, from this day forward.

Laura collapsed from her joyful exhaustion and struggled to catch her breath. In this exquisite moment, she was deeply entranced and under John's titillating spell.

CHAPTER 16

After dinner at Mama Lena's Italian Restaurant, Joe and Sara returned to her house. A note from Anna rested on the counter.

Sara read it. "We just missed Anna. She went to the gym to work out. Then she booked a two-hour massage."

"I could go for a two-hour massage."

"I'm sure." She paused. "You know, Laura is over at John's. She won't be home at all tonight."

Joe slipped his arms around Sara. "Oh really?"

"Really."

Realizing their good fortune, Joe said, "That means we've got the place to ourselves. At least for a few hours."

"Uh huh."

Joe raised his eyebrows. "Are you thinking what I'm thinking?"

Sara smiled. "Since you surprised me today, I think I'll surprise you. I was going to do this on your birthday, but I think today is a better day."

"Really? What?"

"For me to know and you to find out!"

Joe grasped Sara's hand and attempted to lead her to her bedroom. Sara resisted.

Puzzled, he asked, "What's the problem?"

"There's no problem. Stay here. I have to get ready."

"Ready for what? I'm ready. You look like you're ready. What's the big deal?"

"Trust me."

He shrugged. "Okay."

Sara went into the kitchen and filled a glass with ice. As she disappeared into the hallway, she said, "I will call for you when I'm ready."

"Don't take too long."

"It will be worth the wait."

Joe turned on the television, sat on the mauve couch, put his feet up on the coffee table, and watched sports highlights.

After fifteen minutes, in a sing-songy voice, Sara called out, "Joe, I'm ready."

Joe did not need to be called twice. He turned off the television as he sprang from the couch.

Sara's bedroom door was open. Her desk chair was positioned between the doorway and the bed. Peppermint-scented candles illuminated the room.

"Hello? I'm here."

From the bathroom, Sara directed, "Sit in the chair."

Joe sat. His heart raced in anticipation. *This should be good.*

Within moments, Sara strutted through the door in black thigh high boots. Her long brown hair fell in loose, relaxed curls upon her shoulders and breasts. Black eyeliner outlined her bright blue eyes. And her full pouty lips glistened with a warm pink lip gloss. Her curves were accentuated by a black leather corset and matching thong.

Joe was speechless. His mouth hung agape. Overwhelmed, he tried to take in every inch of her. *Wow! She is so hot! That corset makes her breasts look huge. And those boots! God! Those boots!*

"Well?" Sara asked in a sultry tone.

Joe uttered, "Wow!"

I look hot, and I'm driving him crazy. Good!

Wanting to show his appreciation, Joe stood.

"I don't think so." Sara lifted her right foot and used it to push him back into the chair. "I said, 'Sit!'"

"Yes, ma'am." He felt adrenaline rush through his body.

Hands on her hips, Sara stated, "You have been a bad, bad boy."

"Yes! Yes, I have!"

Strutting around him, she posed the question, "What *am* I going to do with you?"

With gusto, he suggested, "Punish me! I need to be punished."

"You think so?" She leaned over his shoulders from behind, ran her hands down his chest, and bit his earlobe.

Insistent, he reiterated, "Yes. I need to be punished."

"I agree." She positioned herself in front of Joe and turned away from him. She leaned over, her hands on her thighs. Then she swayed her hips back and forth. She arched her back as she swayed.

Joe's eyes tracked Sara's ass as if it was a pendulum.

As she rolled her hips, Sara looked over her shoulder to gauge Joe's reaction.

Joe commented, "I like how this is going so far."

Sara placed her right index finger on his lips. "I didn't tell you that you could speak."

He mouthed, "Sorry." His hands grasped her hips.

"I didn't tell you that you could touch me either. Hands down. Hold the seat of the chair."

Joe complied readily, although the desire built within him.

Sara turned toward him and flipped her hair to give it a sexier, messed up look. With bedroom eyes, she slowly straddled him.

He kissed her breasts as they hovered in front of his face.

"Naughty boy!"

"Guilty as charged."

"Shhh!"

It took every ounce of strength Joe possessed not to stand up, throw her on the bed, and make mad, unbridled love to her.

He closed his eyes as she brushed her leather-bound chest against his face. But they flew open when she sat down and grinded on him.

She smiled at the mixed expressions of pleasure and sexual frustration on his face. "Let's move you to the bed."

"Thank you. It's about time." He breathed a sigh of relief, then wrapped his arms around her and kissed her.

She pushed him away. "Not yet," she scolded.

"I'm *dying* here."

"Too bad. Take off your shirt."

He did so.

She commanded, "Lie down on the bed."

Joe unbuttoned his pants.

"No. Keep your pants on. Button them back up."

"But …"

"Just do it!"

Exhaling loudly, he obliged. Ready, willing, and able, Joe spread out on the bed.

Sara obtained a package from her nightstand that was next to the glass of ice. The plastic made crinkling noises.

Curiosity piqued, Joe asked, "What's that?"

"Strawberry licorice whips."

"Ooooo! Are you going to whip me with them?"

She unwound the licorice strands. "No. I am tying you to the bed-posts."

"Either way, it's kinky. And I like it!" He scooted higher, closer to the headboard.

"Thought you would." Sara wrapped the licorice whips around each wrist and post. Then she straddled him again. She leaned over and whispered, "I hope you are enjoying yourself."

"I am, but I know how I would enjoy this more."

"Patience, Joe." She popped the button of his jeans and unzipped them.

He inhaled deeply.

Returning her attention to his neck, she kissed it. Then she kissed down his chest to his navel. There, she placed wet kisses in a line, right above the waistband of his underwear.

He squirmed. "Oh, come on! Have a heart."

"Aw, poor baby." She kissed his lips and ran her hands from his neck, down his muscular chest, to his taut abdomen. She lingered for a moment. Then she slipped her fingers between his underwear and skin.

He whimpered, "Oh, God!"

She felt all eight inches of his hardness. "Nice."

"I'll give you *nice*."

He groaned as she massaged him. His willpower waned.

Sara slowly removed his jeans. They ended up on the floor at the end of the bed. She tormented him for several minutes before pulling off his underwear. They suffered the same fate as the jeans.

Joe exhaled, "Thank you."

"Patience, Joe. Patience."

Before rejoining him on the bed, she plucked an ice cube out of the glass. She sucked on it as she mounted him.

Joe watched her pink lips and tongue doing glorious things to that ice cube. Reflexively, he licked his own lips.

Sara took the cube and slowly touched her neck with it. "It's so hot in here. I need to cool off."

Joe was mesmerized as the trickles of water flowed down her long neck to her firm breasts. All of this was just too much to take. The pent up desire overwhelmed him. With one jerking motion, he snapped the licorice whips that bound him to the bed.

He grabbed Sara by her corseted waist and flipped her over on her back.

Teasing, she asked, "Couldn't take it anymore?"

Hovering over her, on his hands and knees, he replied, "No. I'm in charge now. And you're going to get it good."

"Oh, really?"

His answer came in the form of a steamy, urgent kiss.

She melted more quickly than the ice cube. It was easy to get caught up in him.

Joe's fingers quickly unlaced the thong that stood between him and ecstasy. With a flick of his wrist, the thong flew. It hit their engagement picture on the dresser and hung precariously off one corner.

For a moment, Joe gazed at Sara like a hungry animal. She was sexy and sultry. "You are mine now."

She giggled. "I'm ready."

As Joe's hand moved lower and his fingers delved into her, he agreed, "Yes, you are."

Their lovemaking session was extraordinarily powerful. Climaxing together, she allowed him only moments of rest before coaxing him back to life.

Invigorated by Sara's raw insatiable needs, Joe powered on. However, eventually, he collapsed from sheer exhaustion, completely spent.

So wrapped up in their sexual escapades, the lovers failed to hear Anna return.

Although sex-starved Anna could not help but overhear their throes of passion. She found a pair of ear plugs and wore them to bed. She would be glad when they got married and lived in their own place.

Around sunrise the next morning, Joe awakened. He gazed at his lover. *I don't deserve you.*

Sara slept peacefully.

In days, we will finally be married. We'll be together forever. Waking up with you by my side every morning will be a dream come true.

Parted slightly, Sara's full lips were irresistible. He felt compelled to kiss them. As he did so, she awoke.

She stretched and yawned. "Did I oversleep?"

"No," he replied. Not able to control himself, he brushed his hand across her breasts.

She perked up. "Still want more?"

He confessed, "I can never get enough of you."

She rolled toward him. "Me either. But I have morning breath."

"Do I look like I care about morning breath?"

She felt his hardness pressed against her. "No, I guess not."

Joe grabbed her ass. His need was urgent. He pulled her on top of him.

Sara's morning urges were as primal as Joe's. No foreplay was needed. As he slid inside her, she groaned. That excited him even more. He held her hips as she grinded, knowing he was massaging her G spot. He knew those orgasms were the most powerful for her. And he wanted to push her right over the edge. Sara's moans spoke to him. She was close.

Then he felt the familiar tightening of muscles. This was it.

With unfettered abandon, Sara rode Joe hard, bearing down as she came. He loved watching her lose control. Her hair was messy and sexy, her pale skin flushed. He loved that she kept her eyes closed throughout, heightening her other senses.

Admiring such a beautiful sight, he could not hold his orgasm any longer. He exploded into her.

Thrilled to feel his eruption, she clenched and milked him until he was utterly spent.

The energy expended as they climaxed was palpable.

Out of breath, Joe confessed, "Wow! That was amazing."

Glistening with sweat, Sara agreed, "Wow is right! And yes, it was."

CHAPTER 17

SIX team members suited up for their late night operation. They were dressed completely in black, equipped with body armor, night vision video cameras, Tasers, tear gas, and firearms with extra magazines. Lee stayed behind to monitor communications.

They positioned themselves at the tree line near the front of the house. The narrow gravel road separated them from the structure. They were hidden by the brush and foliage. Turning their cameras to record mode, they waited and watched. Staying sharp was vital to any mission.

They each went through audio and visual checks. They were ready.

Sully asked, "Lee? Do you have eyes in the sky?"

"Yes. There are six heat signatures in the house. Four on the main level, clustered together in the back of the house. Two on the upper level. Separate rooms, on either end of the house."

"Roger."

The team split off in pairs and covered the three exits—the front door, the back door, and the garage.

Sully gave the signal. They kicked in the doors simultaneously and breached the house.

The two men that had served as perimeter sentinels jumped up, weapons aimed at the team.

Al Fuentes scrambled under the kitchen table for cover. "Don't shoot! I'm unarmed."

Esmeralda Fuentes sat at the far end of the table. She did not flinch. The disdain she felt for her son's actions was evident on her face.

Sully ordered, "Drop your weapons!"

The older tattooed sentinel replied, "No chance in hell, old man!"

"I'm not going to tell you again. Drop your weapons!"

The sentinels' answers came in the form of gunfire. Their aim was accurate. However, the bulletproof vests worn by all team members protected them from harm.

Spaulding and Sully fired back at the assailants with deadly force. Both hostiles were mortally wounded.

Throughout the exchange, Esmeralda sat stoically.

Al, on the other hand, cowered under the kitchen table.

Pounding on the table, Tony directed, "You can come out now, Fuentes. Slowly. Hands behind your head."

Al Fuentes crawled out from his hiding place. He lied, "Those men are the culprits. My mother and I are innocent. We came by to check on the renovations to the house. We found them here. They were holding us hostage."

Tony ensured the zip ties were tight around Al's wrists. "Save your breath. We're not buying it."

Georgopoulos secured Esmeralda before getting her on her feet. "Do you have anything to say for yourself?"

Esmeralda remained silent.

Spaulding and Sully cleared the rest of the main floor. Repeatedly, they barked, "Clear."

After the main floor was secured, White and Ashby headed up the stairs, guns at the ready. They knew two people were on that level. Although the odds were that they were captives, the team never assumed anything.

The door to the first room was slightly ajar. A pregnant girl crouched in the corner. She was shackled to the bed by one ankle. White recognized Tina Robb from the pictures of Sabrina's missing friends.

White approached the girl, reassuring her, "Tina, you're safe now. We've come to take you home."

Tina cried, "Thank you!"

They helped her stand and freed her from the leg restraint.

The team discovered Amber Vaughn in the same predicament at the other end of the hallway. They freed her as well.

In the kitchen, Al Fuentes reiterated, "My mother and I were just checking on the progress of the house. I was negotiating for our lives when you arrived. We had no idea what was going on."

Tony maintained, "Again, no one's buying what you're selling, Fuentes."

Recognizing Tony and Dee, Al smiled. "So, it appears the antique business is more of a hobby then, as this is your real job, Anthony."

Tony refused to acknowledge him.

Turning his attention to Dee, Al said, "I know who Mr. Lazaro is, but you, my dear, remain a mystery. If I decided to send you flowers to thank you for saving us, to whom shall I address the card?"

Dee's nostrils flared. She did not dignify his remark with an answer.

Enjoying himself, Al continued, "You can't believe I had anything to do with this. I'm an upstanding citizen, a pillar of the community. My mother is a modest hotel owner and loving matriarch."

Annoyed, Dee replied, "You were offering us a baby in days or weeks. I'd say you're fingerprints are all over this."

"Circumstantial. We were at the wrong place at the wrong time. You could have asked the gunmen, but you killed them."

Georgopoulos remarked, "Convenient for you."

"If you don't believe me, ask the girls. They'll tell you that we had nothing to do with any of this."

Tony and Dee hauled off Al and Esmeralda before the girls were led downstairs. There was no reason to inflict further emotional trauma on them.

The girls were thoroughly examined at the hospital. As a precaution, they were required to stay overnight.

In the morning, from their hospital beds, the teens identified the two dead men as their captors. Both girls relayed the same story—word for word. Even to an untrained bystander, their statements were obviously well-rehearsed.

They denied that Al Fuentes and his mother had anything to do with their kidnappings. The fathers of their babies were boys they met at a college party. They did not know the boys' names.

The only portions of their testimonies that rang true were that they were thrilled to be free and with their families again.

Down at the jail, Al Fuentes continued to claim his innocence. Esmeralda refused to speak, other than to ask for representation. They were booked while they waited for their lawyers.

Leaving the station, Tony said to Dee, "What a scum bag. I can't believe he claimed to be investigating the lack of progress on the house. He blamed the dead guys, who coincidentally happened to be his third cousins."

Sarcastically, Dee added, "Because of all the things those guys could have chosen to do, trafficking babies was the best fit. Not. They seemed more like drug runners to me."

"Your powers of deduction are dead on. I pulled their rap sheets. Aside from various assault charges, they had a list of drug charges a mile long. But since they're dead, they're easy patsies."

"We know it was Fuentes. We just have to prove it."

Tony shrugged. "The girls aren't talking, and they've been reunited with their families. So, case closed."

Defiant, Dee argued, "Not in my book. And how about that mother? She doesn't talk at all. Whose mother stays completely silent?"

Shaking his head, he said, "I have no experience with that one. But technically, our part in the case is over."

"We can follow up on it off the books."

He tormented, "I just can't get rid of you, can I? I know you really enjoyed being married to me."

Facetiously, Dee said, "Oh yeah, that was the best part."

He jabbed back, "Being married to you was like living in paradise, sweetheart."

"Uh huh, especially since I made you sleep in the chair."

He rubbed his neck. "Uh huh. Thanks again for that."

Dee laughed.

He pulled into the parking lot of the apartment complex. "Here you are."

"Thanks for the ride."

"My pleasure."

Tony released the trunk and pulled out her luggage. "Let me help you with these."

Dee argued, "I can do it myself."

"It's not a problem."

"Fine. Suit yourself."

He hoisted a bag on his shoulder as they wheeled the other pieces up the sidewalk.

Once inside, he asked, "Where do you want these?"

"You can just leave them here in the hall."

He followed her directions. "Okay."

"Thanks."

"You're welcome." As Tony turned to leave, his cell phone rang. It was Sully's ringtone. He answered, "Yeah?"

"Fuentes and his mother made bail."

"You gotta be kidding me."

"No. He already knows your real identity. It's a matter of time before he discovers Georgie's. Take precautionary measures. Leave town."

"Can't. But thanks for the heads-up."

As Tony hung up the phone, Dee asked, "What?"

"Fuentes and his mother made bail. So, I'm not leaving you alone."

"I'll be fine."

Tony argued, "Our cover was compromised. He knows my name. He'll know yours soon. For the time being, I'm sticking to you like glue."

"Wonderful."

"I know you're not going to like this, but you're going to have to come with me today to my brother's bridal shower."

She gave him the deer in the headlights look. Meeting his family had not been on the day's agenda. "Hell no!"

He insisted, "You really don't have a choice."

"Meet your family? You've got to be kidding."

"No. I'm not. We're stuck together."

"You're crazy."

Looking at the time, he noted, "We don't have time to argue."

"I don't know details that I should know if we were dating. It's one thing to pass as a couple in front of strangers. It's entirely different in front of family. For instance, we've only kissed a few times as part of our cover. It would have to look natural."

"We could fix that pretty easily. We do have a certain kind of chemistry."

"I don't know what kind of food you like or music you like. And then there's sex. For all I know, you want a 'wham-bam-thank you-ma'am' thing in a woman. That's not the kind of woman you bring home to meet your mother."

Noting this was an odd comment, he answered, "Not by a long shot. But maybe that's *your* thing."

"Why would you say that?"

Rubbing his forehead, he replied, "Because of the way you rode me in the hotel and just walked away like nothing happened."

She glared at him for mentioning the incident again.

Aware he touched a nerve, he said, "Dee, I'm a romantic. Think about everything I did all weekend. You can talk about those things. And how I do romantic things for you all the time. It's the exact opposite of the 'wham-bam' thing."

"I still think it's a bad idea."

"Good God, woman! Why?"

"Maybe they won't like me."

Incredulously, he asked, "Why do you care? We're not really dating."

"Oh, right."

He threatened, "Don't make me handcuff you."

Assuming a protective stance, she replied, "You wouldn't dare!"

"Watch me. We're going to be late."

To prove it was not an idle threat, he produced his handcuffs and swung them in front of her like a pendulum.

She pushed them away. "You're relentless! I'll go! I'll go! But if it's a disaster, it's your fault."

"I'll take full responsibility."

"I'm just not a bridal shower kind of girl."

"With the right guy, you might be."

She reluctantly admitted to herself, *You may be right*.

Glancing at the time, he stressed, "We'd better get going. Ma will kill me if I'm late."

After being released from jail, Al and Esmeralda returned to the hotel. In her private parlor, they discussed their predicament.

Esmeralda questioned, "So, you're going to make all of this go away?"

He leaned back in his chair and put his feet up on the coffee table. "Yes, everything is circumstantial. The girls didn't give us up. They identified Raul and Rico as their captors. We're off the hook."

Disgusted, Esmeralda knocked his feet off the table. "You're too cocky. That's when you make mistakes."

Brushing off her concerns, he disagreed, "We're clean. Trust me."

Esmeralda warned, "You need to tie up loose ends."

Al replied, "The girls gave their statements. And I assure you Sabrina won't say a word. I have her under my thumb."

Wary, she said, "I wouldn't be so sure of that."

"I can keep her in line. Don't worry."

"Your cousins died and took the rap for your filthy business. You owe their families."

"I'll take care of the families. Don't worry."

She shook her head. "I have to worry with you. You're impulsive and irresponsible. I'm tired of cleaning up your messes. This is it! Do you hear me?"

"Yes, Mother."

Aggressively, she threatened, "No more of this disgusting behavior, or I'll take matters into my own hands. Am I making myself clear?"

"Crystal."

CHAPTER 18

MITA awoke to the smell of bacon, eggs, and homemade waffles. For a minute, she forgot where she was staying. She glanced over at Flora's bed. It was empty, and the bedroom door was ajar.

She resigned herself to the fact that she would not fall back to sleep. So, she kicked off the sheets, stretched, and shuffled down the hallway to the kitchen.

Walking directly to the coffee maker, she poured herself a cup of coffee.

Helen greeted her, "Good morning, Mita. How did you sleep?"

Mita had slept surprisingly well. But she would not admit it. Instead, she grunted.

"I see you're still a cheerful morning person."

Mita ignored the comment and sat at the other end of the table.

Flora arranged the food on her plate to look like a face. The eggs were eyes, the bacon became hair, and she cut up the waffles into tiny pieces to serve as teeth.

Helen smiled at Flora's creativity.

Mita did not notice. She drank her black coffee while scanning the local newspaper's Classified section.

"Do you have a plan for today?" Helen asked her daughter.

Without looking up, Mita answered, "You're looking at it."

Helen joined them at the table. "In that case, you are both coming with me to church."

Mita argued, "No, I'm not."

Helen sipped her orange juice. "This isn't up for debate. You're going."

With an annoyed look, she proclaimed, "I don't do church."

Not to be deterred by her daughter's bad attitude, Helen retorted, "You are starting a new life. And it includes church."

Recalcitrant, Mita protested, "No."

"As long as you're living under my roof, you're going to church."

Pushing back from the table, Mita asked, "Are you seriously pulling that shit on me?"

Cutting her waffle into bite-sized pieces, Helen calmly replied, "Language, Mita. Yes. Deal with it."

Flora's fork held a piece of waffle dripping with syrup. Innocently, she interrupted, "Can I wear my favorite blue dress?"

Smiling, Helen replied, "Of course you may, Flora. Finish up your breakfast, and then you can get dressed."

Chewing, Flora celebrated, "Goody! I love my blue dress."

Helen ordered, "Mita, deal with it. We're leaving in thirty minutes."

They attended Mass at St. Peter's Catholic Church, the predominant Catholic Church in the town of Clear Brook. The church had established itself as an educational powerhouse from elementary school level to college university level.

The church was situated on the corner of Main Street and Third Avenue. A large parking lot separated the church from the mission. The mission strived to provide vital services to the entire community. The elementary school and high school resided on Third Avenue, across from the church. The university campus stretched across five city blocks and was located on Seventh Avenue.

Flora insisted they sit in the front of the church. She wanted to get a better look at the statues and stained glass windows.

After Mass was over, Helen introduced Mita and Flora to Father Francis, the church's pastor.

"Mita, this is Father Francis. He baptized you."

Mita said, "Hi."

Father Francis replied, "I'm so glad that you've come back to us after all of these years."

Helen nudged Flora forward. "And this is my granddaughter, Flora."

With a big smile, he said, "Nice to meet you, Flora."

Flora smiled back. "Nice to meet you."

Father Francis addressed Mita, "We have several volunteer opportunities over at the mission. It would be a marvelous way for you to meet people in the community. And you would be helping the less fortunate in the process."

Brushing the priest off, she remarked, "I need to find a paying job."

In a sympathetic tone, he replied, "I understand. But you could volunteer in your spare time. We all should give back in some small way."

Annoyed with his persistence, she answered, "I'll think about it."

Making excuses for her daughter, Helen said, "She's always been shy. It was like pulling teeth to get her to join things as a child. But I'm sure once she's been here for a little while, she'll feel right at home and join in. Won't you, Mita?"

Unenthusiastically, she agreed, "Sure."

Focusing on the angelic child, Father Francis inquired, "Is Flora enrolled in school yet? We have a wonderful program here."

Bored, Mita replied, "No. We just got here. I haven't thought about it."

Father Francis assured her, "The school year is barely under way. She could catch up quite easily."

Flora piped up, "I already know my numbers and letters, and I can read too!"

Smiling, Father Francis said, "That's wonderful, Flora. You're quite precocious, aren't you?"

Flora beamed and nodded, despite not knowing what he meant. She assumed it was a compliment.

Helen answered, "Yes, she is. We are proud of her. Aren't we, Mita?"

Wearing a disingenuous smile, Mita agreed half-heartedly, "Yes. Very proud."

Father Francis informed them, "The number for the school office is in the bulletin. Just call and make an appointment to complete the enrollment paperwork."

Helen responded, "Thank you, Father. We'll do that."

"Excellent. We'll see you soon then. Have a blessed day."

"Thank you. You too, Father."

On the drive home, Mita pretended to read the bulletin to avoid talking with her mother.

Helen admonished her daughter, "Would it kill you to be nice to people? I mean really, Mita. He's a priest for Christ's sake."

Mita whined, "I didn't want to be there in the first place. You dragged me there."

"Stop acting like a five-year-old."

Furrowing her brow, Flora questioned, "What's wrong with being five? I'm five."

Helen reassured her, "You're a good girl, Flora. I was just trying to tell your mother to act her own age."

Flora replied, "Oh."

Mita complained, "Can you quit nagging me for five damn minutes? Let me read this stupid bulletin in peace."

Pointing out the obvious, Helen said, "Like you care about what's in the bulletin. You can't avoid talking to me forever."

Mita held the bulletin up between them. "But I can sure as hell try."

Helen shook her head in disgust.

The last page contained the engagement and wedding announcements. One of the pictures caught Mita's eye.

Helen proposed, "I was thinking we could all go to the lake this afternoon."

From the backseat, Flora excitedly asked, "A lake? Is it big? Is it deep? Are there fish in it? Are there sharks? Can I go swimming?"

Before Helen could answer the myriad of questions, Mita said, "We're not going to the lake."

Flora pouted, "But why?"

Mita slapped the bulletin down on the seat. "Because I said so."

Unsure of her daughter's objections to the lake, Helen said, "It's a little cool out for a swim, Flora. But we could take a boat ride another day if you would like."

"A boat ride? I've never been on a boat before! Promise?" Flora asked.

Helen replied, "Yes, I promise."

Clapping, Flora cheered, "Yay!"

Helen inquired, "So what are we going to do today?"

Mita corrected, "*We* aren't doing anything. Flora and I are going sightseeing."

Surprised, but encouraged, Helen suggested, "I can drive you around."

Mita declined the offer, "No. We'll do fine on our own."

"But you don't have a New York State driver's license or a car. And

I'm not giving you mine."

Agitated, Mita said, "Well, of course not. Wouldn't want you to be put out. We'll take a cab."

Attempting to reason with her daughter, Helen continued, "That's a huge waste of money. I can show you around."

"No."

Puzzled, Helen said, "You're being ridiculous."

Her anger building by the second, Mita demanded, "Get off me!"

Recognizing the argument would escalate even further without a rational resolution, Helen backed down. Turning into the apartment complex parking lot, she said, "Fine. Suit yourself."

Mita searched for some names and addresses on her phone. When the cab arrived, Mita yelled, "Flora! We're leaving."

Flora appeared within seconds, clapping her hands excitedly. "Where are we going?"

"It'll be a surprise."

Helen asked, "Will you be home for dinner?"

Mita replied, "Maybe."

Helen hugged and kissed Flora.

Flora cheerily chirped, "Bye, Nana."

"Good-bye, honey."

Addressing Mita, Helen said, "Call or text me later."

"Uh huh."

Helen wished them well, "Have a good time."

Mita ignored her.

Flora said, "Thank you, Nana. See you later."

As they departed, Helen wondered what her daughter had planned. She had hoped a change of scenery would improve the girl's mood.

That remained to be seen.

Mita and Flora arrived at the first address. She paid the driver and approached the condominium door. Mita knocked. A large cranky woman answered, "What? You from the cable company? I've been waiting for you people for hours. I've been without cable since I moved in last night. Last tenant cut everything off. Bastard."

Flatly, Mita stated, "I'm not from the cable company. I've got the wrong place."

Disgusted, the woman replied, "Well, if you see that cable guy, send him here."

Strike one.

Luckily, the taxi driver was checking his messages on his cell phone and had not left yet. Mita opened the rear door and pushed Flora in.

The driver commented, "That was quick. Where to now?"

Mita announced, "St. Peter's University."

The driver informed her, "The main academic building is on Seventh Avenue. The campus itself stretches five city blocks. Which building do you need?"

"I don't know."

"Well, I can drop you off at the main academic building. That's where I drop most people."

"Fine."

As they rounded the next corner, Mita saw a liquor store. "Driver, pull over. I want to stop here first."

When it was safe to do so, the taxi driver parked in front of the liquor store.

Mita instructed, "Flora, stay here. I'll be right out."

He warned, "Lady, you can't leave your kid unattended."

She opened the door. "You're here, aren't you?"

"I'm just a cab driver."

"You're an adult. I'll just be a minute." Mita slammed the door before the driver could respond.

Uncomfortable, the driver glanced back at Flora. "So, how old are you?"

Flora held up her hand, fingers splayed. "Five."

"Wow, five! That's great."

She volunteered, "I know all of my numbers and letters. I can even read too."

"I'm impressed."

Mita did not have to go far to locate a vodka display. It contained miniature bottles, most commonly found in hotel rooms and on airplanes. They would also be easily concealed in a purse.

She placed eight bottles on the counter.

The clerk recommended, "It's cheaper if you buy a bigger bottle."

Biting the clerk's head off, Mita shouted, "Do I tell you what to do? Maybe it's easier for me to carry around small bottles. Did you ever think of that?"

The clerk was used to dealing with drunks and difficult customers. So he ignored her rant and asked for her identification.

"You think I look under twenty-one?"

"Lady, I have to proof everybody. No matter what. You could be one of those undercover cops."

She laughed hysterically. "Me? A cop? Not a snowball's chance in hell, kid." She showed him her passport since she did not have a driver's license.

"No driver's license?"

"You asked for ID, I'm showing you ID."

He held his hands up, "Okay, chill out, lady."

While he entered the information into the computer, she twisted off the top of one of the bottles and guzzled the contents.

He exclaimed, "Lady! You can't do that! You haven't even paid for them yet."

Pulling out some cash, she slapped it on the counter. Placing the empty bottle next to it, she said, "I just did."

As he rang up the sale, she twisted the top off a second bottle and emptied it.

Annoyed that she ignored his previous objection, he asked, "You need a bag? Or are you going to drink them all here?"

She opened her purse and rested it against the edge of the counter. With one sweeping motion, she corralled them. And one by one, they fell into the open purse. "I got it. Thanks."

When they arrived at the campus, the driver announced, "St. Peter's University."

Flora peered out the window. "Oh! It's really, really big."

"Yeah," Mita agreed, pulling out her wallet. She had exchanged her currency before the trip, but after forking over cash at the liquor store, she decided to switch to plastic. She attempted to hand the driver her card.

The driver commented, "You do it yourself. The machine back there takes credit and debit."

"Fantastic."

"Just slide the card through the reader in front of you." He turned to face her. "You meeting someone?"

Sliding her card, Mita replied, in a standoffish manner, "It's none of your damn business."

"You're right. But it's Sunday. So, whoever you're looking for might not be here."

Mita thought about it.

The cabbie turned back around.

She asked, "Can you wait?"

"Yeah, but I charge even if I'm not moving."

Not having another choice, she responded, "I'll pay. Stay."

"It's your dollar."

Mita opened the curbside door and exited the taxi. Flora followed close behind. Mita marched up the steps.

Flora soaked in her surroundings. She proclaimed, "When I'm grown up, I want to go to a school just like this."

"If we play our cards right, kid, you'll do exactly that."

Mita and Flora entered the building. Mita scanned the directory. She found the office number for which she was searching. She led Flora through the main corridor. They stopped once they reached Room Number 180.

Mita tried the doorknob. The door was locked. She peered into the window. Darkness cloaked the room.

A female student stopped. A wadded up ball of paper hit the girl in the side of the head. She turned. "You dork!" she shouted after the running male student. Addressing Mita, she informed her, "Professors aren't in on Sundays."

"Thanks."

Strike two.

As they walked back down the hall, Flora was mesmerized with all of the art on the walls.

Taking advantage of the situation, Mita removed one of the bottles from her purse. She gulped down the vodka and tossed the empty bottle in a nearby trash can. It clanged against the metal.

Startled by the noise, Flora asked, "What was that Mama?"

Mita lied, "Nothing. Just threw out a medicine bottle."

Concerned, Flora inquired, "Are you sick?"

"No. I'm fine. Keep walking."

As they exited the building, Mita lit a cigarette.

Flora ran to the taxi and jumped in while waiting for her mother to finish smoking.

With her back to the taxi, Mita downed another bottle of vodka. With no trash can available, she shoved it back into her purse. Then she flicked the cigarette butt on the ground, stepped on it, and exhaled as she opened the taxi door.

When she closed the door, the driver asked, "Find who you were looking for?"

"No."

"Where to now?"

CHAPTER 19

ROSE Lazaro scurried around the dining room table, straightening the lace tablecloth. Everything had to be perfect for her son's and future daughter-in-law's bridal shower.

Rose was a dynamo and a force to be reckoned with, despite standing only five feet, two inches tall. Her short black hair was always styled to perfection. Her head tilted from side to side as her blue-green eyes examined the fabric for any ripples.

Joe had just finished adding the extra leaves to the table. He stood in the doorway, awaiting additional instructions. During the lull, Joe received a text from his older brother, Tony. He relayed the message to his mother, "Tony says he's running late, but he'll be here shortly. He says he has a surprise for you."

Throwing up her hands, she complained, "Of all days not to be here! And to be late! I told him to postpone that silly trip of his. I knew this would happen. Doesn't he know how important today is? I've got a slew of people coming, and he's not here to help. I can't believe this. Of all days! And a surprise? I don't need any surprises today. What is he thinking?"

Attempting to put his mother at ease, Joe said, "Ma, it's okay. Dad and I have got it covered for now. He'll be here soon."

Pulling two large serving platters from the china hutch, she ordered, "Take these to the kitchen."

Joe relieved his mother of the china.

She continued, "Anthony should be here already. When he gets home, I'm going to give him a piece of my mind!"

Joe placed the platters on the counter. "Until then, what do you need us to do?"

Joining him in the kitchen, Rose answered, "Bring up the chairs from the basement and arrange them nicely in the living room."

"Got it."

Joe's father, Salvatore, a sturdy man, standing five feet, eight inches tall, entered the kitchen. "Reporting for duty."

"Since Anthony isn't here, we're short-handed. I've got Joey bringing up the chairs from the basement."

Sal acknowledged, "I'll help him finish that, then we'll set up the backyard."

"Okay, fine."

Sal descended into the basement. He and Joe hauled up the folding chairs, four at a time.

In the kitchen, Rose's sister, Carm, and their mother, Marie, were busy with food preparation.

Carm and Rose bore striking resemblances to their mother. The only differences were their ages and heights. Marie was the shortest, standing just under five feet tall. Carm was the tallest at five feet, five inches.

Rose looked at her watch. "The guests will be here soon. How are we doing?"

Carm reassured her, "We're in good shape. Don't worry."

"I'd worry less if Anthony was here to help."

On cue, the door opened. Anthony announced, "I'm home."

Hands planted firmly on her hips, Rose criticized, "Well, it's about time!"

Tony apologized, "Sorry I'm late, Ma."

She scolded, "You know how important today is for your brother. I can't believe you're so late. What do you have to say for yourself?"

Tony moved aside.

Dee emerged from behind him.

Tony introduced her, "Ma, I'd like you to meet Dee."

For a brief moment, Rose stood speechless.

Carm and Marie stopped working and looked up. They could not believe their eyes and ears.

Dee approached Rose. "Hello, Mrs. Lazaro. It's a pleasure to meet you."

Stunned, but thrilled, Rose hugged and welcomed Dee warmly. "The pleasure is all mine."

Carm whispered to Marie, "Oh my God, Anthony brought a girl home."

Marie replied in a normal voice, "Thank God. I thought he was gay."

Everyone turned to look at Marie.

Brushing it off, Marie responded, "What? There's nothing wrong with being gay. But this is the first time he's brought home a girl."

Dee looked at Tony. She asked incredulously, "I'm the first girl you've ever brought home?"

Tony confirmed, "Yes."

Astonished, Dee murmured, "Oh, God."

Tony said, "Aunt Carm, Grandma, this is Dee."

Marie remarked, "We heard." She stood and hugged Dee. "Very nice to meet you."

Carm hugged her as well. "Nice to meet you."

"Nice to meet you both."

Tony asked, "Want anything to drink?"

Dee thought, *Something really strong.* But instead, she replied, "Water's fine."

Amazed to see her son doting on a woman, Rose was overjoyed to see this new side of him.

Rose offered Dee a chair, "Dee, come sit. We'll talk while we work."

Dee sat and crossed her legs.

Rose ordered, "Anthony, get those chairs they're bringing up and set them up in the living room."

Tony replied, "Okay, Ma." He turned to Dee, "Are you going to be okay?"

Dee plastered on a smile. "I'll be fine. You better do what your mother says."

He kissed her on the cheek. "Okay."

Rose yelled down the cellar stairs, "Sal!"

Sal appeared at the bottom of the staircase. He craned his neck up to meet her gaze.

"Joey can carry up the rest of the chairs. I need you to set up for bocce in the backyard. After that, you can take care of the outside tables and chairs."

He answered, "Yes, dear. I'll grab one last load. No sense coming up empty-handed."

She turned and called out, "Anthony!"

Tony leaned into the kitchen. "Yeah, Ma?"

"When you are done inside, help your father set up the outside tables and chairs."

"Okay, Ma."

Dee offered, "I can help them set up."

All three women answered, "No."

Dee anticipated the reaction would have been the same at her mother's house, but figured it was worth a try.

Patting Dee, Rose said, "Let the men do the lifting. We're just getting acquainted."

"Can I help with the food then? I feel like I should be doing something."

Pleased with the offer, Rose declined, "No, you're a guest. Just sit there and relax."

Marie inquired, "So, how did the two of you meet?"

Dee thought quickly. "We met through online dating."

Rose questioned, "Really? I didn't realize Anthony was doing that. He doesn't spend a lot of time on the computer."

Dee responded, "You can do it from your cell phone too."

Carm asked, "Are you from here?"

"I grew up in Rochester."

Marie asked, "Are you Italian?"

"I'm Greek."

Marie commented, "Eh, close enough."

Dee grinned.

Rose pried, "You get along well with your mother?"

"Yes, and with my whole family. We have dinner every Sunday at my grandmother's house."

Marie pointed out, "Today is Sunday. And you're here with us."

"Yes, I know. We'll stop by afterward."

Encouraged, Rose asked, "So you're introducing Anthony to your family during Sunday dinner?"

Keeping up the charade, Dee responded, "Yes."

This news pleased Rose. "That's wonderful!"

Sal ambled up the stairs with his last load of chairs. After leaning them against a wall, he announced, "I'm headed out to set up for bocce."

Rose stopped him. "Hold on a minute, Sal."

Sal pulled a handkerchief out of his back pocket and wiped the sweat off his brow.

Excitedly, Rose introduced Dee, "This is Dee, Anthony's girlfriend."

Questioning what he heard, "Anthony's what?"

Slowly, Rose repeated, "Girlfriend."

Astonished, he asked, "Girlfriend? He brought home a girl?"

Rose gestured with her eyes and head. "Yes. This is Dee."

Stunned, he extended his hand. "Nice to meet you, Dee."

"Nice to meet you, Mr. Lazaro."

Joe carried up the last remaining chairs. He saw Dee and hesitated. He looked at her puzzled, unsure how to react.

Dee smiled and took the lead. "Hi, I'm Dee."

"Hi, I'm Joe."

Rose finished the introduction, "Joey, this is Anthony's girlfriend."

Pretending they had not already met, Joe said, "Wow! Hey, nice to meet you."

Dee returned the pleasantry, "Nice to meet you. Congratulations, by the way."

"Thanks."

Sal stood transfixed, not believing his eyes. Hell was freezing over. His eldest son finally had a girlfriend.

Rose broke the silence, "Okay, then. Move it out. There's a lot of work to be done."

Sal and Joe walked out together.

Sal asked, "Did you know he had a girlfriend?"

Joe replied, "No."

"I wonder what she does for a living."

Joe was dying to blurt out the truth, *She's an undercover spy.* Instead, he responded, "I'm sure Ma will badger it out of her.

Sal chuckled in agreement. "She's a really pretty girl."

"Yup. She is."

Carm mixed the punch in an extra-large punchbowl, while Marie finished up with the cold cut and cheese trays.

Rose asked, "What's left to be done?"

As she rolled slices of capicola, Marie replied, "I'm almost done with the cold cuts. The potato salad and macaroni salad need to be made. The potatoes should be cool enough now."

Tony traversed through the kitchen over to Dee. "How's it going?"

She answered, "Great."

He leaned over and kissed her cheek.

She whispered, "I think a firing squad might be less painful."

He laughed.

She patted his back. "Go ahead, laugh it up. You're meeting my family tonight."

"Huh?"

"A nice, big Greek Sunday dinner. I was just telling them about it."

"Sounds delicious!"

He kissed Dee's cheek again before sneaking a few pieces of salami off of the tray his grandmother prepared.

Marie slapped his hand. "Your hands are filthy! Don't touch the food with those hands. And that's all of the salami we have. Now, I'll have to add more ham."

With his mouth full, he apologized, "Sorry. We were really busy earlier and didn't have a chance to eat."

Rose tilted her head slightly. "I see."

He winked at Dee.

Dee's initial instinct was to hit him. But she thought better of it.

Rose admonished him, "Hands off of the food, Anthony. It's for the party guests."

Dee knew that although these women might not be packing heat, in a blink of an eye, a rolling pin could suffice as an effective weapon.

Using her hands in a shooing motion, Rose directed, "Get out there. Help your father and brother. And don't come back in until everything's done."

He kissed the top of her head. "Yes, Ma."

While their father set up for bocce, Joe asked Tony, "So, she's your girlfriend now?"

Tony replied, "For today, yes. Long story."

Joe shook his head. "I have a feeling everything with you is a long story."

They placed a table in the grass and began to arrange the chairs around it.

Observing them from the kitchen window, Rose yelled, "The tables don't go there. That's too close to the bocce court. Someone could get hurt. Move them farther over." She waved her hands in the direction they should follow.

Joe waved back. "Yes, Ma."

Tony said to his brother, "On three."

Joe nodded. "One, two, three."

They moved the first table closer to the fence line.

Joe shouted, "Here?"

Pointing, Rose yelled back, "No! No! No! Put them in the shade. Over there! We are not going to be responsible for causing someone to get skin cancer."

Rose spoke to Carm and Marie, "Nobody wants to sit in the sun anymore. Am I right?"

The women agreed.

Rose watched from the window with her hands on her hips. "What are they thinking?"

To Dee, this kitchen felt just like home.

After setting up for bocce, Sal joined his sons.

Joe whispered to his father, "We'll end up moving these ten times before it's over."

Sal smirked as they moved the table into the shade. They looked in Rose's direction for approval.

Sal shouted, "How's this?"

With a wave of her hand, she approved, "Good. Carry on."

Sal asked Tony, "So, this girl you brought home, she's not pregnant is she?"

Flabbergasted, Tony responded, "Dad! Come on! That's the first question you ask?"

Sal looked his son in the eye. "Anthony, this is the first girl you've ever brought home. So, yes, it's the first thing that came to mind."

"No. She's not pregnant."

"Good. So is she the one?"

Pondering the question, he answered truthfully, "I really think she might be, Dad."

"Good. Glad to hear it."

"Thanks."

Sal did not bother to ask any additional questions. He knew he would get a detailed account from his wife after the party. He imagined the girl was being interrogated thoroughly by the kitchen patrol. He pitied her.

When the men finished, they reported to the kitchen for any remaining instructions.

Sal stated, "We're done setting up all of the tables and chairs."

Rose asked, "In the shade?"

Sal replied, "Yes, they all fit in the shade. I'm going to take a shower now."

Rose nodded. "Good. Thank you."

Tony reported, "The fridge in the garage is stocked with beer, pop, and ice."

Joe walked over to the cold cut tray and swiped a few pieces of ham.

Marie swatted her grandson's hand away.

Tony put his arm around Dee.

Wrinkling her nose, Dee complained, "You're hot and sweaty."

He squeezed her. "You doing okay?"

Leaning away from his pungent, sweaty body, she answered, "Yes."

Tony kissed her on the head and walked toward the pantry.

Joe opened the refrigerator door. "What can we eat?" He spied the olive tray and popped a few olives into his mouth before his mother could intervene.

Rose tried to stop him, but he outmaneuvered her.

Tony grabbed a bag of potato chips out of the pantry. He held them up. "These okay to eat?"

Exasperated, Rose questioned, "Potato chips? You are going to ruin your appetite."

Tony complained, "We're starving. We'll eat plenty later. Don't worry."

Joe shoved his hand into the bag. "So, Dee, how'd you guys meet?"

Tony and Joe were both curious to hear the answer.

"Online dating. Isn't that right, Tony?"

Playing along, Tony agreed, "Yeah, online dating."

Joe commented, "Huh! You swore you'd never do that."

With a mouth full of potato chips, Tony claimed, "I changed my mind."

In a snarky tone, Joe replied, "Apparently."

Rose asked, "Was it love at first sight?"

Dee shook her head. "No. He grew on me."

Under his breath, Joe muttered, "Like mold."

Tony puffed up his chest. "I was persistent."

Dee agreed, "If nothing else, he's definitely persistent."

Rose inquired, "What about children? How many do you want?"

Tony objected, "Ma!"

Rose threw up her hands, "What? It's a simple question. I want to know her thoughts on children. Is that a crime?"

Joe chuckled. He enjoyed not being on the receiving end of these probing questions for a change.

Dee answered, "We haven't discussed it yet."

Dissatisfied, Rose asked, "How long have you been dating that it hasn't come up yet?"

Tony protested, "Ma!"

Knowing what Rose wanted to hear, Dee recovered, "I would like to have two or three children after I get married."

Directing her answer to Tony, Rose beamed, "See, that wasn't so terrible, was it?"

As the brothers munched on potato chips, several crumbs landed on the floor.

Rose pointed to the floor as her right foot tapped it. Her right index finger punctuated her words as she spoke, "I cleaned this floor on my hands and knees this morning. I am not doing it again. Did I raise you two in a barn?"

Joe quickly bent over and cleaned up the mess. "Sorry."

She pursed her lips and crossed her arms. "Uh huh."

Her boys stared at her.

Peeved, Rose asked, "Well, what are you two waiting for?"

Tony blurted, "Directions."

Rose waved them off. "You're done. Go upstairs and get cleaned up. The guests will be here before you know it. Go!"

Dee stifled her laughter. She really liked Rose.

Sara, Laura, and Anna arrived thirty minutes before the party was to start. They wore bright, colorful dresses for the occasion. Their arms were full, carrying boxes of party favors.

Sara said, "Thank you so much for throwing me this shower, Mrs. Lazaro."

"You're welcome. I'm thrilled to do it."

Sara acknowledged Dee, "Hi."

Dee replied, "Hi."

Rose quickly made an introduction, "Oh girls, this is Anthony's girlfriend, Dee."

The girls exchanged glances. A flurry of "nice to meet you's" followed.

Laura asked Rose, "Where would you like the shower favors?"

"On the end table in the family room, next to the fireplace. There should be enough room."

Sara asked Dee, "Would you like to help us set up?"

Relieved, Dee answered, "Yes, I'd love to."

A steady stream of guests descended upon the house. Sara felt introductions were unnecessary. She had spent years attending family gatherings with Joe's relatives.

However, Rose insisted. Luckily, it did not take long. The introductions were crammed into a span of approximately thirty minutes. Sara estimated there were thirty-five adults and twenty children mulling around. After she received hugs and air kisses from all of them, the men and children were directed to go outside.

The conversations were loud and boisterous.

Anna made small talk with Sal's eighty-four-year-old aunt, Jo, "How are you?"

The elderly woman placed her hand on Anna's arm. "Oh, my hip is just terrible. This cooler weather is killing me. I went to the doctor. He says it's arthritis, and I have to live with it. Can you believe the nerve?"

"That's a shame."

Jo ranted, "Telling me I have to live with this pain. Can you believe it? He's crazy if he thinks I am going to just let this go. He needs to do something. He needs to fix this."

Anna said, "I'm sure there is some medicine you can take."

Jo complained, "Medicine? I hate medicine! I am eighty-four years old, and I am not about to start taking any damn pills now. I am not going to become a pill-popping junkie."

Not to be left out, her eighty-six-year-old sister, Serena, chimed in, "That's nothing. I shrunk another inch. That makes it almost three inches now."

Refusing to be upstaged, Jo added, "I got cataracts in my good eye."

Serena said, "Big deal. I had that last year. Quit complaining about it and have the surgery. I told you I have almost perfect vision."

Jo dismissed her. "Eh! I don't like your doctor."

With indignation, Serena asked, "What's wrong with my doctor?"

"He's not Italian."

Serena threw up her hands. "So what?"

Jo crossed her arms. "I want an Italian doctor."

As the sisters bickered, Anna slipped away. As she passed the front door, the bell rang. She answered it and greeted Emily, one of Sara's friends from work.

Emily brought a homemade gluten-free salad. Anna took it and carried it into the kitchen.

Marie asked, "What's this?"

Anna explained, "It's a quinoa veggie salad. One of Sara's friends from work brought it. It's healthy and gluten-free."

Marie directed, "Put it on the counter."

Anna did so and rejoined the others in the living room.

Marie eyed the dish suspiciously.

Skeptical, Rose observed, "It looks colorful."

Marie declared, "In my day, people ate gluten."

Carm interjected, "Ma, some people have allergies now."

Marie replied, "Uh huh. Sounds like a fad to me. Who's going to taste it before we put it out?"

Carm stated, "If the girl has a gluten allergy, we have to put it out. She made it. She'll eat it."

Rose extracted a small spoonful and tasted it.

The women waited while Rose chewed.

The suspense was too much for Marie. "Well? How is it?"

Definitively, Rose responded, "It needs gluten."

In the backyard, the men played games of bocce and cards while the children played tag.

Mario, Sal's older brother, asked, "Aren't we supposed to be in there?"

Sal questioned, "Are you volunteering?"

"No. But I thought we were dragged here to participate."

"If you want to watch that girl open boxes of towels and kitchen doodads, be my guest."

Mario held up his hands in protest. "No, thank you. I'm sure I'll get the rundown later tonight from my wife."

The men laughed.

Joe interjected, "We started picking at the food before everybody showed up. After that, Ma had a change of heart."

Mario laughed, "Good work."

Sal said, "Quit your yapping and take your turn."

Serena asked incredulously, "So, Sara's parents couldn't make it for their own daughter's shower?"

Disgusted, Marie said, "They're helping some poor people somewhere."

Serena expressed her sentiments, "They're more concerned about strangers than their own daughter? What kind of people are they?"

Rose answered, "They're not Italian."

Serena rolled her eyes. "Obviously. They have no sense of family."

Carm asked, "What is more important than your only daughter's bridal shower? They can help other people any time. Your daughter only gets married once."

Rose testified, "I left three messages before Sara's mother finally called back. And it was the shortest phone call I've ever had in my life. There was no reasoning with that woman. Supposedly, they will be here for the wedding."

Serena said, "Well, I would hope so. Could you imagine missing your own daughter's wedding?"

Marie responded, "Wild horses couldn't drag me away."

Rose replied, "Not in a million years. I'd have to be in a coma dying in a hospital before I'd miss it. And even then, I would expect one of you to wheel me there."

Carm testified, "I might smack you into a wall or two in the process, but I would get you there."

Marie stated, "Rose, the lasagna should be done."

As Rose got up, the oven timer beeped. She loved the accuracy of her mother's internal clock.

Carm and Marie joined her in the kitchen.

Rose removed the lasagna trays from the oven and positioned them across the burners on top of the stove.

Carm and Marie pulled food out of the refrigerator and lined up the containers on the counters.

Rose relocated some of the dishes to the dining room table. She peeled off aluminum foil and plastic wrap as she went. When she was satisfied with the food placement, she informed the women that it was time to eat.

Once all of the women fixed their plates, Rose hollered out the door to the men and children, "Time to eat!"

They did not have to be called twice. They lined up, piled food high on their plates, and returned to the backyard.

Tony devoured the last forkful of lasagna when his cell phone vibrated in his pocket. He pulled it out and swiped the screen. Dumbfounded, he stared at the image and the short text message that accompanied it.

Tony stared at the picture of Rita Fuentes. The woman was dead.

The message read: Mother murdered. Girl missing. War room. ASAP.

Vinnie sat next to him. Observing his cousin's reaction, he glanced over and saw the image. He uttered, "What the hell? Is that some kind of prank?"

Tony ignored his cousin and shoved the phone back into his pocket. He stood up, leaving his plate on the table.

Concerned, Vinnie grabbed his cousin's arm. "Tony, I'm talking to you."

Tony jerked his arm away and headed to the front yard. "It's nothing. Like you said, it's a prank."

Not to be deterred, Vinnie followed. "I don't believe you."

Tony removed his phone from his pocket. He typed as he approached his car. He pressed the send button when he reached the vehicle.

Vinnie snatched the phone out of his cousin's hand. "Tony, talk to me. What's going on?"

Tony grabbed for his phone. He demanded, "Give it back."

"Not until you answer my questions."

Tony held out his hand. "Don't do this. Give it back."

"Who's the woman? What's going on?"

Pressed for time, Tony replied, "I don't have time to explain everything. I'm working undercover."

Vinnie's disbelief showed on his face. He returned the phone.

Tony pocketed it. "I'm serious. I work for an agency."

"What kind of agency?"

Tony gave him a look. "It's need-to-know."

"I think I need to know. I'm a cop and your cousin. I can help."

"No, you can't."

Vinnie blocked Tony's car door. "Why not?"

"This is serious, Vinnie. I'm not fooling around. If I could tell you, I would. But I can't. But there is something you can do for me."

"What's that?"

"Cover for me. I just texted my partner, Dee. She's in there with the women."

"So she's not your girlfriend?"

"No, she's my partner."

"Aunt Rose isn't going to be happy that she's not your girlfriend."

"That's the least of my problems. Dee can't leave without raising suspicion. But I need to meet with the rest of my team. So cover for me, and keep an eye out for her."

"I can do more than that."

Unlocking his car door, Tony disagreed, "Not right now. I have to go."

Vinnie stepped aside. "This conversation isn't over."

Tony hopped into the car. "I know. I'll explain more later."

"You'll have to. In the meantime, I got your back. If you need anything, let me know."

"I will. Thanks, Vinnie."

CHAPTER 20

WHILE Tony drove, he checked his mirrors constantly. In hindsight, accepting an assignment this close to home was risky and more trouble than it was worth.

After confirming he was not being followed, he drove to headquarters. He pulled into the parking lot of the non-descript office building. He approached the revolving door, swiped his badge, and pushed hard.

Spaulding met Tony outside the war room. They walked in together.

Sully noted, "All team members accounted for except Georgie."

Tony stated, "She's safe but unavailable at the moment. Report."

Spaulding rattled off the facts, "Al Fuentes was friends with the judge. No surprise there. He and the mother made bail. That pushed the girl over the edge. She made a video and uploaded it to the Internet."

Tony joined the rest of the team at the table.

Lee loaded the video. The team watched it on the main screen.

Sabrina appeared distraught and disheveled. A handgun was positioned next to her on the bed. She clutched a bottle of whiskey. She took a drink straight from the bottle. She grimaced as it went down.

She professed, "I have to tell the truth. Everyone needs to know what a lying horrible piece of shit Al Fuentes is. That monster gets away with everything! I thought he would be locked up with his bitch of a mother. But they're out! This nightmare is never-ending!"

Mascara ran down her cheeks as she cried.

"I'm tired of keeping his dirty secrets. Every time Mom went out of town, he'd score drugs. We'd get high and have sex. It was our little secret." She used air quotes.

"He got really good stuff for my birthday. He told me to invite a bunch of friends over for a party. He took like ten of us to the lake house for a long weekend. We were all dancing and partying the day we got there. But I can't remember the rest of the weekend. I'm not just talking part of it, like the whole thing. I had a couple of flashes. Everyone was passed out. I don't even remember the drive home. I asked him about it later. He told me I had an active imagination."

She drank from the bottle and shuddered.

"When I asked my friends about the party, everybody said they had a great time. But they all told different stories. I know it's because nobody remembers."

She raised the bottle to her lips again and drank.

"A few weeks later, Tina, Amber, and I felt sick. At first, we thought we had the flu or something. But it didn't go away. We got sicker. So I went to the doctor. He told me I was pregnant. Amber and Tina took home pregnancy tests. They were positive. So, we confronted him, and he totally freaked out. Said we'd ruin him."

She held her pillow tightly to her chest while she sobbed.

"We didn't get kidnapped from any sleepover. He locked us up! He threatened Amber and Tina that he'd destroy their parents' lives if they say anything. So, they're not talking. If you don't believe me, do DNA tests on their babies. That will prove everything!"

She took another swig of whiskey and made a face that clearly indicated she loathed its taste. "His bitch of a mother cooked for us and checked in on us. I begged her to let us go. She wouldn't."

She wept, "I had a baby girl. They wouldn't even let me hold her. I don't know where she is! I can't live like this. With him! I just can't."

Off camera, Rita Fuentes was heard yelling, "Sabrina! That's not true!"

Sabrina looked in the direction of the voice. "Yes, it is!"

Outraged, Rita questioned, "Who are you talking to?"

Sabrina gestured toward the computer. "The whole world."

Rita screamed, "Take all of that back right now! You're making this up."

Sabrina cried, "No, I'm not! It's all true. Every last word. You married a child molester and rapist!"

"I did not! Oh, God! You're filming this? What do you think you're doing?"

Rita entered the frame. She attempted to shut off the camera. "How do you shut this off?" She turned and approached her daughter. She demanded, "Shut it off!"

Sabrina raised the gun, pointed it at her mother, and shot twice.

Rita went down with a definitive thud.

The remaining part of the video showed Sabrina resting the gun on the bed. She stared at her mother's body for about a minute. Then reality hit. She jumped up and shut off the camera.

Lee switched off the video. "That's it. She had posted to her Twitter and Facebook accounts earlier that she was going to post a video. She touted it as a must-see. She was live-streaming it. Someone notified the police. By the time they got to the house, the mother was dead. Sabrina was gone. From what they could tell, she took her car, the gun, and the whiskey."

Shaking his head in disbelief, Tony insisted, "We have to get justice for her and those girls."

Spaulding pointed out, "They're allegations of a suicidal girl who killed her mother."

White added, "They'll paint her as troubled, crazy, and unstable. Without proof or corroborating testimony from the other girls, Fuentes might go free. And she's on the run and wanted for murder now."

Frustrated with the situation, Ashby said, "We have to be able to prove what Fuentes did."

Sully stated, "With no one talking that looks unlikely."

Tony complained, "It just burns me that he's getting away with something this huge."

White remarked, "He'll slip up eventually."

Sully barked, "Lee, keep an eye out for any bank or credit card activity and plane, train, or bus tickets. Basically anything."

Lee acknowledged, "On it." He paused. "Wait a sec. Remember that juvie record that was sealed?"

Sully asked, "What about it?"

"It's unsealed now."

Curious, Sully pressed, "What's it say?"

Lee read quickly, "Al Fuentes has done this before. He was charged with raping several girls when he was younger. All of the cases were eventually settled out of court for an obscene amount of money."

"Good job, Lee. That's all I need as proof. White and Ashby, keep tabs on Fuentes' brother and family. They might decide to help them."

They nodded.

"Spaulding, you track Fuentes' secretary."

Sully continued, "TJ, you and Georgopoulos lay low."

Protesting, Tony questioned, "So we're not part of the mission?"

"I'm not going to explain myself again. I can't risk losing you both. Stay under the radar."

"But …"

"That's an order."

"I don't like it, and Georgie won't either."

"I don't give a damn what either of you like. You've been compromised. I want you out of town immediately."

"If we were anywhere but here, I would do just that. But my brother is getting married this week. I can't miss his wedding. The full force of my mother's wrath is more life-threatening than anything Fuentes can dream up. Trust me."

Sully rolled his eyes.

Looking at the time, Tony said, "And speaking of Ma, I gotta get back before she misses me."

Sully teased, "Fine. Go back to your *frou-frou* party. Just keep a low profile."

Standing up, Tony retorted, "It might be *frou-frou*, but you can't beat the food. Keep me posted."

Tony left the building and drove back to his parents' house.

Excited, Lee hopped a little in his chair. "Wait, there's breaking news. Hold on to your seats."

The team listened intently.

"The police have issued APBs for Al and Esmeralda Fuentes. The other two girls watched the video and went to the police with everything they knew. They corroborated Sabrina's story completely."

Sully ordered, "Everybody roll out. We've got to find these bastards."

Al Fuentes and his mother, Esmeralda, fled the city. In a silver Mercedes, they headed north on Interstate 81.

Being short on time and resources, Al had emptied his main savings account. His mother withdrew a substantial sum from one of her accounts as well.

Driving the speed limit to avoid unwanted attention, Al said, "This is temporary until I can straighten this out."

Esmeralda replied, "I thought you were going to handle it. This is how you handle things? The loose ends are all unravelling."

"The loose ends will be tied up soon."

"What does that mean?"

"The agents and the girls won't be problems for long."

"You had better straighten this out quickly and properly. I will not hide on some island for the rest of my life. You slipped up one too many times."

"Trust me. It's being taken care of permanently."

"Forgive me if I'll believe it when I see it."

"You'll be proud, Mother."

"I'll be the judge of that."

Apologetically, he said, "I'm sorry."

Disappointed, she responded, "I'm the one who's sorry. I bailed you out years ago with all those girls. I made it all go away, didn't I?"

"Yes, you did."

She chided, "And when you came to me this time, you groveled on your hands and knees. You begged me to save you again. And look where it's gotten me. I am a fugitive! A fugitive! I did not scrape and fight my way from poverty in Columbia to spend my life in prison in the United States. You *will* fix this."

"I promise, I will."

Disgusted with his lack of control, she continued, "I even told you to stay away from that girl. You just couldn't help yourself, could you? And you made it worse by involving other girls. What kind of idiot does that? Besides you and your lousy good-for-nothing father. Always a taste for the young girls."

"I'm sorry."

"You should be."

CHAPTER 21

MITA and Flora Scotto stood on Rose Lazaro's front porch. Flora pleaded, "Can I ring the bell? Please?"

"All right."

Flora pressed the button.

Anna was closest to the door. She got up and answered it, "Hi! Come on in. The party is in full swing."

Flora exclaimed, "A party! It's my first American party!"

Surprised, Anna replied, "Your first American party? Oh!"

Anna knew a few relatives from Italy were coming for the wedding. She did not realize any of them would be coming in for the shower.

Flora bounded into the house.

"Flora!" Mita snapped, to no avail.

The women in the living room looked at the child.

Marie greeted her, "And who do we have here?"

Proudly, she answered, "I'm Flora."

Marie complimented, "Well, Flora, that is a pretty dress you are wearing."

Flora twirled around to show off her dress. "Thank you. I picked it out all by myself."

Carm leaned over and whispered in Rose's ear, "Who's got a daughter named Flora?"

Puzzled, Rose whispered back, "I don't know."

Marie asked, "Flora, would you like a cookie? I made them myself this morning."

Eagerly, she responded, "Yes, please."

Marie directed, "They are in the next room. Put some on a plate, and come back in here with us."

Flora dashed to the dining room.

Mita entered the room.

Anna followed.

Rose greeted Mita, "Well, hello!"

"Hello," Mita responded, flashing her dingy cigarette-stained teeth.

Rose said, "So wonderful to see you."

Mita offered, "Mita."

"Yes, Mita. Please join us."

Marie whispered to Carm, "Mita? Must be Salvatore's side."

Carm replied, "I guess." She gave her the once-over. "Not too pretty. Spends too much time in the sun. Definitely not our side."

Marie commented, "Not with that nose."

Flora returned, sat cross-legged on the floor, and munched on homemade chocolate chip cookies as Sara resumed opening presents.

Fishing for details, Marie asked, "So, did you have to come far?"

Flora answered, "The flight from Italy was really long."

Surprised, Marie said, "Oh, you came from Italy."

Enjoying her cookie, Flora answered, "Yes!"

Rose inquired, "Did you have a good flight?"

Mita said, "Yes. It was fine."

"You don't seem to have an accent," Rose observed.

Mita shrugged and responded, "I was born here."

Rose's mind worked overtime trying to figure out how this woman was related to the family. "I see."

Marie asked, "So you are one of Salvatore's relatives?"

Assuming it was a safe ruse, Mita nodded.

Marie said, "So glad you arrived in time for the party. We didn't realize you were coming today, or we would have sent someone to get you."

"Is this a birthday party?" Flora eagerly asked.

Carm replied, "No honey, it's a bridal shower."

Flora asked, "Who's getting married?"

Marie answered, "Your cousin, Joe, and his girlfriend, Sara."

Out of the blue, Serena asked, "Why are all the men outside? I thought this was supposed to be one of those co-ed showers."

Rose replied, "We decided against it this morning. They were eating all of the food as we were trying to prepare it. It's better for them to play bocce and cards. We don't want them to ruin the shower. Let them be."

Laura and Anna picked up the brightly wrapped gifts and handed them to Sara. They noted on a sheet of paper who gave which gift. The pile of unwrapped gifts grew steadily.

The majority of women gave practical gifts such as pots, pans, bed sheets, towels, china, silverware, and an outdoor grill. However, some of the women had different, more playful gift ideas.

Laura taunted, "Oh, this box is small and light. I wonder what this could be!"

Sara accepted and opened the box. She recognized the pink tissue paper. She peeled back the tissue, revealing a white and pink lace-up corset and matching G-string. She tried to put the cover back on the box without displaying the contents.

The crowd protested.

Cousin Gina shouted, "Let everyone see it. I paid good money for that. Show it off!"

Sara blushed.

Gina took the box from her and held up the corset for all to see. "And with a pair of white lacy thigh highs and some stilettos, you'll blow Joe's mind!"

A chorus of "ooohs" and "aaahs" from the younger women filled the room.

The older women just smiled.

The next present was oddly-shaped. Sara ripped the paper and saw fuzzy handcuffs. She looked at Laura.

Laura put up her hands. "I didn't buy that."

Squinting, Jo shouted, "I can't see! Hold it up!"

As Sara ripped off the remaining wrapping paper, she realized it was worse than she originally thought. Reluctantly, she displayed the gift.

The giggling was contagious as the women looked at the fantasy kit. It contained pink fuzzy handcuffs, a blindfold, a miniature whip, edible underwear, flavored body paint, and massage oils.

Still squinting, Jo asked, "What the hell is that?"

Serena replied, "It's a fantasy sex kit."

Confused, Jo questioned, "You need a kit to have sex now?"

"No, Jo. It's to have more fun, if you know what I mean."

Jo loudly stated, "I don't know what you mean. In my day, you didn't need a kit. You just took off your clothes. There would be a lot of groping and kissing, he'd poke around for a while, and if you were lucky, he'd hit the right spot, and then it was over."

The older women smiled. The younger girls laughed.

Jo continued, "If he didn't hit the right spot, then I'd do a load of laundry."

Perplexed, Anna asked, "Is that a euphemism for something?"

Jo schooled her, "No, dear. I would do a load of laundry that would be unbalanced, and I'd sit on the washing machine until I was satisfied. One time, I got a bit carried away and forgot to hold on. I fell off. He heard the noise and came to investigate. I was using the washing machine to stand back up. My naked backside was facing him. When he saw me bent over, that floppy penis of his sprang to life. Boy, oh boy! That was some of the best sex I ever had. And I got exactly what I needed after all." She winked.

Not knowing how to reply, Anna sat there stunned.

Rose fanned herself. "Holy Mary, Jesus, and Joseph!"

Serena admonished her, "Oh, Rose, don't be such a prude."

Rose gave her a look.

Jo called Rose out, "Like you never tried the washing machine trick?"

Mortified, Rose exclaimed, "Good Lord, no!"

Steering the conversation back to her, Serena announced, "Anyway, I wanted to make sure the kids had some fun."

Flabbergasted, Rose asked Serena, "*You* bought that?"

Proudly, Serena replied, "Yes, I did. I even bought one for myself."

Rose held her head. "For the love of God and all that is holy."

Serena declared, "I might be old. But I'm not dead. Eighty-six is the new fifty."

Excited, Jo piped up, "So, that makes me forty-eight. I like this new math. I don't know what everybody is complaining about."

Carm corrected, "That's not what the new math controversy is about, Jo."

Ignoring her, Jo remarked, "Who would have thought it? I'm forty-eight again! I'm all for this new math."

Continuing her original conversation, Serena explained, "The edible underwear is popular with the younger boys. One said it tasted like one of those strawberry fruit roll-up snacks."

Rose felt a headache coming on. She protested, "I don't want to hear this. This is not appropriate conversation for a bridal shower."

Serena laughed, "God, Rose! Live a little! Don't be such a prude. Have some fun."

Indignant, Rose stated, "I have *plenty* of fun. Thank you, very much."

Serena disagreed, "You seem a bit uptight to me."

Rose fumed, "We are *not* having this conversation."

Hands extended, Gina demanded, "Sara, pass it around. I want to take a look at it."

Anna sighed. "That eighty-six-year-old woman is getting more sex than I am."

Laura whispered, "Weird fruit roll-up sex."

"Hey, sex is sex. She's *old*, and she's getting some. I'm young, and I'm not. This is a nightmare."

Laura consoled her, "Hang in there. It will happen, sooner or later."

"Uh huh."

Laura joked, "And don't forget, there's always the washing machine."

Astonished, Anna said, "Oh my God! You just had to go there! Ugh!"

Laura laughed. "Sorry. I had to."

Flora questioned, "Mama, did we bring a present?"

Marie maintained, "Just having you here is present enough. You came across an entire ocean."

Flora smiled and bit into another cookie.

Since Mita had consumed several small bottles of vodka prior to their arrival, the numerous glasses of punch she drank pushed her over the edge. She slipped off her chair, onto the floor. She roared with laughter.

It was not a pleasant laugh. It sounded harsh, over the top.

Flora rushed over to her mother. "Mama?"

Mita used the chair to pull herself up. "I'm fine." She waved off any help.

Marie, Carm, and Rose exchanged glances.

Marie shook her head. "Definitely not our side. We can hold our liquor."

Rose added, "I can't remember all of the cousins. Maybe it's Nino's daughter."

"Who knows? At least the little one is cute."

Stealthily, Dee stood and approached Mita. "Why don't we freshen up a little?" She manhandled Mita and escorted her out of the room.

Everyone expressed surprise and relief at Dee's actions.

Jo asked, "Who's that girl in charge?"

Happily, Rose responded, "That's Anthony's girlfriend, Dee."

Astonished, she questioned, "Anthony has a girlfriend?"

Proudly, Rose confirmed, "Yes. She seems very nice."

Serena observed, "And she's definitely a take-charge kind of gal."

Turning to Serena, Jo deadpanned, "I thought we decided he was gay."

Serena admitted, "Guess we were wrong."

Jo slapped her knee. "There's a first time for everything."

After all of the discarded wrapping paper was stuffed into garbage bags, Laura asked Rose, "Do you want us to carry the stuff to the car now?"

Rose replied, "No, we'll have the boys do it later. It's time to cut the cake."

"Okay."

Rose marched through the house to the kitchen. She opened the back door and ordered, "Everybody in!"

Joe complained, "We're in the middle of a game."

Rose stated, "This is your shower. You're lucky we let you stay out there in the first place. Play time is over. It's time to cut the cake. Everybody inside. Now!"

Grumbling, the men filed into the house. The kids rushed in. They were excited about eating cake.

As her husband entered the house, Rose directed, "Sal, go back out, and get the cake. It's in the garage fridge."

Turning around, he replied, "Yes, dear."

Sal balanced the cake masterfully as he weaved through the sea of children into the dining room.

Rose lifted the cake out of the box and placed it in front of Joe and Sara.

Sara exclaimed, "What a beautiful cake!"

Laura concurred, "Wow! It's like a miniature wedding cake."

Anna asked, "Did you make it, Mrs. Lazaro?"

Rose confessed, "I have to admit I did not make this one. I bought it at Roselli's."

Laura added, "Their cakes are to die for!"

Rose handed Sara the knife and stepped aside. Joe joined Sara next to the cake.

Holding up her cell phone, Laura shouted, "Wait! Let me get a picture."

Joe and Sara held the knife and posed for the picture.

Anna said, "Me next. Look at me. Say cheese!"

"Cheese," Joe and Sara said in unison.

Flipping his cell phone sideways, John announced, "I'm rolling video. You can start any time."

From the hallway, Mita fumbled with her purse and yelled, "Wait! Did I miss it?"

Joe and Sara stopped, believing they were posing for another picture. They plastered the smiles back on their faces and waited.

When Joe saw Mita, his smile melted away.

Inches from the couple, Mita stumbled. She recovered and exhaled in his face, "Hi, Joe! Miss me?"

Initially, he was repulsed and recoiled. But his shock rapidly transformed to anger. Joe grabbed Mita's upper arm. He pulled her out of the room and into the hallway.

Confused, Sara looked to Rose for an explanation.

Rose threw up her hands and shook her head, equally confused.

Jo asked loudly, "What's going on?"

Craning her neck, Serena replied, "I don't know."

Jo followed up, "Where'd he go?"

Pushing her way toward the hallway, through the sea of guests, Serena remarked, "How the hell do I know?"

Low conversations started amongst the guests.

In the hallway, Joe growled, "I don't know how you found me, but you're leaving. Now!"

Mita protested, "But I'm having *so* much fun!"

Disgusted, Joe observed, "You're drunk and reek of smoke. Go back to the hole you crawled out of."

"Fuck you. I'm staying. I've been hanging with your family. Should've met them sooner."

His grip tightened as he dragged her toward the door. In a strong voice, he demanded, "Get out!"

Sara appeared. "What's going on?" She saw the vice grip he had on Mita's arm. "Joe?"

Rose slipped into the hall. "Joey, your cousin is drunk. Don't let this ruin the day."

Dee joined them in the hall. She attempted to defuse the situation. "I'll take her to the guestroom. She can sleep it off in there."

"She needs to leave now," Joe insisted.

Dee detected more in Joe's tone. *This woman might not be a drunken cousin after all.*

Flora weaved through the adults' legs. She peered up at her mother. "Mama? What's going on?"

Mita patted her daughter's head. "Don't worry, baby. Mama's just ruining Daddy's day."

A shock wave hit the crowd in the hallway.

Dee's mind assessed the situation, *Jilted lover. Escalation and a highly volatile exchange are guaranteed.*

The word, "daddy," rippled from the hallway into the dining room and beyond.

Sara pressed Mita, "What did you just say?"

Rose demanded, "Who the hell are you?"

The hallway quickly became overcrowded with curious relatives.

Basking in the spotlight, Mita proclaimed, "I am the woman he left this bitch for. We had a great time in Italy. Isn't that right, Joe?"

Joe seethed in anger.

Stunned, Sara stood transfixed.

Looking directly at Sara, Mita continued, "I read your pathetic letters. 'Oh Joe, I love you and miss you. Please come home.' Ha! What a joke."

Furious, Sara glared at Joe. Astonished, she asked, "You let her read my letters?"

"I didn't know she read them."

Mita continued, "He's not too bright. He left them out where anyone could see them. And after reading them, I knew exactly what to say to convince him that we were soulmates. He was meant to find me. It was fate." She cackled.

Laura pushed through the crowd to reach Sara.

Mita taunted, "Hey, someone had to keep him warm at night. And it wasn't you, princess."

Sara lunged at her. "You bitch!"

Laura intervened and grabbed Sara.

Sara pleaded, "Let me go! I'm going to scratch her eyes out!"

Laura restrained Sara and attempted to reason with her. "She's white trash. She's just goading you. She's not worth it, Sara."

Mita tormented, "A man can only go so long without sex. What did you think he was going to do? Live like a monk?" She laughed. It was an ugly, evil laugh.

Joe pushed Mita toward the door. "Get out!"

Shaking, Sara wanted the truth. She asked, "Joe, is this true? Is what she said true?"

He had no words for Sara. Instead he screamed at Mita, "Get out!"

Worried and confused, Flora whispered, "Mama?"

Carm took the child by the hand. "Come on, honey. We're going to go in the kitchen for a few minutes."

Looking over her shoulder, Flora left with Carm.

Mita continued, "I gave him everything he wanted and taught him a few tricks too." She thrust herself at him and started grinding her hips.

Joe pushed her away. "Get the hell away from me!"

Mita clung and would not let go. "Funny. You never said that when we were together. You couldn't get enough of me, could you?"

Dee pried Mita off Joe.

All of the color drained from Sara's face. She stopped fighting Laura's hold on her.

Laura asked Sara, "What can I do?"

Slowly, Sara said, "Kill me."

Furious, Laura countered, "I could kill *him* instead."

Mita yelled at Dee, "Get off me!" She struggled to break free of Dee's powerful grip.

Dee held firmly and ignored her.

Mita licked the left side of Joe's face. Dee jerked her away.

Rose shouted, "That's it! Get this tramp out of my house now! Or God help me!"

The fantasy sex kit was on the end table. Dee asked Serena, "Can you get the cuffs out of that box for me?"

Serena smiled. "Sure thing." She opened the box, peeled back the plastic and handed the pink fuzzy cuffs to Dee. "Who knew we'd have to use them during the shower?"

Dee stated, "Stranger things have happened."

Serena continued, "If I had known, I could have brought mine from home. They're regulation police issue you know. Much heavier duty than these. I've never needed them at a bridal shower before. I better start carrying them to family gatherings. You can't be too prepared I guess."

Dee accepted the cuffs and tried to process what the octogenarian just said. "Thanks."

Dee slapped the cuffs on Mita.

Serena said, "From now on, I'll bring my personal handcuffs everywhere I go. I need to be prepared."

Mita spat at Dee, "You bitch! Take these off!"

"Not on your life, sister."

Mita yelled, "Don't you people want to hear the best part?"

All eyes and ears were on Mita.

She answered her own question, "You do. You're dying to know. I can see it in your eyes."

Sara swallowed and braced herself.

Locking eyes with Sara, Mita declared, "The love of your life wasn't into safe sex."

Sara bristled.

Mita elaborated, "And I didn't mind one bit. You know it feels much better that way. And I did things to him you wouldn't do." Mita smirked. "And if you have unprotected sex enough times, you know what happens."

The room was silent.

Mita paused for dramatic effect. "And Flora is living proof!"

Audible gasps rippled like waves across the house.

Sara leaned against the wall.

Mita laughed her horrible, evil laugh. It sent shivers down Sara's spine.

Mita rubbed salt in Sara's wounds. "Joe and I will always be connected through our baby."

Feeling ill, Sara uttered, "I'm going to throw up."

Dee decided everyone had had enough. She dragged Mita out of the house.

Joe reached for Sara's hand. "Sara, I'm sorry. But it's all in the past."

Sara pulled away. Stunned, she asked, "How could you?"

Joe stammered, "I was stupid."

Searching his eyes for a reason, she repeated, "How could you do this to me?"

"It was a long time ago. She doesn't mean anything to me. I swear."

Rose interrupted with the question no one else dared to ask, "Is that child really your daughter?"

Joe replied truthfully, "It's possible. I don't know for sure. I didn't have a paternity test. I assumed she was mine."

Rose slapped him hard across the face.

Outrage joined the sick feeling in Sara's stomach. She screamed, "You left me for her? She's not even pretty!"

Joe begged, "Sara, please let me explain."

"Explain what? How you loved screwing her? How you just couldn't go without sex?"

Silence.

She grilled him. "How long did it take? A year?"

Silence.

Sara pressed, "Months?"

No answer.

Sara persisted, "Weeks? Days?"

After a long pause, he replied, "It was just about sex. It didn't mean anything."

"How long?"

"It doesn't matter."

"Yes, it does! How long?"

He admitted, "A few months."

"A few months? Are you kidding me? You couldn't last a few months? You didn't break up with me for two years. You were calling me and sending me letters telling me you loved me. And the entire time, you were screwing that whore and raising a child with her? How could you do that?"

He choked, "It wasn't like that exactly."

Sara berated him, "How stupid are you? The rich, young college guy sweeps into town. You were probably flashing your money around, buying drinks for everybody. Partying it up. Having a great time."

He hung his head.

"I'm betting she targeted you from the moment she saw you."

"I told her I had a girlfriend back home."

"A lot of good that did! She figured she just had to bide her time. She knew eventually you'd cave. She lent you an ear. Poor pitiful you. All alone and no one to comfort you."

Joe shoved his hands in his pockets and shifted his weight from foot to foot.

"Were you at least drunk when you did her for the first time? I can't believe you had sex with her. Have you actually looked at her? You are so stupid!"

"I screwed up."

With both hands on his chest, Sara pushed him. "You threw everything away for an ugly, crazy whore."

Meekly, he said, "I don't know what to say."

She pushed him harder. "I stayed faithful to you the entire two years. I missed you. I longed for you. I wanted you so badly. My heart ached for you. Did I go out and screw some other guy? No! I didn't."

Tears rolled down Joe's face.

With clenched fists, she pounded his chest. "I don't even know you."

He grabbed her wrists and held them. "Sara, please listen to me."

Jerking away, she yelled, "Let go of me. Don't you touch me!"

Keeping his distance, he begged, "But I came back for you."

"But you left your daughter!"

"I'm not sure she's mine."

Sara just stared.

"Sara, I came back for you."

Sara shook her head in disbelief. Her life unraveled before her eyes.

Joe explained, "She was nuts. She was drinking all the time, and we had a huge fight. She threatened to kill me. That's when I realized my mistake. I am so ashamed of what I did. If I could go back and change everything, I would."

"Wait. So you realized she was a psycho-bitch, and *that's* what finally convinced you she was wrong for you?"

Knowing there was no right answer to that question, he remained silent.

Sara's heart palpitated so fast she thought it would explode. "Oh my God! But you can't go back. You can't undo any of it. She had to threaten to kill you for you to realize that you belonged with me instead! Oh my God!"

"I'm so sorry."

The gravity of the situation became heavier with each exchange.

"And that little girl could be yours. You might have fathered a child with that crazy bitch. She will *always* be in your life. You will *never* be able to get rid of her."

"I'm sorry."

"You are a selfish, lying, cheating son of a bitch!"

He grabbed her hand. "I only love you. Can't you see that?"

She pulled her hand away. "I told you not to touch me!" Sara stormed out, cutting through the kitchen. There she saw Flora's big, tearful eyes looking up at her. Overwhelmed, Sara ran out the back door.

Laura followed her.

Sara ran to the largest tree in the far side of the backyard and leaned against it. She sobbed as she slid to the ground.

Laura knelt beside Sara and held her.

Joe tried to push his way through the crowd to follow Sara.

Rose wrenched her son's arm. "No, you don't!"

"I have to go after her."

"No! You have done quite enough."

"Ma, let me go."

Rose slapped her son right across the face for the second time. "I don't know you. I did not raise you to be like this. What's the matter with you?"

Sal concurred, "I am disappointed in you, son. More disappointed than I have ever been in my whole life."

That comment from his father hit hard. Joe was used to getting yelled at and lectured to by his mother. But his father's words stung.

Rose released Joe and crossed her arms, primarily so she did not slap her son again. "I don't even know where to start with you. I am so upset right now, I am almost speechless."

He defended, "But it happened years ago. That woman means nothing to me."

Sal questioned, "Do you not understand the repercussions? There's a child involved."

Joe received disgusted looks from all the women in the house. The men shook their heads in dismay and were glad they were not in his shoes.

Carm attempted to distract Flora with more cookies and milk.

As Dee dragged Mita down the driveway, Vinnie followed.

He said, "You're Dee, I presume?"

Sticking with their cover story, she responded, "Yeah. I'm Tony's girlfriend."

Vinnie revealed, "I know you're his partner. He told me to keep an eye on you."

Surprised, she answered, "Really?"

He noticed the pink fuzzy cuffs Mita wore. He teased, "Nice handcuffs. Is that what undercover operatives use now?"

"Hey, I had to make due. I didn't bring mine to the shower. These were part of a shower gift. That aunt of Tony's—Serena—she's a riot."

"She can be, whether she tries or not. By the way, I'm Vinnie, Tony's cousin."

"I know. Nice to meet you."

Cocking his head toward Mita, he asked, "Mind if I read this one her Miranda Rights?"

"Be my guest."

She handed over Mita. "Mita, this nice officer is going to read you your rights now. Try to behave."

When Vinnie finished reading Mita her rights, she spat.

Tony had parked his car down the first side street from his parents' house. As he exited the vehicle, he received a call. He answered, "Yeah?"

Lee said, "Here's a heads-up. I know you're not on the case, but thought you'd like to know that the two girls came forward after seeing Sabrina's video. They were scared to death and corroborated her story. The local police issued APBs for Fuentes and his mother."

"Good. Thanks."

"No problem. Stay safe."

"Will do."

That news was of little comfort. However, some progress was better than nothing.

As Tony approached the driveway, he was curious with the odd scene. He asked Dee, "What's going on?"

"We're taking out the trash."

Puzzled, he inquired, "You need help?"

Vinnie responded, "No. We're good."

Dee asked Vinnie, "What about the kid?"

"She's fine for now. I'll come back for her later."

Dee replied, "Okay."

Scratching his head, Tony commented, "Obviously, I missed something."

Dee laughed. "You sure did."

Restraining a struggling Mita, Vinnie suggested, "You two should go back inside."

Dee said, "If you're sure."

"I'm sure."

Dee asked Tony, "So, what did I miss at the briefing?"

"I'll tell you later."

Tony and Dee walked toward the house. He asked, "Who was that?"

Dee replied, "From what I could gather, one of Joe's ex-girlfriends. She crashed the shower."

Shocked, Tony asked, "And I missed it?"

"It was ugly. But the good news is that no one noticed you were gone."

Mita argued with Vinnie, "I'm not going anywhere with you."

"Yes, you are."

She kicked him in the shin. "How do I know you're a real cop? You could just be saying that."

Vinnie jerked her arm. "Aside from the patrol car I'm about to put you in, you'll know when you see the new charges of resisting arrest and assaulting a police officer to the other charges I'm filing."

Defiant, she claimed, "I didn't do anything."

"That's what they all say. I'm charging you with disorderly conduct. That right there can get you fifteen days in jail and a fine."

"Screw you! I just told the truth. It's not my fault they couldn't handle it."

He checked her pockets. They were empty.

"Assuming Mita is your first name, what's your last name?"

"Fuck you."

"Lady, we can do this the hard way or the easy way. Your choice."

He pushed her into the back seat of his police car and slammed the door. She kicked the doors, the windows, and the bulletproof glass that separated them.

He settled into the driver's seat. "You're a live one, aren't you? Let's try this one more time. Name?"

She ignored his request.

When they arrived at the police station, Vinnie extracted Mita from the vehicle and pulled her along. He ushered her into one of the interrogation rooms.

"Pig!" Mita yelled. "You can't hold me here."

"You're a terrorist to my family, lady. So, you'll enjoy the amenities of this place until the judge says so. Deal with it."

"I want a lawyer."

"You'll get one. Where are you staying?"

"None of your business."

Vinnie persisted, "Is there anyone who can watch your daughter, or do we turn her over to Child Protective Services?"

Through clenched teeth, she replied, "My mother."

Sara wept. "I just can't believe Joe did this to me."

Laura could not conceal her contempt. "He's an ass. He's a stupid, selfish, narcissistic ass."

She picked at her dress. "And I love him. Why?"

"Because your heart wants what your heart wants. It sucks."

"What am I going to do?"

Laura brushed Sara's tears away and the hair out of her face. "You have to decide if you can forgive him or not."

Blinking through bleary, tear-soaked eyes, she said, "He cheated, and he lied. Why didn't I know? I should have known."

"Love is blind. And you guys were an ocean apart. How could you have possibly known?"

"I don't think I can live without him. But how can I ever trust him again?"

"You don't have to make a decision right now. Take some time to process all of this."

Hysterical, she cried, "I don't have time! The wedding is in less than a week!"

Laura reassured her, "Don't worry about it."

"How can I not worry about it? Oh, God! All I can think of is him having sex with her." She shuddered. "And she wasn't even pretty!"

Laura calmly asked, "So if she was pretty, that would have made it all right?"

Sara shot her a look. "No! But at least *then* I could rationalize it. How do I rationalize that he left me for that ugly, crazy bitch? It makes me physically ill."

"I'm sorry, Sara."

"I can't go back in there and face all of those people."

In a reassuring tone, Laura said, "Sara, those people love you. They're on your side. Hell, his mother is on your side. I think she is going to kill him."

"Good! He deserves it."

Laura observed the guests departing. "It looks like people are leaving. Let's sit out here a little while."

Shattered, Sara wiped away tears. "Okay."

"I'm going to get you some water. I'll be right back."

"Thanks."

Laura hurried back to the house to get Sara a bottle of water.

As Sara sat alone, she thought, *How did this happen? Why wasn't I enough for him? Am I enough for him now? Will I ever be enough? And how can I deal with that bitch and her daughter? Their daughter.*

When Laura opened the kitchen door, the women turned.

Anxious, Rose asked, "How is she?"

Laura shook her head. "Not good. She's beyond devastated. I'm getting her some water."

Rose rushed to the refrigerator, extracted a bottle, and handed it to Laura.

Laura accepted it. "Thank you."

Wringing her hands, Rose inquired, "What can I do?"

At a loss for ideas, Laura responded, "I really don't know. She's beside herself. I need to get back out there. I don't want to leave her alone."

Rose shooed Laura away. "Go! Go already!"

From the window, Joe saw Sara sitting alone. He ran into the kitchen. His mother, Rose, stood between him and the door.

Offensively, she inquired, "Where do you think you're going?"

Anxious and desperate, he replied, "I need to go outside and talk to Sara."

Rose contradicted him, "No, you don't."

He attempted to go around her.

Rose blocked him, stood firm, and assumed a wide stance, hands on her hips. "You're going to have to go through me."

"What the hell, Ma?"

Infuriated, Rose reprimanded, "Don't you dare speak to me that way! Are you insane? Haven't you done enough? You are *not* going anywhere near that poor girl. You have put her through enough for one day. Go to your room!"

He stared at his mother in disbelief.

Pointing her index finger at him, she spoke slowly and sternly, "Don't you give me that look! You will not bother her. And you better pray to God Almighty that she finds it somewhere in her heart to forgive you and take you back. You better pray like you have never prayed before."

"But …"

Rose spoke deliberately, "I do not want to hear so much of a peep out of you."

Joe pressed his lips together and pouted.

Rose grabbed him by the ear and pinched hard.

He winced, "Ma!"

"Go! And God help you! He is the only one who can right now. Get out of my sight!"

When she released him, he glanced around the room for support. His gaze was met by his grandmother and aunt, both with scowls on their faces and their arms crossed. Dejected, Joe obeyed his mother's directions.

Rose plucked the box of tissues off the counter and headed outside toward Sara and Laura.

Sara sipped water from the bottle Laura provided.

Both girls looked up at Rose when she joined them.

Rose asked, "Laura, won't you be a dear and bring your car up into the driveway?"

"Sure thing, Mrs. Lazaro."

Rose knelt in front of Sara and embraced her tightly. "I am so sorry. I had no idea. I apologize for my lousy son. You did not deserve this, especially not today of all days."

Sara's body trembled. "He ripped my heart out."

"I know. I'm sorry he broke your heart. He's stupid. I told him not to bother you."

Sara cried, "I can't breathe. I feel like I am going to die."

Rose rocked her. "You're not going to die. God will help you through this. You know I have always thought you and Joey belong together. But if this is too much to bear and forgive, I understand. This is for you to decide and no one else."

"I know. That's the worst part."

Chapter 22

AFTER Mita was processed and booked, Vinnie drove to Helen Scotto's apartment. He rang the bell.

Helen answered the door. She was shocked to find an officer on her doorstep. "Yes?"

"Good evening, ma'am, I'm Officer Vincent Varone. Do you have a daughter, Mita?"

Helen tensed up. "Yes. What has she done? Oh, God, what about Flora? Where's Flora?"

"Flora's fine, ma'am. May I come in?"

She stepped aside and allowed him entry. "Yes."

Vinnie relayed the events that occurred at the shower.

Helen was mortified and shocked. "I am so sorry. I had no idea. Where's Flora now?"

"She's safe at my aunt's house. I didn't want to drag her down to the station. She didn't need to see her mother getting hauled off to jail and get booked."

Grateful that Flora had been spared that ordeal, she responded, "Thank you for that."

"No need to traumatize her any more than she has been. Are you willing to care for her while your daughter is in custody?"

She nodded. "Of course, I am. What do I need to do?"

"Why don't you get your purse? I'll take you to her."

"Thank you, officer."

By the time Vinnie escorted Helen to his aunt's house, the guests had departed. Carm and Marie comforted the worried child.

Rose paced the kitchen floor as she prepared another lecture for her son. Dee, Tony, and Sal cleaned up the party mess.

158

Flora's eyes lit up when Helen walked into the kitchen. She ran to her. "Nana!"

Helen reassured the child, "You're okay, Flora. I'm here."

Speaking rapidly, Flora said, "I don't know where Mama is, but Auntie Carm gave me milk and cookies and told me funny stories."

Helen looked at the women. "Thank you."

Carm responded, "My pleasure."

Awkwardness filled the air.

Rose approached Helen. "I'm not sure what you were told."

Helen replied, "I understand Mita ruined a bridal shower. I'm so terribly sorry."

Rose added, "She also claimed that Flora is my son's child. I need to know for sure."

Helen agreed, "I would feel the same way."

Rose stated, "We need to run a paternity test as soon as possible."

Vinnie interjected, "I can get the DNA sample from Flora now. I've got a kit in my trunk. I just need to swab the inside of her cheek."

Helen agreed, "That would be fine."

Rose turned to him. "Well? What are you waiting for? Go get it!"

Vinnie raced out to retrieve the kit.

Rose addressed Helen, "Would you like anything? Water? Tea?"

"No, thank you. I think we've inconvenienced you enough."

"It's no bother."

"Really, I'm fine. Thank you."

Vinnie returned with the kit and swabbed the inside of Flora's mouth.

Rose instructed Vinnie, "Joey's in his room. Go get his sample while you're at it. This needs to be resolved once and for all."

Vinnie picked up the kit and headed for Joe's bedroom. "Yes, Aunt Rose."

When he reached the door, he knocked.

An angry Joe asked, "What?"

"It's me, Vinnie."

"What do you want?"

"I have to swab you."

"You have to what?"

Vinnie repeated, "Swab you. Open the door."

"You've got to be kidding."

"No. Open up."

Joe opened the door. "Geez."

"It will only take a second. Open your mouth."

Joe opened wide.

Vinnie swabbed Joe's cheek and deposited the sample in a collection tube. "All done."

"Good. Get out."

As he left, Vinnie said, "Sorry."

Joe shut the door.

Vinnie returned to the kitchen, where he assured the women, "As soon as the results come in, I'll let you know."

Helen apologized, "Again, I'm very sorry. I didn't raise Mita to be this way. I apologize for the damage she's done."

Accepting the apology, Rose said, "Thank you for saying that."

Vinnie concluded, "I think we're done here. I'll take you home now."

Without prompting, Flora said, "Thank you for the milk and cookies."

Rose replied, "You're welcome, dear."

Flora took her grandmother's hand. "Bye!"

As Rose watched them depart, she wondered if the beautiful child was her granddaughter.

CHAPTER 23

STILL in her party dress, Sara sat at the kitchen table. Hunched over, she concentrated on the pad of paper in front of her.

As Anna and Laura joined her, she put her pen down.

Anna inquired, "What are you doing?"

In a low voice, Sara revealed, "Making a list of pros and cons."

Laura asked, "How's it going?"

Pushing the pad toward her, Sara replied, "The list of cons is longer."

Laura glanced at the list. "How do you feel about that?"

"Not good."

Attempting to be optimistic, Anna asked, "Are you sure you listed everything?"

"Yes."

Laura pushed the pad aside. "Maybe you shouldn't be so analytical about it. Maybe listen to your heart a little."

Sara agonized, "My heart is broken, and it's bleeding to death. My head feels like it's going to explode. And I want to throw up."

Laura suggested, "Maybe you'll feel better after you sleep on it."

Sara disagreed, "I doubt it. What's to sleep on?"

In an attempt to comfort her, Anna noted, "It's been a long, stressful day. You need time to let it work itself out."

Frazzled, Sara replied, "I don't *have* time. And what's to work out?"

Laura suggested, "Maybe the little girl isn't his. That makes a big difference."

"Okay, for argument's sake, let's say she's not his. He still cheated on me and lied about it."

Laura said, "Yes, he did. But it was years ago. He said he's sorry."

Anna added, "I don't think he'll do it again."

Sara threw up her hands. "Maybe, maybe not. He's done it once. He could do it again."

Laura replied, "Technically, yes. But I don't think he would."

"But who knows for sure?"

Patting Sara's shoulder, Anna suggested, "I think the key is to try to be positive."

Sara shrugged her off. "I can pretend to be positive, but how about if the child is his? Then I'm stuck with the constant reminder of what he did. And I'll have to deal with that crazy bitch for the rest of my life. You know she's going to make my life a living hell."

Anna reminded her, "But you're soulmates. You and Joe are meant to be together."

Sara disagreed, "Maybe not. Things keep pulling us apart."

"But you find your way back to one another."

Sara explained, "Because it's our default position. We think we should be together, so we try desperately to force it. I think God, the universe, fate, destiny, or whatever it is, keeps intervening for a reason."

Solemnly, Laura said, "Sounds like you've made a decision."

Sorrowfully, Sara replied, "Yeah. I don't think I'm meant to be with Joe. I don't trust him. I don't think I ever will. I'll always be wondering if he's telling me the truth. And I can't live like that. I don't want to live like that."

Chapter 24

After Mita was booked, she was taken to a holding cell. As the female officer locked the cell, Mita yelled, "You can't keep me here! I didn't do anything. I want a lawyer."

The officer chuckled. "Of course you do. I'll get right on that."

"Filthy pig!"

Taking a step back, the officer asked, "Now, is that any way to get what you want?"

Mita bellowed, "I have rights! I want a lawyer."

In a condescending tone, she stated, "It's Sunday night, sweetheart. They'll get to you tomorrow. In the meantime, you can cool down and dry out."

Mita paced in the cell.

A large woman on the far bench ordered, "Sit down. You're annoying me."

Mita refused, "No."

The woman insisted, "Sit your ugly ass down. I'm not going to tell you again."

"What are you going to do if I don't?"

The woman stood. She towered over Mita. "I'm in for trying to kill my husband. He managed to run. But you have nowhere to go, and I bet I could snap your neck in seconds."

The woman's threat appeared to be genuine. So, Mita stopped pacing and sat on the bench farthest from the woman.

Mita's cravings for a cigarette and a bottle of vodka raged as time dragged on.

Thrilled she ruined Joe's engagement party, she congratulated herself in her mind, *I showed him. I crashed his perfect party with his perfect little fiancé. What a stupid whiny bitch she was. I'm going to bleed him dry. I'm going to get every last penny he owes me. He screwed up my life. It's high time I screwed up his. He had it coming. Stupid son of a bitch.*

This resentment had dominated the last five years of her life. *It's time for retribution, Joe Lazaro. And as soon as I get out of this dump, I'm going to take exactly what's mine and then some.*

The female officer returned, pushing a cart with meal trays for the women. She announced, "Come and get it. Dinner's served."

The other women collected their trays and sat down to eat.

Mita shouted, "I don't want dinner. I want out. Where's my lawyer?"

"Like I said, it's Sunday night. Deal with it."

"This is bullshit."

"You better relax. You're spending the night regardless. So suck it up, buttercup."

Mita met with the public defender in the morning. She refused a plea bargain. As a result, the judge set bail at fifty thousand dollars.

Mita yelled, "Where the hell am I going to get that kind of money?"

Calmly, the public defender replied, "And that's why I told you to accept the plea deal."

She grumbled as they returned her to jail.

CHAPTER 25

A FTER Tony and Dee finished cleaning up the house, Tony announced, "I'm driving Dee home."

Distracted, Rose said, "Dee, it was nice meeting you."

"You too, Mrs. Lazaro. I'm sure everything will work out fine."

Appreciative of the girl's positive attitude, Rose replied, "I'm not too sure about that. But you never know."

As Tony and Dee left the house, Dee asked, "Remember when I said I wasn't the bridal shower kind of girl?"

Tony opened the car door for her. "Yeah."

She sat in the passenger seat. "Well, after that fiasco, I'm sure of it."

He closed the door and walked to the driver's side of the vehicle. After getting comfortable in his seat, he said, "From what I know about showers, this was an anomaly."

"Uh huh."

"I'm glad you were there to help though. God knows what could have happened if you weren't there to intervene and slap on those pink fuzzy handcuffs."

Shaking her head in dismay, Dee commented, "I still can't believe your Aunt Serena bought those. And you should have heard the other sex stuff she and her sister were talking about. I thought your mother was going to lose her mind."

He started the car. "I can only imagine." Tony pulled out of the street. "Am I really going to meet your family now?"

"Ha! You worked up an appetite and want a big Greek meal? Sorry, no. I think we've both had enough family drama for one day."

As Tony turned into Dee's apartment complex, a black Chevy Suburban with tinted windows pulled out of the lot.

When they arrived at Dee's apartment, the door was ajar.

On alert, Tony and Dee nodded to one another and pulled their weapons. Tony nudged the door open fully with his foot.

There were signs of intrusion. Pictures were knocked over. Couch cushions and throw pillows were scattered on the floor. Papers were strewn on the countertops.

The pair quickly cleared each room.

Tony observed, "I don't believe this was just a random burglary. Fuentes is sending a message."

Dee concurred, "Message received. And I'll bet it was the guys in the black Suburban. We just missed them."

"Agreed. Anything missing?"

Shaking her head, she assessed the mayhem. "Doesn't look like it. They just tossed the place."

Suspicious, Tony said, "Maybe they left something behind instead."

Following this thought process, she asked, "You think they might have planted a bomb?"

"Can't be too sure these days. Better safe than sorry."

Tony called Sully. "We have a situation."

As they exited the unit, Tony pulled the fire alarm. Tenants teemed out of the building and congregated in the parking lot. Sully and the rest of the team assembled onsite in less than five minutes. They established a perimeter and moved everyone away from the building.

The fire department arrived two minutes later.

Sully immediately identified himself to the firemen as being with Homeland Security. He quickly flashed a badge and told the fire crew to stay back. A bomb threat was being investigated.

Ashby and Spaulding were the bomb experts. Outfitted with protective gear, they entered the building. They conducted an extensive search of the apartment and adjoining areas.

When Ashby and Spaulding emerged, Ashby reported, "All clear. Heads-up though, the walls now have ears. They planted a bug."

Sully acknowledged, "Good job." Turning to the fire chief, he said, "Premises are secure. You're free to conduct a sweep if you'd like. We're moving out."

Never having encountered this type of situation before, the chief responded, "Okay. Thanks."

Tony instructed Dee, "Grab some things. You're going on vacation."

Peeved at the inconvenience, Dee said, "I have a feeling I'm not going to enjoy myself much on this vacation."

Tony stated, "Your place is bugged now. They probably have eyes on us too. We'll discuss it when we're out of here. And just in case, bring a dress for my brother's wedding."

Petulantly, Dee asked, "Do I have to?"

"Yes."

Tony stood guard while Dee packed some necessities. After all of the residents returned to their units, there was no unusual activity on the street.

Carrying two bags, she announced, "I'm ready."

Tony inquired, "Before we go, do you have any scissors or wire cutters?"

Dee smiled. "I know what you're thinking." She pulled the back off her phone and removed the SIM card. "I have an industrial shredder. It'll do the trick."

Tony extracted his SIM card and handed it to Dee.

She shoved her card into the slot. The shredder ate through her card. She repeated the process with Tony's card. "We'll get burners on the way."

"I love how you can read my mind."

After obtaining new cell phones, food, and supplies, Tony and Dee drove around on the outskirts of town to spot any tails. They were not being followed. So, Tony drove to a remote location. It was heavily wooded. Trees canopied the narrow road. There was a small house in the woods at the end of the road.

As she surveyed the landscape, Dee quipped, "I'm beginning to hear banjo music."

"Ha! No, this is not *Deliverance*, smart ass."

Dee wrinkled her nose. "Sure looks like it."

He reassured her, "It's safe here. The trees shelter us from prying eyes in the sky. There's no way to track us."

"How about the GPS on your car?"

Shutting off the vehicle, he said, "Disabled as soon as I got it. We're completely off the grid."

Opening her door, she replied, "I should have known you would have thought of that."

They approached the house together.

Unlocking the door, he said, "Welcome to my home away from home."

She crossed the threshold. Scanning the primitive surroundings, she observed, "Pretty sparse accommodations."

Sarcastically, he responded, "Next time, I'll book you a room at a Hilton. You'll just have to make due with the two hundred thread count sheets."

She joked, "Just two hundred? Talk about roughing it."

Tony volleyed back, "Interesting comment coming from someone with stories about having to use leaves for a blanket and a rock for a pillow."

"I'm just messing with you."

He knew she was joking, but he enjoyed tormenting her when the opportunity presented itself.

"How long are you planning on being here?"

"Until Fuentes and his mother are apprehended or my brother's wedding, whichever comes first."

"You're joking."

"Nope. It's been a long day. We should get some shut-eye."

Dee questioned, "Shouldn't one of us stand watch?"

Tony opened a door that revealed a security room, complete with monitors. "The system will stand guard for us. If anyone gets within a mile, we'll know about it."

Testing him, she asked, "Then what?"

"Then, we can use the cache of weapons I have on hand, under these floorboards." He stomped over the access spot.

Dee saw one board was slightly offset from the others. Still, she questioned, "If that fails?"

Proud to show off his preparedness, he proclaimed, "Oh ye, of little faith! In the event that fails, I do have an underground escape tunnel."

Secretly impressed with his resourcefulness, she asked, "Seriously?"

"Dead serious, Georgie."

Satisfied, she stated, "You thought of everything."

"It must have been the Boy Scout training of my youth. I'm always prepared."

"That you are."

CHAPTER 26

SARA sat quietly, bent over at the kitchen table, her head rested on her crossed arms. Damp used tissues were strewn across the tabletop.

Laura rubbed her eyes and yawned as she entered the kitchen. She greeted Sara flatly, "Morning." She rubbed Sara's back as she passed her, not knowing what else to do.

Sounding nasally from bouts of crying, she answered, "Morning."

Laura poured herself a glass of orange juice. "Did you get any sleep at all?"

Despondent, she replied, "No."

"You should have gotten me up. I would have kept you company."

"No. You're pregnant. You need your sleep."

"Then you could have woken Anna up."

"No. She has a big presentation at work today. And I needed to think. I finally made my decision."

Laura sat next to her. "Okay. Whatever you decide, I'll support you."

"Thanks."

Laura waited.

Sara lifted her head up and sighed. Her face was puffy and splotchy from crying. "I'm positive I can't go back to Joe. I'm calling off the wedding."

"Oh, Sara, I'm sorry."

Tears flowed again. "So am I."

Empathizing, Laura asked, "Is there anything I can do?"

Weakly, Sara said, "Yes."

"Just name it."

"I thought about it all night." She paused. "I can't get the deposits back for the flowers or the caterer. I want you and John to get married on Saturday instead."

Flabbergasted, Laura said, "Sara, that's generous, but I couldn't. I don't feel right about it."

Sara pulled a tissue from the box. "It's the only thing to do at this point."

Laura suggested, "Maybe Mrs. Lazaro can do something to get the money back."

Sara wiped her nose. "I don't want her help. Don't you understand? You getting married is the only thing that makes any sense right now. Everything else in my life is a mess. I have a church reserved and food ordered. It's stupid to let it go to waste. You have to. You're pregnant."

Hemming and hawing, Laura said, "I don't know. It doesn't seem right."

"Please, Laura. I want you guys to be happy."

"Oh, Sara, I want *you* to be happy. I wish I could erase the past twenty-four hours."

Physically and mentally exhausted, Sara said, "Nobody wishes that more than me."

"I'm so sorry, Sara."

"Thanks. Just say that you'll get married on Saturday."

"I'll talk to John about it. But I feel guilty being happy and celebrating when you're hurting so much."

Sara wiped away tears with the back of her hand. "Just because I'm not happy doesn't mean you can't be happy. Something good needs to come out of this."

"I'm still going to feel guilty."

"Forget it. You're pregnant. This is going to be a wonderful time for you and John. You two deserve to be happy."

Laura hugged Sara. "Thank you."

"You're welcome." Sara blew her nose.

"I'm guessing it's too much to ask for you to be my maid of honor."

Sara laughed painfully. "If this was a soap opera, I'd do it. I'd stand there across the aisle in my bridesmaid's dress, looking at Joe, wishing it was the two of us exchanging vows." She paused and sighed heavily. "But this isn't a soap opera. Although, it does feel like one."

Laura apologized, "I'm sorry for even bringing it up."

"Don't be sorry. I know we swore to be best friends forever and stand up for each other. But honestly, I just can't do that right now."

"Don't worry about it."

Crying, Sara lamented, "I really wish I could."

As Laura hugged Sara, she said, "I wish I could take this pain away from you."

"Me too." She pulled away and reached for a tissue from the almost empty box. Sara blew her nose. "I've decided to go away."

"Where?"

"I don't know. I just have to get out of here, or I'm going to lose it. I need some time alone to figure things out. A road trip might clear my head."

Concerned, Laura questioned, "A road trip alone?"

"Why not? I have a cell phone. I have AAA if anything happens to the car. I'll be fine."

"If you can wait a couple weeks, I can schedule vacation and go with you."

"No. Thanks, but no. I need to be alone."

"I know I already asked, but where are you going to go? You have to have some idea."

The pile of used tissues on the table finally registered in Sara's brain. She gathered them up and threw them in the trash. "I don't have any set plans. I'm just going to drive and see where the road takes me."

"That's not like you. You make itineraries and reservations." Laura sipped her orange juice.

"I'm just going to wing it."

Laura choked on her juice and coughed. "Wing it? You don't wing anything."

She held her arms open wide. "Well, we see what planning everything got me."

The doorbell rang, interrupting their conversation.

Laura jumped up. "I'll get it." As she opened the door, she thought, *Oh crap.*

Before Laura breathed a word, Joe noted, "I know everyone in this house hates me. I get it. I hate me. But I have to talk to her. Please, I'm begging you."

From the kitchen, Sara yelled, "Let him in."

Laura stepped aside and allowed Joe to enter.

Sara met them in the family room and sat on the far end of the couch.

Joe sat on the opposite end of the couch, careful to leave a couch cushion between them. He had dark circles under his eyes.

Laura informed Sara, "I'll be in my room if you need me."

Sara nodded.

Tension saturated the air.

Grateful, Joe said, "Thank you for agreeing to see me."

Awkwardly, Sara replied, "You're welcome."

Joe began, "I know I was stupid and reckless. But it was years ago, and I'm different now. I know exactly what I want. I want you. I love you, Sara. I never loved her. You have to believe me. It's always been you."

Sara contradicted him, "Except for all the times you were screwing her and when you were raising a child with her."

He readily admitted, "I'm not perfect. I made a huge mistake."

"One with lasting consequences."

He shifted on the couch cushion. "I'm sorry. I wish I could make you understand how sorry I am."

Sara crossed her arms. "You're sorry you got caught."

The truth hurt. Joe had never planned to tell Sara about his indiscretion. But the truth always had a way of coming out. He especially regretted that the truth came out the way it did.

He continued, "I'm sorry for everything—the way I acted, the lies, the cheating, all of it. Please believe me."

Sara saw the anguish in his eyes. "I believe you're sorry. But it's not enough."

He begged, "Tell me what I can do."

Tears welled in her eyes. "There's nothing you can do. You've broken my heart completely. You're a liar and a cheater. I can't trust you. I don't think I can ever trust you."

He pleaded, "There has to be a way. We're meant to be together. Sara, you're the love of my life."

She confessed, "I will always love you, Joe. Always. But I can't be with you. What if Flora really is yours?"

"We'll deal with it."

"Deal with it? She's a child, not a situation. And that horrible crazy bitch would be a part of our lives forever. I would have to sit in school auditoriums, on ball fields, and God knows what else, with her there too. Constantly reminding me of what you did. Rubbing it in every chance she got."

"Maybe over time …"

Sara interrupted, "It will *not* get better over time. I already resent you, and I will end up resenting your child. I'll end up bitter and negative. I *can't* live like that. I *won't* live like that."

Grasping at straws, he proposed, "I'll relinquish custody."

Disgusted, she asked, "And leave that poor child to grow up with only that witch? How could you do that?"

He shrugged.

Disappointed with him as a man, she answered for him. "That's right, you already did it once by leaving Italy. I don't know how you can so easily dismiss your own child. And who's to say you wouldn't do the same to me and our children one day?"

He promised, "I wouldn't."

"But you could. You've already demonstrated that you can. It was easy for you. And you're willing to do it *again*. You just said so."

"It's different. Our children will be conceived in love. I won't leave you or them. I swear." He crossed his heart.

His gesture was lost on her. "Your words don't mean anything anymore. And get real. Your mother won't let you give up that child if she's yours."

Joe knew that to be true.

Summoning all of the courage she possessed, she removed the engagement ring from her finger. Hand trembling, she held it out to him. "The wedding is off, Joe. I can't marry you."

Joe's stomach dropped. His mind refused to process her words. *This can't be happening.* "I won't take the ring back. Flora might not be mine."

"It doesn't matter. This has made me realize that we don't belong together."

Joe insisted, "That's not true. We do."

She disagreed, "No, we don't. Fate keeps intervening. I have to take this as a sign."

Feeling his true love slip away, he begged, "Please don't."

Her tears flowed as she spoke, "I have no other choice. I need to reevaluate everything and figure out what I want to do now."

"There's nothing to figure out. I love you. You admitted you love me. What more is there?"

"So many things, like respect, trust, honesty, integrity. I need to move on."

Since he refused to take the ring from her, she laid it on the coffee table.

Desperate, he begged, "Please, Sara, I'll make it up to you somehow. I swear. Even if it takes the rest of my life."

"I'm done, Joe. It's killing me to say this, but I'm done with you. I'm done with us."

In utter disbelief, he questioned, "How? How can this be the end?"

She sobbed, "It has to be. I'm sorry."

He reached out to her and held her face in his hands. "But you love me, and I love you."

Her bottom lip quivered as she whispered, "I do love you, but I just can't be with you anymore."

Joe embraced Sara. Feeling their bond slip away and their hearts break, they held each other tightly and sobbed.

This felt worse than death—an emptiness, a wound that would never heal.

With tear-stained faces, they relaxed their embrace. Looking into each other's eyes, they kissed one final time—an insufficient end to such a passionate, tumultuous love story.

They sat in silence, attempting to absorb their new reality.

After a few moments, she quietly confessed, "I'm going away."

"Going away? To where?"

She wiped her tears away. "I don't know. I need to clear my head."

"It's too dangerous to go alone. I know you don't want me, but take Laura or Anna."

Focusing on the facts, she revealed, "Laura and John are getting married Saturday instead of us. She's pregnant, and the church is already booked. Anna's standing up for her because I just can't bring myself to do it."

Trying to process this news, he muttered, "Laura's pregnant? If you're not going to the wedding because you think I'll be there, I won't go. It's more important that you be there."

Smiling at the absurdity of this conversation, she said, "It doesn't matter if you were going to be there or not. It was supposed to be *our* wedding day. There's no way I can stand in that church on that day. I'm just not strong enough."

CHAPTER 27

LAURA watched for John at the window. She opened the front door before he reached it.

Surprised, John asked, "Can't wait to see me?"

She put her index finger to her lips, indicating he should be quiet. She whispered, "Thanks for coming over here. I didn't want to leave Sara alone. I gave her a sleeping pill. Hopefully, she'll get some sleep. But I want to be here when she wakes up. I don't want her to be alone."

Speaking softly, he replied, "I get it. Where's Anna?"

"At work. I told her she might as well go since Sara's sleeping. I can handle things until she gets back."

Astonished, John remarked, "I still can't believe what happened at the shower. I mean, Joe might be a father. But what really blows my mind is that he cut off all contact with her. That's so unreal."

"Well, we don't know for sure she's his daughter yet."

"Still though. He thought she was, and he left."

"So, he never mentioned anything about it to you before?"

He shook his head. "No. I thought I knew him better than that. We've been friends since we were kids. I have to say the whole thing surprised me."

"Do you want something to drink?"

"No. What I want is a kiss."

She kissed him tenderly.

"That's better. How's Sara?"

She led him by the hand to the love seat. They sat.

Laura sighed. "Not good. Not good at all. She's done with Joe. She told him a little while ago. He's not doing well either."

Dumbfounded, he exclaimed, "She's *done*, done?"

She confirmed, "Yes. She's completely done. I overheard the breakup. It was the saddest thing I've ever heard."

The dismay resounded in his words. "Wow! I always thought they'd be together."

Laura draped her leg over John's leg to get more comfortable. "So did she. But she can't get past the lies and the cheating."

He rested his hands on her leg. "Can't say that I blame her. It's just hard to believe. Everything changed in an instant."

"Yes, it did. And Sara can't get the deposits back on anything."

He leaned into her and kissed her neck, just below her ear. "That sucks."

"Yes. But there's a silver lining of sorts."

He placed delicate kisses down the length of her neck. "Really? What's that?"

Struggling to focus, she said, "She offered us everything."

Clearly not paying attention, he replied, "That's nice."

Laura spelled it out for him. "We can get married on Saturday instead."

His kisses stopped. "Huh?"

She repeated, "We can get married Saturday."

With a quizzical expression on his face, he asked, "Why would you want to do that?"

Not liking his answer, she pushed away from him. "You don't want to?"

"Well, I didn't say that. It's just a bit sudden. What's the rush?"

Laura's stomach flipped. Panic overcame her. "Are you saying that you don't want to marry me?"

John noticed the drastic change in her demeanor. He patted her. "Laura, calm down."

Trembling, she asked, "Calm down? Why did you propose if you don't want to get married?"

Attempting to soothe her, John said, "I didn't say that. You're jumping to the wrong conclusion. I *want* to marry you. I just thought we'd take our time to plan everything, so it's the perfect wedding you've always dreamed of."

Laura protested, "We don't have time!"

"Sweetheart, we have all the time in the world."

"No, we don't!"

Confused, he asked, "Why not? Because of what happened with Joe and Sara? That's not going to happen with us."

Hormones raging, Laura shouted, "No! Because I'm pregnant!"

Stunned, the words slowly tumbled out of his mouth, "You're pregnant?"

Shaking, she confirmed, "Yes."

Laura did not want to tell John in this fashion, but she could not take back her words.

"Oh, wow!" He ran his fingers through his hair. "Are you sure?"

Although she did not have the definitive proof of a blood test, she knew her body. She responded, "Yes." She waited anxiously for the news to soak in.

He repeated, "Wow!"

She felt queasy. She knew the news would shock him, but she hoped his reaction would be positive.

Finally regaining his faculties, John realized, "So that pregnancy test Sara was holding, that was for you, not her?"

Laura admitted, "Yes, I panicked when I saw you."

He took her hands in his. "Why?"

"You have to ask?"

"Okay. I get it. And that explains why you wanted cider instead of wine. Duh! I should have figured it out."

"How could you have guessed? We used protection. And it's not like I'm showing yet or anything."

Shaking any doubts from his own mind, he looked directly into her eyes. "I want to spend the rest of my life with you. If you want to get married on Saturday, we'll get married on Saturday."

Worried, she said, "Now you're just saying that because of the baby."

Gently, he rested his hand on her abdomen. "Baby or no baby, I want to start our life together. If we could get the church today, I'd marry you today."

Still doubtful, Laura questioned, "You mean it? You're not just saying that?"

John slipped his right hand behind her head. He leaned in and pulled her to him. The kiss that followed was the only answer Laura needed.

CHAPTER 28

TUESDAY and Wednesday were rainy and gloomy days. The weather only exacerbated Sara's melancholy mood. She refused to eat and stayed in bed most of the time.

Sara had called her mother on Tuesday. The call went straight to voice mail. In a weak voice, she left a message. "Hi, Mom. It's Sara. I'm calling to tell you that the wedding is off. Joe and I aren't getting married. He betrayed me. It all came out at the shower. It was horrible. I'm totally devastated. I really need to talk to you. Please call me as soon as you get this. Love you."

Her mother failed to return Sara's call. Instead, on Wednesday, she received an e-mail.

Sara emerged from her room. She yelled, "Oh my God!"

Anna questioned, "What? What happened?"

Laura rushed in from the other room. "What?"

Holding her cell phone, Sara answered, "My mother! My own mother couldn't be bothered to call me back. She sent me a lousy e-mail. An e-mail! My life is crumbling down around me, and she sends an e-mail!"

Anna and Laura exchanged glances. It was evident they could not believe the callous actions of Sara's mother.

Sara read the e-mail aloud. "Sara, we're so sorry to hear the wedding is off. But you're young and pretty, and you'll find someone else. We've decided to cancel our flight, since there's no wedding. Your dad and I think you should come down and join us instead. It will make you realize that your problem is small compared to others' problems. We'll be in touch soon. Love, Mom."

Sara was stunned. Not only did her mother not call her back, but she minimized her pain. She did not understand how her mother could be so unfeeling and detached.

Dismayed, Anna and Laura responded in unison, "I'm sorry, Sara."

Feeling abandoned, Sara wept. Anna and Laura embraced her. They held the group hug for several minutes until Sara released them.

Sara announced, "I need to go to the bathroom."

When she was out of earshot, Laura whispered, "I can't believe Mrs. Taylor did that."

"I can't either. I guess we're it for her support network."

Laura shook her head. "As if things weren't bad enough already."

"Do you think we should try to call her parents?"

"No. She'll get pissed off that we interfered. And honestly, since her parents are being so selfish right now, I don't want them here. They won't be supportive. They'll just tell her to snap out of it and move on. She needs support and love. And we can give that to her."

"You're right. Her mother never was the loving, nurturing type anyway."

They heard Sara coming back, so they terminated the conversation.

Anna offered, "Would you like me to make you some tea or something?"

Sara carried a box into the room. "No."

Anna mouthed to Laura, "What's the box for?"

Laura mouthed back, "I don't know."

Through her tears, Sara walked through the house taking down pictures. Any picture that contained Joe or her parents was taken down and relegated to the box.

Realizing what she was doing, Laura asked, "Do you want me to do that for you?"

Somberly, Sara replied, "No. I need to do it."

Feeling helpless, Laura and Anna just followed Sara from room to room. Their hearts ached for her.

The final room was her bedroom. The girls knew the entire room, from top to bottom, was filled with pictures and mementos. It would be a daunting task to clear it out, even under the best of circumstances.

Without prompting, Sara said, "I can't go through everything in my room. I'm just going to sweep everything off of my dressers into the box. Can you guys take the pictures off the walls while I do that?"

"Sure. No problem."

Anna ran to get another box while Laura began taking down the pictures.

Laura stacked the pictures face down.

Sara confessed, "My feelings are just too raw to handle the flood of memories and all of the betrayal. I just need to eliminate their faces from my surroundings."

Laura replied, "I understand."

Anna returned with the box. She saw the stack of pictures and quickly placed them in the box.

Once everything was safely in boxes, Sara taped them shut. "I'm going to take these into the basement." Sara lifted the first box.

Grabbing the second box, Anna volunteered, "I'll help you."

After returning to the kitchen, Sara announced, "I'm going to start packing for my trip."

Laura offered, "If you need any help, let us know."

"I think I can pack my own underwear without any help. Thanks."

A long list of tasks to cancel Sara's remaining wedding plans loomed.

Anna said to Laura, "I didn't want to upset Sara any more than she already is, but it's Wednesday. We need to try to cancel whatever you're not going to need for your wedding on Saturday. And we need to notify all of the guests."

"I know. I took her wedding planning guide from her room. I'll be using a lot. But the big thing I really need to get for myself is my wedding gown. I can't wear hers."

"Yeah. That would be too weird."

"Let's split up the guest list and start making calls. I'll call Mrs. Lazaro. She can help."

"Good idea."

Laura made the awkward phone call to Rose. "Mrs. Lazaro, it's Laura."

"Hi, dear. How's Sara?"

Truthfully, Laura answered, "Not good. I hate to call about this, but we need to contact everyone to tell them the wedding's off. Anna and I can take care of Sara's side. I was hoping you'd take care of your side."

Rose replied, "Of course, I'll take care of the guests on our side. It's the least I can do."

"Thank you."

"Do you need me to call the florist or the caterer? They'll probably give you trouble because you're cancelling so late."

"No. We're not cancelling entirely. John and I are going to get married instead."

Flabbergasted, Rose asked, "Really? Pardon me for saying so, but isn't that a bit insensitive on your part?"

"Believe me, I thought that too. But Sara was the one who suggested it and insisted."

Rose recovered, "Huh! Well, congratulations then!"

"Thank you. It's going to be difficult though."

"I can only imagine."

Extending an invitation, Laura said, "Of course, you're all invited to the wedding, if you want to come."

Rose lamented, "Under normal circumstances, I would love to be there. But I'm not leaving Joey alone that day. He's in a bad place right now."

"I understand."

Apologetically, Rose replied, "I'm just sorry that my son was so stupid. If Sara needs anything, let me know. I'm willing to help in any way I can."

"I know you are. I'll tell her. Thank you."

Chapter 29

I N his childhood bedroom, Joe laid in his bed, in the dark, running through scenarios to try to win Sara back. Despondent, he prayed that Flora was not his. *If she's not mine, I have a chance of getting Sara back.*

Rose opened his door without knocking and interrupted his futile musings. "You can't wallow in self-pity forever. I'm sorry it didn't work out. But actions have consequences. I've told you that since you were young."

"I know. You don't have to remind me."

Making a beeline for his drapes, she instructed, "You need to start planning for the future."

"I don't have a future without Sara."

She pulled back his drapes to let the sunshine in. "Yes, you do. You have to think about what you're going to do if that little girl is yours."

"I don't want to think about that." Putting his arm up to shield his eyes, he whined, "Geez, Ma, close the drapes!"

Dismissing his request, she insisted, "You have to think about it. And no, I will not close the drapes."

He pulled the covers over his head. "I'll deal with it when the time comes."

Not to be deterred, she yanked the covers off her son. "Fine then. Get out of that bed."

"No."

Rose's voice went up, "What did you just say?"

Defiant, he refused, "No, Ma. I'm not getting up."

She hovered over him at the side of his bed. One hand rested on her hip as the index finger on her other hand wagged at him. "You're too old for a temper tantrum. Don't make me drag you out of that bed. God knows I'll do it. Don't you test my patience, Joey."

Joe knew his mother was strong enough to physically drag him out of the bed. Petulantly, he sat up and swung his legs over the side of the bed. "Happy?"

"Not even close. Go take a shower. Make yourself presentable. You'll feel better."

Not believing that was true, he stood. "Don't bet on it."

While contemplating whether to follow him to the bathroom or not, the phone rang.

Rose answered, "Hello?"

"Hey, Ma, it's me, Tony."

Relieved to hear from her older son, she exclaimed, "Anthony! Where have you been? We have a major crisis here."

Used to his mother's opinion of what qualified as a crisis, he said, "I'm going to be out of town until the wedding. What's going on? What's the crisis this time?"

Gesturing as she spoke, she replied, "What's going on? Everything! Your brother's wedding is off. Sara broke up with him for good. Now John and Laura are getting married instead. You need to go to their wedding. We were all invited. But obviously, Joey can't go. And I'm not leaving him home alone that day. You need to go to represent the family."

Processing all of the new information, he said, "Sorry to hear about Joe and Sara. That's too bad."

"Your brother could use some support right now. He's moping around and feeling sorry for himself. You should come home and cheer him up."

"I wish I could, Ma. But I have to finish this business first."

Discontent, she responded, "Business! Always this mystery entrepreneur business with you! You need to go into a different line of work. Something respectable, so you can get married to that nice girl, Dee. Don't you let her get away. She'll make a good wife and mother. She looks sturdy."

Tony laughed. "Oh yeah, Dee's sturdy all right."

Perplexed about why he made that statement, Dee looked at him.

Tony winked at Dee.

Rose chided, "Don't be fresh, Anthony."

Wrapping up the conversation, he said, "I hear you, Ma. Gotta go. Love you."

"I love you, Anthony."

He disconnected the call.

Dee asked, "Do I even want to know?"

He laughed. "Probably not. I cut her off before she could comment on your child-bearing hips."

"She's not going to be happy when she finds out we're not a couple."

"You could spare her feelings and marry me."

"Now you've completely lost your mind."

Winking, he joked, "Think of it like taking one for the team."

"In your dreams, Lazaro."

With a gleam in his eye, he replied, "Can't fault a guy for trying."

Dee dialed her parents' phone number.

Her mother answered the phone, "Hello?"

"Hi, Mommy. It's me."

"Hi, honey. How are you?"

"Good, Mommy. I just wanted to let you know I'm going to be out of town this week."

"I'm glad you called when you did. Your father and I are going to Boca for the next two weeks on vacation. You remember my cousin, Benny, the one with the limp?"

"Yes."

"He retired down there and invited us to stay. Isn't that wonderful?"

"That's great."

"We leave tonight. It's so exciting!"

"I'm happy for you. Have a great time. I'll see you when you get back."

"Okay, honey. Love you."

"Love you, Mommy. Tell Daddy I love him too."

"I will. Good-bye."

"Good-bye."

Dee handed the phone back to Tony.

Accepting it, he commented, "That was quick."

"They're leaving for Boca tonight. So, I won't have to worry about them. They'll be out of town for two weeks."

Relieved, he replied, "Plenty of time for this whole mess to get resolved."

"Exactly. So now what?"

"We can play cards or twenty questions."

Facetiously, she asked, "What? No spin the bottle?"

He smirked. "If you want to kiss me, kiss me."

She pushed him away. "Oh, you'd like that wouldn't you?"

"Yes. And you know you would too."

She protested, "Oh, you wish."

He teased, "You brought it up, not me."

She brushed off the comment and walked into the kitchen area.

He followed and cornered her.

She confronted him, "What?"

He leaned in and kissed her.

Her mind urged her, *Go for it. You want him. Take him.*

She pulled back from the kiss.

Tony steeled himself for the slap he anticipated.

Instead, with both hands, Dee grabbed his shirt just above the first button and pulled in opposite directions. Buttons flew every which way.

Tony was stunned but thrilled. He saw the look in her eye—a tigress stalking her prey.

He eagerly played along and moved backward slowly.

She pursued him.

He removed his shirt and tossed it aside. He tempted, "Come and get me."

Loving a challenge, she lunged at him. He fell onto the couch.

Although he was not resisting her advances, she was aggressive and pinned him down.

With the same gusto she possessed when popping the buttons off his shirt, she liberated him of his pants and underwear. She yanked hard enough that his shoes came off with them.

She shed her own clothes as she surveyed his naked body. His full erection beckoned to her.

Gazing up, he took in every inch of her curves with his eyes. His hands were jealous and wanted to feel those perfect curves for themselves.

Without warning, she pounced. Her hands grasped the back of the couch while she mounted him.

He guided her voluptuous hips as he slid deeply into her.

She gasped when his entire shaft was buried within her walls.

Tony wanted to kiss. But Dee was not interested in foreplay or kissing.

Her groaning increased in intensity as she grinded against him. He had found her G spot.

He gave her what she wanted, heaving into her.

Dee's breathing became more labored.

He knew it would not be long now.

With fierce determination, Dee rode him hard and fast.

Guiding her hips, Tony ensured he hit the right spot over and over.

Dee unleashed a guttural moan as she climaxed. Her volume level surpassed any other that Tony had ever heard. He delighted in her expressions of ecstasy.

When she finished, she rolled off of him onto the couch. "Thank you."

Tony laughed. "Thank you?"

Panting, she replied, "Yeah. That was really good."

"Well, sweetheart, I'm not done. So neither are you."

He scooped her up and carried her to the bed.

She attempted to catch her breath.

As he laid her on the bed, he informed her, "We've done it your way. Now we're doing it my way."

CHAPTER 30

L AURA felt a great deal of guilt being happy and preparing for her wedding day. It also brought frustration because everything was so rushed. With such short notice, it would be a small affair with just immediate family and close friends. Laura called her parents in Florida. They booked the next flight.

With the wedding day only two days away, Anna took Laura to Theresa's Bridal to pick out a wedding gown. They scoured the clearance racks until they found a dress in her size. It had more lace on it than she would have liked. But it fit her perfectly, and time was of the essence.

When they returned from shopping, they almost fell over Sara's bags which were staged next to the door.

Anna inquired, "Leaving so soon?"

Sara responded, "I just can't stay here any longer. I need to get out of here, or I'm going to lose what's left of my mind."

Noticing the garment bag draped over Laura's arm, Sara asked, "You found a dress?"

Feeling self-conscious, Laura said, "Yes."

"Can I see it?"

"Of course!"

They walked into the family room.

Laura laid the bag across the sofa. She unzipped it and held up the dress. "What do you think?"

Sara critiqued it, "It's beautiful. I love the mermaid style. But I didn't expect all of that lace."

"It looks better on."

"I don't doubt you look gorgeous in it. You can wear anything. I am just surprised you picked lace."

Putting it back in the bag, Laura confessed, "It basically picked me. It was the only gown that fit without needing alterations."

"I'm glad you found such a pretty gown."

"Thank you. I just wish ..."

Sara interrupted her, "Don't say it. I know."

Laura threw her arms around Sara. "I'm going to miss you."

Sara hugged her. "I'm going to miss you guys too. I really should be going now. I want to drive in daylight."

Getting choked up, Laura nodded.

Anna directed, "Call or text us, and let us know where you are."

Sara confirmed, "I will." Turning to Laura, she said, "You're going to make a beautiful bride. Be happy."

"Thank you. I'll try."

Addressing Anna, Sara stressed, "You're in charge. Take good care of her while I'm gone."

"I'll do my best."

Hating long farewells, Sara picked up her bags. "I'll be back in a couple of weeks. Bye."

They called after her, "Bye."

Sara loaded her bags in the trunk and left for parts unknown.

The girls watched her Impala disappear from the front window.

Anna asked, "Do you think we should have let her go?"

Laura stated, "I don't think we ever had a choice. This is something she has to do."

CHAPTER 31

S ARA drove aimlessly for hours. Her instincts and reflexes operated the vehicle on autopilot. When dusk arrived, she found herself in the Adirondacks. Fatigued, she stopped at a diner to rest and eat.

It was an old-fashioned, hole-in-the-wall type of diner. She guessed it had been built in the 1950s. The place was clean, but everything was faded, from the black and white checkerboard floor to the red vinyl booth seats and counter stools.

The waitress, a spry woman in her 70s, gave Sara a menu and a glass of water as she rattled off the specials.

"Thank you. I'll need a few minutes."

"No problem, hon. I've got all the time in the world. Holler when you're ready." The waitress ambled away, turning her attention to another customer at the counter. She warmed up his coffee.

Sara texted Laura to let her know she was okay and that she would probably spend the next few days in the Adirondacks.

With that task complete, Sara leaned forward and scanned the menu. Although she had not eaten much lately, the smell of bacon that permeated the diner whetted her appetite.

When the waitress returned, Sara noticed her nametag. The waitress' name was Betty.

Pad and pen in hand, Betty asked, "Did you decide yet, hon?"

"Yes." Sara ordered breakfast for dinner—scrambled eggs, limp bacon, and a blueberry muffin. Then she went to the ladies' room to freshen up.

As she slid back into her booth, two men walked in. They looked like they survived a fight in a mud pit.

She gave them the once-over. They were both rugged, well-built men. Their hair was dirty blond, although she laughed internally at the redundancy today. Their blue eyes shone brightly through the grime.

The older one shouted, "Hi there, Betty! How's my favorite girl today?"

Betty winked. "I'm still on the right side of the grass."

As they cozied up to the counter, they greeted all of the men occupying the other counter stools, who Sara assumed to be regulars.

Betty commented, "Looks like another hard day, boys."

The older of the two men replied, "Yes, but we finally finished."

Betty clapped her hands together. "Heavens be praised!"

The younger one chimed in, "And just before the storm. The sky to the west is pretty dark. Clouds are moving fast."

"Then we better get you fed and on your way. The usual?"

In unison, they responded, "Yes, ma'am."

As a mother would, she instructed them, "Go get cleaned up while I put your order in."

When they returned, Sara observed their hands and faces were clean, but their clothes were still covered with what she hoped was just dirt.

The two men tormented each other and roughhoused a bit.

The waitress threatened jokingly, "If you boys don't settle down, I'll call your mother, and she'll straighten you both out."

The older brother complained, "Don't call her; she'll just side with Tommy. She always sides with Tommy, because he's the baby."

Tommy shoved his older brother.

Betty picked up Sara's meal while she chided the men. "Don't make me separate the two of you."

The men laughed.

The waitress served Sara's meal, hot off the grill. The bacon smelled heavenly.

Sara said, "Thank you."

Betty asked, "Can I get you anything else?"

Eyeing the older brother, she answered, "No, I'm good."

He had a certain *je ne sais quoi* about him.

The waitress noticed Sara staring and raised her right eyebrow. "That's Phil Potter. He's real easy on the eyes. If you're going to be sticking around, I can introduce you."

Embarrassed, Sara put her hands up and declined, "No. I'm just passing through."

Betty smirked knowingly. "Let me know if you change your mind. He's quite a catch."

Sara continued to stare at the Potter brothers. The other patrons in the diner were boring compared to them. And the more she watched, the more she fixated on Phil.

As if he felt her eyes on him, Phil turned around.

She averted her gaze until he faced forward again. Then she resumed staring.

He spoke to Betty, who glanced in her direction and smiled.

Sara picked up a piece of bacon with her fingers and devoured it. The sweet and salty mix awakened her taste buds. She chased the bacon with a forkful of scrambled eggs.

Phil glanced Sara's way and winked at her.

Reflexively, she smiled. Then she split her blueberry muffin in half. The warmth of the muffin soaked up the butter she spread across it.

Biting into it, blueberries popped in her mouth. This was one of the freshest muffins she had ever tasted.

So engrossed in her meal, Sara did not see Phil leave his stool.

Savoring the last morsel of muffin and licking her fingers, Sara was mortified when Phil appeared in front of her.

With a winning smile, Phil said, "Hi there."

Wiping her fingers on the napkin in her lap, she replied, "Hi."

"Mind if I sit?"

Before she could answer, he slid into the booth seat across from her.

She stammered, "I was just about to leave."

He stretched his arm out across the top of the seat. "So soon? I was hoping to buy you a piece of pie."

She dabbed her lips with her napkin and placed it on the table. "I have someplace I have to be. I have reservations at a lodge in the mountains," she lied. "Thanks anyway."

Persistent, he attested, "Betty makes the best apple pie you've ever had. Trust me."

She thought, *Trust you?*

At the moment, she did not trust anyone, including herself, especially when it came to men.

Phil glanced out the window at the dark clouds. "The nearest lodge isn't that close, and the storm is moving in fast."

Nervous, her right leg bounced. "Then I better leave now."

Phil disagreed, "It might be safer to ride out the storm here."

Uncomfortable, she insisted, "No. I'll be fine. I really should be going."

"Suit yourself. You're missing out on some really good pie. Maybe next time."

Hurriedly, Sara replied, "Yeah. Maybe."

He winked as he pushed off the tabletop with his right hand and returned to his brother.

Relieved, Sara scooted out of the booth, hastily paid her check, and left.

The storm clouds moved quickly. She hoped to reach the lodge she had programmed on her GPS before the storm hit.

No such luck. The storm hit hard. The rounds of thunder and lightning were wicked. As she approached a curve, a deer jumped out into her path. She slammed on her brakes. However, due to the high volume of water on the road's surface, she hydroplaned. Screaming, she careened right off the road. When she hit the gravel and mud shoulder, the car stopped abruptly.

Shaken but not injured, Sara tried to catch her breath. Her heart pounded.

Praying there was enough gravel to provide traction, she threw the car into reverse. The car did not move. She actually felt the vehicle sink deeper into the mud. She knew she could not push it out without help. Stuck, she turned her hazard lights on. *For all the good that will do.*

She pulled her cell phone out of her purse. It registered no signal. *Wonderful. Just wonderful.*

She tossed the useless phone on the passenger seat.

Thinking her situation could not get any worse, she heard the unmistakable sound of hail hitting metal. Sara started to laugh at her lousy luck. Laughter quickly turned to tears as she realized her predicament. She screamed and beat the steering wheel with her hands until they hurt.

Then she leaned forward, draped her arms over the steering wheel, and rested her head against it. *What am I going to do? God, you have to help me. I just don't know what to do anymore.*

Although the wind gusts were strong, the car did not sway much due to the mud's suction. The hail came in waves. At times, she could barely see the hood of her car.

After what seemed an eternity, she saw the glowing red of brake lights.

She exclaimed, "Thank you, God!"

The Good Samaritan turned on his hazard lights before wading through the mud to reach her.

He wore a hard hat and a hoodie. He kept his head down.

She tried to open her door, but the mud prevented it. She powered down the window.

He shouted, "You okay?"

She cringed as the hail bounced off his hard hat. "Yes. But I'm stuck."

"From what I can see, you're stuck really good. There's no way I can get you out in the middle of this storm. Come with me, and we'll get the car out when the storm dies down."

Sara hesitated, "I don't know."

He yelled, "Lady, I'm standing here in the middle of a thunder and lightning storm, knee-deep in mud, getting pelted by hail, offering to help. What other option do you have?"

Sara furrowed her brow. He had a point. "Okay. But I can't open the door. It's stuck."

The stranger placed one hand on the door handle. He grabbed the door frame through the open window with the other. He steeled himself and heaved hard. The door opened enough for her to squeeze through.

She pressed the button to raise her window, turned off the car, and threw her keys in her purse. Then she slung her purse across her body diagonally, so she would not drop it.

The helpful man assisted her out of the car.

As they trudged on, she wished he had brought her a hard hat to wear. The hail hurt as it hit her head and body.

Halfway to the street, the mud sucked off one of her shoes. "Oh my God!"

"What?" He turned around and saw her bare foot and laughed.

"This isn't funny!" She attempted to balance on one leg to reach down to get her stuck shoe. Instead, she pinwheeled and toppled over into the mud. Sara screamed.

Her body weight shifted the mud. In a split second, the shoe was lost to her. She struggled to stand but fell again. Defeated and plastered in mud from head to toe, she cried.

Without a word, he bent over, put his hands under her arms and lifted her up. Now in a standing position, he swept her up in his arms.

Sara was too exhausted to protest.

He carried her to his truck. After managing to open the door, he slid her onto the seat. He slammed the door before running to his side of the truck.

Sara felt like a drowned muddy rat and assumed she looked like one too. Tears streaked her filthy face.

Once he was safely inside, he pulled off his hood and hard hat.

She recognized him immediately. "Geez."

Before looking fully at her, he asked, "What? Are you okay?"

She shivered. "I think so."

Facing her now, he laughed. "It's you! Guess you didn't quite make it to that lodge, did you?"

"No, but thanks for pointing out the obvious, Phil."

Surprised, he replied, "Um, I don't remember telling you my name."

Embarrassed, she confessed, "Betty told me."

He smirked. "Did she now?"

"Oh my God! Don't get any ideas!"

He held up his hands. "Don't worry. I have no ideas at all."

"Ugh!"

He noticed her tears. "Are you sure you're okay?"

Frustrated, she unloaded, "Except for the fact that my entire life is one freaking epic disaster after another, I'm just *fantastic*."

Offering consolation, he remarked, "Well, I can't fix your whole life. But I sure can get you someplace warm and dry. And I can get your car out when the storm subsides."

Grateful, she responded, "Thanks."

Curious, he asked, "Which lodge were you headed to in this storm anyway?"

She felt glops of mud ooze from her shirt into her lap. She cringed. "The Happy Bass Lodge."

Apprehensively, he said, "I hate to tell you, but it closed last year."

Teeth chattering, she replied, "Great. Of course it did."

He reached into the back seat and grabbed a coat. "Here, put this over you. I'll crank up the heat too."

Objecting, she put her hands up. "Thanks, but I don't want to ruin it."

He chuckled. "I think you've done more damage to my truck's seat than you could ever do to that old coat. I can wash the coat."

Realizing what her mud-covered body was doing to his upholstery, she apologized, "I'm sorry. I'll pay to have your truck detailed."

"No need to be sorry. It's not the first time, nor the last. Shit happens, honey."

No kidding! Welcome to my life!

Phil reassured her, "Don't worry about anything. And the good news is that I've got plenty of room at my place."

Sara silently shook her head. *Of course you do.*

After setting the heat to the highest setting, he inquired, "Can I ask you a question without you getting mad?"

She turned and gave him an annoyed look.

He grinned. "Well, I guess I'll risk it anyway."

"Go ahead."

"What's your name?"

Relieved that was all he asked, she answered, "Sara."

"Nice to meet you, Sara. I promise I'm not a serial killer. It wouldn't be good for business."

She shivered despite the coat and blowing heat. She felt soaked to the bone. "That's comforting."

In an effort to ameliorate her worries, he urged, "Just relax. Everything will be just fine."

Sara quipped, "Famous last words."

He shook his head. *It's going to be a long night.*

They pulled up to a large cabin. "Welcome to my humble abode."

She slid out of the truck and limped along behind him.

He ushered her into the mudroom. He grabbed a towel from a nearby shelf.

She removed her purse from around her neck and slipped off her single remaining shoe.

Handing her the towel, he directed, "Here, use this to wipe off the excess glops of mud. I don't want you tracking it through the house."

She wiped herself off the best she could.

He observed the frustration on her face. "Okay. Good enough."

Taking the towel from her, Phil stated, "I know you're not comfortable not knowing me. My room is on this side of the house. You can stay on the opposite side. You'll have your own bathroom and everything. My brother went back down the mountain, so you won't have to worry about him lurking around." He threw the towel in the washing machine.

"Okay. Thanks."

Phil peeled off his filthy clothes and threw each piece directly into the washer. "I'm going to get a fire started to warm up the place. In the meantime, why don't you take a shower and get cleaned up?"

He stood before her in a T-shirt and underwear. His physique was solid from his head to his toes.

Sara looked down at the floor, feeling slightly embarrassed. Then she noticed his feet. They were long and wide.

She tried not to think about what that might mean. Although that proved difficult since he had just stripped in front of her.

Regaining eye contact, she stated the obvious, "I don't have any clothes to change into."

Removing his T-shirt, he replied, "There should be some shirts and sweats in one of the drawers in the bedroom. Help yourself to whatever fits. Just go straight through the great room into the hall on the opposite side of the cabin. The bathroom is on the left. The bedroom is directly across from it. You can't miss them."

She was taken with his muscular chest. Its magnificence was covered in a light layer of blond hair. His arms were beautifully sculpted, undoubtedly from hours and hours of manual labor.

The darker trail of hair that extended from his navel into the low-riding waistband of his underwear led her eyes and her mind on a fantastic journey.

She thought, *That is definitely one path I wouldn't mind following all the way to the end.*

She faintly heard him say, "If you need anything else, let me know."

Catching herself gawking, she responded, "I'm sure I'll be fine. Thanks."

Sara took a long, hot shower. The bath gel smelled heavenly, and the towels were super plush.

With a towel wrapped around her, she scampered to the bedroom across the hall and closed the door.

The quilt and pillows on the bed appeared warm and inviting. Opening the top dresser drawer, she discovered an assortment of shirts and sweatpants. She selected a gray sweatshirt and matching sweatpants. They were big, but they were clean and dry. She thought under different circumstances, she would consider this a spa day.

After towel-drying her hair, she entered the great room. The fire roared. She sat on the hearth, with her back to the fire, in an attempt to further dry her wet hair. She ran her fingers through her hair a few times.

Music blasted from another room. Bachman-Turner Overdrive insisted, "You ain't seen nothin' yet."

The wind whipped wildly outside and briefly caused a backdraft. She felt it against her back and jumped up.

Smoke backed up into the room and triggered the smoke detector.

Gazing heavenward, she exclaimed, "Seriously? Come on!"

The ceiling was too high for her to reach the unit and shut it off. She looked in the pantry for a broom but did not find one.

She returned to the great room to open the windows. But it was raining sideways and the rain drove incessantly against the windows. So she ran back into the kitchen and turned on the exhaust fan.

That was when she noticed a tin of cocoa and a sugar bowl on the counter. Milk simmered in a saucepan on the stove.

Cocoa does sound good right about now.

Not knowing what else to do, she walked toward the music. She intended to ask Phil what he wanted her to do about the smoke.

She turned the corner and heard Phil singing along to the music. He had a nice singing voice.

When she turned the next corner, she was in Phil's bathroom. His shower door was clear, and he was in the process of taking a shower.

Despite only having a side view, she realized that his feet did not lie. She found herself leaning on the doorjamb for support as she watched his hands soap up the most private and intimate parts of his body. They were the only parts of his body she had not seen in the mudroom.

The song had changed while she lingered. Phil belted out, "Takin' care of business every day. Takin' care of business every way."

Sara did not think this was the kind of business Bachman-Turner Overdrive was referring to, but she realized Phil's shower was about to end.

Not wanting to be caught as a voyeur, she quietly slipped out of the bathroom.

After the water shut off, she yelled, "Hey, the smoke detector's going off! What should I do?"

He shouted out, "Just a sec!"

A few moments later, Phil zipped out into the hall wearing a pair of shorts and a sweatshirt. "Oh crap! How'd that smoke get in here? I opened the flue."

Sara noticed Phil's hair was a lot lighter than she originally thought. But his eyes were the same azure blue.

She answered, "The wind is crazy. It backed up. The rain is driving sideways, so I didn't want to open the windows."

Nonchalantly, he made his way to the door. "Well, I'll open the front door for a few minutes. We need to clear the smoke out. Stand there in the doorway and make sure no critters come in."

Sara was not sure if he was joking or not. She swung the door back and forth repeatedly, trying to clear out some of the smoke.

Phil grabbed one of the fireplace tools, stretched, then turned off the smoke detector. "Problem solved!"

Disgusted with missing such an obvious solution, she thought, *Duh, Sara! Why didn't I think of that?*

Pleasantly, Phil announced, "I think it's time for cocoa. Want some?"

"Yes, please."

As he poured the milk from the pan into mugs, he said, "You can close the door now. Take a seat in front of the fire."

She followed his directions and curled up on a big brown leather chair. She gazed into the flickering flames.

Phil carried two mugs. He offered her one, "Here's yours."

Tired, she accepted it. "Thank you."

Phil took a seat on the matching brown leather couch. "It's my grandmother's recipe. She loved cinnamon."

Sara sipped her cocoa as she listened to the popping and crackling of the fire. It was soothing.

Phil's grandmother knew how to make cocoa.

She complimented, "This is delicious."

He stretched out, taking up the entire couch. "Glad you like it."

She looked at the pictures on the mantel. There was a pretty girl with him in most of the shots. "I'm sure your girlfriend wouldn't like the idea of you being up here alone with me."

Sipping from his mug, he informed her, "I don't have a girlfriend. The woman in the pictures was my wife. She died two years ago."

Feeling stupid for assuming, she meekly said, "Sorry."

"Thanks. It was cancer."

Ugh! Way to go, Sara. "I'm so sorry."

"We had twelve good years. I'm grateful for those. What about you? Anyone wondering where you are on this dark and stormy night?"

"No. I was engaged. But it ended badly. This Saturday was supposed to be my wedding day." Tears welled in her eyes.

"Bummer. Sorry to hear that."

She wiped the tears on her sleeve. "Thanks."

He knew he could not leave it at that, so he asked, "Want to talk about it?"

Before she could answer, a brilliant flash of light illuminated the room. In addition to the sound of rolling thunder, it was followed by a loud crashing noise. The windows rattled, and the ground shook.

Sara jumped and screamed.

He laughed.

"What was that?"

Thankful for the reprieve, Phil hurried to the window and peered out into the darkness. The next flash of lightning revealed the culprit. "Wow! Lightning hit and toppled one of the enormous trees out front."

"No!"

He motioned to her. "Come see for yourself."

Curious, she joined him. "Did it hit the house?"

He pointed. "No. It just missed the garage. But it's blocking the driveway completely."

Alarmed, she asked, "We're trapped?"

Optimistically, he responded, "Don't worry. I'm sure it won't look so bad in the morning. And there's plenty of food here to last days."

Overwhelmed, she questioned, "*Days? We could be stuck days?*"

Unfazed, he answered, "Maybe. Not definitely. I won't know until morning."

Sara plopped back into the chair.

Phil observed she looked distraught. "Let's get your mind off of it. You want to play a game or read or something?"

Resigning herself to the situation, she said, "No. I just want some sleep. Do you mind if I sleep out here in front of the fire? I don't want to be alone on that side of the house."

"No problem. I'll keep you company."

"You don't have to do that."

He stretched out on the couch again. "I know. But truth be told, I'd rather sleep in front of the fire too."

She curled up in the chair.

Phil pulled a blanket off the back of the couch. "Here's a blanket." He tossed it to her.

She caught it easily and covered herself.

He closed his eyes and pulled another blanket over himself.

Sara was restless and could not sleep. She worried about her car, the storm, and the possibility of being stuck in a cabin with a stranger for days. She longed to be home in her own bed.

Then she replayed the last week in her mind. She ached for the love of her life, although her mind knew that chapter was over. Her heart still pined for him, and her body yearned for him. Feeling sorry for herself, she cried silently.

Sleep eluded Phil as well. After tossing and turning for the good part of an hour, he glanced in Sara's direction and saw tears glistening on her face.

He kicked his blanket off and walked over to her.

She lifted her head. Her face was red from crying.

Phil shook his head, scooped her up, and carried her to the couch. He sat next to her, pulled the lever to raise the footrest, and raised his arm. "No strings attached cuddling. I think we both might find it easier to sleep."

Physically and emotionally spent, Sara nestled against him. After the week she had had, she needed to be held by someone. Even a stranger.

He lowered his arm and pulled her closer. He exuded a warm, safe, protective vibe.

Sara relaxed completely and rested her head and one hand on his chest.

He pulled a blanket over them.

She could hear his heartbeat. It was strong and steady.

He gently stroked her hair.

Within minutes, she was fast asleep.

Sleep found Phil moments later.

Peaceful for the first time all week, Sara was able to dream. In her dream, Sara walked down a wooded path in the rain. She tripped and landed in a large mud puddle. As she attempted to stand, the suction pulled her down, like quicksand.

The more she struggled, the lower she sank. She cried for help.

Swinging from above, suspended from a vine, Phil reached out to her.

She stretched up with both arms.

He swept her up, rescuing her. Holding her close, he declared, "I've got you."

She clung to him.

When they reached safety, he released her. "You're safe now."

At that moment, she realized he looked like Tarzan, sporting only a small loincloth. Mud was smeared across his torso.

She stammered, "Thank you."

Taking her by the hand, he said, "Come with me."

Blindly, she followed him to a lovely secluded oasis.

The first thing Sara saw was an intimate table, illuminated by candlelight, covered with fresh fruit and chocolate. Next to the table was an inviting king-size bed, turned down for the evening.

He led her to a luxury tiled shower with multiple showerheads.

Phil commented, "You're covered in mud, and so am I. There's only one thing left to do with you, dirty girl."

His loincloth dropped to the ground like magic.

Although Sara lusted after his gorgeous body, she desired to be pampered and be treated well. He was going to have to work for her.

As if he had read her mind, he removed her soiled clothes, and led her into the waterfall of water. Their muddy bodies were mere inches away from one another.

The water from one of the showerheads rained over her. She slicked back her hair.

As he stood under another showerhead, he said, "You're a dirty girl who likes to watch. So, watch."

With her heart beating rapidly, Sara gave him her full attention.

With deliberation, he soaped up his beautiful body in front of her.

She watched him slowly wash away the mud on his muscular arms, chest, and torso. She felt her temperature rising.

As Phil's hands moved lower, he encouraged, "Keep your eyes on the prize, sweetheart."

She focused her gaze as his hands expertly cleaned his family jewels. His technique was extremely thorough and sensual.

Unconsciously, she licked her lips. Her pulse raced, and her nipples hardened.

Taking his time, he asked, "Do you like what you see?"

She nodded. "Oh, yes."

He smirked. "Good. Now turn around, close your eyes, and tilt your head back."

She did as she was told.

Sara felt Phil's fingers lathering her hair with shampoo. She allowed her head to fall back as he massaged her scalp. After rinsing her hair, he clipped it up, so it would stay out of the way. She was speechless as she turned to face him.

Phil worked up a lather with the soap. He whispered, "Trust me. I'm going to take care of you. You're in very good hands."

Sara felt weak in the knees, anticipating what might happen next.

He gently washed her face, taking great care to trace her lips with both of his thumbs. Then he washed her neck, arms, and back. His hands followed the curvature of her buttocks, down her legs, then back up, lingering at her inner thighs.

She moaned softly.

He directed, "Turn around."

She faced the wall as his confident hands soaped up her breasts and torso. He took great pleasure kneading her firm, perky breasts. She sighed as he tugged at her nipples.

He pulled her to him, her back against his chest. His hands danced around her lower abdomen and hips, slipping occasionally to her inner thighs. He kept returning to her breasts, massaging them.

Her head rested against his shoulder.

His sense of urgency building, Phil spun her around and kissed her. He boosted her up, and she wrapped her legs around his waist.

Warm water rushed over their dewy bodies.

Phil backed Sara up against the shower wall.

His muscular chest pressed against her heaving breasts.

She felt his hardness resting underneath her. She thought if she could squirm and push him away ever so slightly, he would slip inside her. And she would envelop him completely.

As if he read her mind, he instructed, "Stop wiggling."

Sara pouted.

Amused with her frustration, he whispered, "Tell me what you want."

Sara confessed, "I want you."

He urged, "Louder."

She shouted, "I want you!"

He demanded, "Beg for it, dirty girl."

"Please, Phil!"

"Beg! Say it like you mean it."

Clutching his back, she begged, "Oh, Phil, I want you. Please give it to me! Give it to me good!"

"You want it now?"

She pleaded, "Yes! Now! I'll do anything. Please!"

"Anything?"

Desperate to have him, she confessed, "Yes, absolutely anything."

Phil smiled. "I'll hold you to that." Satisfied, he entered her swiftly.

She moaned deeply as she felt the depth and breadth of him.

Looking directly into her eyes, he thrust slowly, deliberately.

Loving it, she implored, "Don't stop!"

Happily, he obliged. "There's no rush, baby. I can go all night long."

That declaration pushed Sara over the edge.

Phil maintained the slow steady rhythm as she squirmed and writhed. When her muscles relaxed, he shut off the water. Gently, he dried her off with a plush fluffy towel and carried her to the bed.

The sheets felt soft, cool, and inviting.

Sara looked up at him. "That was wonderful."

"Glad you enjoyed it. But I wasn't joking when I said I can go all night long."

"Good because I'm not close to being done with you yet."

He promised, "This is just the beginning. I'm planning on ravishing you until you tell me to stop."

When Sara awoke, it was still pouring outside.

Phil stoked the fire.

They made eye contact.

He commented, "Well, good morning, sunshine! That was one heck of a nightmare you had."

Disoriented, she asked, "What?"

"The dream you had. It was quite a doozy from the way you were thrashing around and yelling."

Sitting up, she muttered, "You have no idea."

"Would you care to enlighten me?"

She lied, "I don't remember it."

"Probably better that way. Are you hungry?"

Truthfully, she replied, "Starving."

"Okay. Let's make some breakfast then."

The weather finally broke in the late afternoon. Phil ventured out to assess the damage. Fallen limbs and branches littered the yard.

He reported, "Well that tree is totally blocking the garage and driveway. There's no way to get out until the tree's gone. And my brother has my chainsaw."

"Don't you have a backup chainsaw?"

"Sorry, no."

Ever the problem solver, she asked, "Do you have an ax?"

"I have an ax, but there's no way I'm tackling a tree of that size with a small ax. I'm going to check out the condition of the road. I'll be back in a few minutes."

"Okay."

When Phil returned, he stated, "A good part of the road is under water. I think we're going to be stuck here for a day or two before the water recedes."

"You're kidding."

Unfazed, he said, "No. This happens when we have big storms. That's why I always have this place stocked. You never know."

Disappointed, she muttered, "Wonderful."

"From what you told me last night, you're not going anywhere in particular. So, relax and enjoy yourself."

Pacing, she said, "Easy for you to say."

"You could do a lot worse than Phil Potter's Bed and Breakfast."

"You're right. I should be grateful."

"I'm stuck here the same as you. At least you're not on the side of the road freezing to death with no food or water."

"Point taken. Thank you."

"You're welcome. Are you up for a hike?"

Lifting up a bare foot, she reminded him, "I don't have any socks or shoes."

He laughed. "You can wear my brother's boots with some thick socks."

She considered it. "Sure. What else do I have to do?"

"That's the spirit! There's something I want to show you on one of the trails."

Phil insisted Sara wear one of his heavier work jackets. The coat was several sizes too big. Rolling up the sleeves, she appeared to be a child wearing an adult's coat.

Sara complained, "I look ridiculous."

Phil poked fun at her, "I'm sure the birds and the squirrels are going to notice. You'll make their worst dressed list for sure."

She pushed him playfully. "Let's just go."

He winked. "Yes, ma'am."

They slogged through the mud and around the larger puddles. A stream overflowed its banks to the left. Tree branches and other debris floated downstream rapidly.

Turning the corner, Phil urged, "Get ready."

"For what?"

He pointed. "Just look."

The waterfall stopped her in her tracks. Awestruck, she uttered, "Wow! I didn't realize we were that close to a waterfall."

"Told you it was worth the hike in all of this muck. It's not a big waterfall, but the extra tier makes it special in my opinion."

"It's breathtaking."

"The rain has increased the volume of water. So it's more impressive after a big rain. I love how the water cascades over that last edge into the pool below. Of course, the pool is murky right now. Normally it's blue-green."

Wanting to hear the roar of the water, she asked, "Can we go closer?"

"Sure, if you're up for it."

The path was very slick. It was difficult to maintain their footing.

After ten minutes of navigating the treacherous terrain, Phil stopped. "I know you wanted to go closer, but the trail isn't really hikeable past this point."

Disappointed, she said, "I know. But I was really hoping to get a closer look."

"We can come back another day. It's not safe. We need to go back."

The hike chilled them to the bone. Phil threw more logs on the fire.

Rattling off the contents of the pantry, he said, "I've got canned stew, a bunch of soups, tuna fish, and mac and cheese."

"What a yummy selection to choose from."

Shaking his head, he said, "It is what it is."

"I know. Beggars can't be choosers. Stew's fine."

"Coming right up!"

After eating the warmed-up stew, they sat on the couch, in front of the fire.

Phil inquired, "So, what do you do?"

She rolled down the sleeves of her sweatshirt. "Up until last week, I was an engineer. But I quit."

"Why?"

She admitted, "I hated it. I wanted to do something more meaningful with my life."

He probed, "Like what?"

"I was going to work for the church. But now, I don't know. I'm not sure about anything anymore."

Curious, he asked, "Does that tie in with your broken engagement?"

She responded, "That's a long story. The short version is he lied and cheated, and there's a woman claiming that he's the father of her daughter."

Scratching the stubble on his chin, he said, "Bummer. That sucks. I'm sorry."

"Thanks. I'm just really lost right now."

"Literally and figuratively."

"Uh huh."

Phil offered, "Well, you can stay here as long as you want to figure things out. Once the trails dry up a bit, you can hike. It's amazing how much clarity you can get after hiking around for a few hours."

"I don't know. Maybe."

"You don't have to decide now. It's time to go to sleep anyway."

Hesitantly, she asked, "Can we sleep like we did last night?"

He nodded. "Sure."

"Thank you."

"You're welcome."

Sara confessed, "This probably sounds stupid, and I know we just met, but you're really nice. And I like spending time with you. You make me feel safe."

Phil smiled. "Good because I like spending time with you. Come here." He raised his arm.

Sara cuddled against him.

He pulled the blanket over them and held her close.

The previous night, they were both exhausted. So the only thing on their minds was sleep. Tonight, however, their minds wandered into different territory.

Phil kissed her on the head as he stroked her hair.

His touch comforted Sara. She snuggled closer against him. He responded by kissing the top of her head again.

The kiss struck a chord in her. She pulled back slightly and gazed up at him.

It had been a long time since Phil held a woman. Instinct took over, and he kissed her. Not knowing if his boldness would be well-received, he was pleasantly surprised when she kissed him back. He pulled her closer.

Sara yielded to him. She enjoyed his taste.

Phil was an older man, a man's man. He had strong, calloused hands, but he touched her gently. She felt as if testosterone oozed from his pores. He was more rugged and raw than any other man she had ever kissed.

She kissed him sensually, wanting to lose herself in him.

He returned the sensual nature of her affection.

As the intensity increased, hands and fingers wandered, explored, and lingered over curves and muscles. It made him feel like a teenager again. It was exhilarating and exciting.

Phil finally had to come up for air.

Bluntly, Sara said, "We're not having sex."

Astonished, he questioned, "Who said anything about having sex?"

"Well, we're kissing, and one thing leads to another."

Although sufficiently aroused, Phil reassured her, "Relax. You just ended a serious relationship. You're not ready yet. And I haven't dated anyone since my wife died. So, I'm in no hurry."

Sara looked at him unbelievingly.

Phil promised, "I'm being serious here. If this is to go anywhere, then let's take it slow. You know, get to know each other as friends. It's important to me to build a solid relationship. Once you start having sex, it clouds your judgment."

Sara agreed, "Yes, it does."

He confessed, "Don't get me wrong. I definitely want to have sex with you. Your kisses are driving me crazy, but we're going to wait. It's the right thing to do. And I have a feeling that it'll be worth it."

Sara knew he was right. And she was glad he was a gentleman. She now felt even more safe and secure with him.

He kissed the top of her head and drew her to him. They embraced and fell asleep in each other's arms.

CHAPTER 32

As the sun rose, light peeked through the window. Already awake, Tony and Dee spooned in bed.

Dee remarked, "I can't believe we've spent most of the week in bed."

Tony corrected, "In bed, on the couch, on the kitchen counter, in the shower, and on the back porch railing."

"I didn't hear you complaining."

"No complaints here. It was all good."

"You know, I thought I was going to hate this mandatory vacation. But it turned out to be pretty good."

He switched positions to lie on his back. "Pretty good? Honey, from what I witnessed, you had a fantastic time."

She flipped over to face him. "Orgasmic would probably be a better word."

"My thoughts precisely."

She ran her fingers through his chest hair. "So, how about one more time before we go to your friend's wedding?"

Checking his watch, he answered, "We're short on time. So, I guess we'll be doing it your way."

Before he finished his sentence, she slithered between his legs. Her lips and tongue got the ball rolling as she stroked him.

He moaned, "Oh, baby."

"Mmm hmm?"

With his hand on her head, he encouraged, "Honey, that's good. Keep doing that."

With a devilish grin, she asked, "You like that don't you?"

"My God, yes! You've done it enough times to know I do."

Tony watched as her tongue licked every inch. Then she circled around and around. In under a minute, he was ready for active duty.

With a sultry look in her eye, Dee completely devoured him.

He ran both of his hands through her hair. But soon, he found himself holding her head in place.

With unmatched vigor, she lured Tony to the edge. And when he was ready to explode, quick as lightning, Dee switched positions and pounced. She loved the feeling of her walls vibrating uncontrollably with him buried deep inside her. She had a very quick trigger and rode his wave of pleasure with him. Bucking and moaning, they climaxed together.

Before he could wrap his arms around her, she dismounted. "While you're recovering, I'm going to take a shower."

Catching his breath, he thought, *If I don't get in better physical shape, she's going to kill me. Although, this would be an awesome way to go.*

Chapter 33

O
N what would have been his wedding day, Joe sat on his parents' couch and drank another beer. It was his third, and it was not yet noon.

Rose entered the room and saw the empty beer bottles. "What do you think you're doing?"

Depressed, he answered, "What does it look like?"

Marching across the room, she reprimanded, "Don't you dare be fresh with me!"

Moving only his eyes, he asked, "What do you want me to say?"

She grabbed the bottle out of his hand.

He objected, "Hey, I wasn't done with that."

Fired up, she responded, "Oh yes you are! No son of mine is going to become an alcoholic. I'm cutting you off. You're done. Do you hear me? Done!"

He protested, "I'm a grown man now. You can't do that."

Gesturing and with eyebrows raised, she said, "Oh really? Some grown man you are—sitting on your mother's couch, drinking your father's beer."

His mother had a point, but he did not want to admit it.

After she removed the bottles from the room, she sat down next to her son.

Looking helplessly at her, Joe broke down. "Ma, I don't know what I'm going to do." He sobbed. "I miss her. I love her. What am I going to do?"

She embraced her son. "I know, Joey. Don't worry. We'll figure it out. You'll be okay. I'll take good care of you." She pulled a tissue from her pocket and wiped his nose.

Joe fussed, "Ma! Geez! Come on!" He squirmed away. "I'm not a baby."

Triumphant, Rose joked, "No. You're not. But at least I got you to move."

Joe wiped his eyes on his shirt.

Rose patted his leg. "You're going to be okay. I promise."

Joe's cell phone rang. The display indicated it was his cousin, Vinnie. He answered, "Yeah?"

Hurriedly, Vinnie said, "I'm on my way to the church. But I had to let you know that the paternity test results are in. Sorry, Joe, but you're that little girl's father."

Devastated, Joe failed to respond.

"Joe, did you hear me?"

Weakly, Joe replied, "Yeah."

"Sorry, man. I know you were hoping for a different outcome."

Joe disconnected the call.

Curious, Rose asked, "What was that about?"

"Nothing."

Joe felt as if he had been hit by a truck. It was the worst possible news.

Almost immediately, the house phone rang. Rose rushed to the kitchen to answer it. When she returned to the family room, she accosted her son. "Nothing? Finding out you're a father is nothing?"

The depression converted to anger in a split second. "You're right, Ma. It's not nothing. It's an absolute total disaster! My life is *completely* over! I'll *never* get Sara back now. And I'm stuck dealing with that crazy bitch for the rest of my life."

Pointing out the positive in the situation, in her opinion, Rose noted, "But you have a daughter."

Joe yelled, "What's it going to take for you to understand that I don't care?"

Refusing to accept his statement, she argued, "You don't mean that."

Joe screamed, "Yes I do! It's what *you* want. It's not what *I* want. I couldn't care less!"

CHAPTER 34

MITA'S bond was posted. She lit a cigarette as soon as she exited the jail. She hired a taxi to take her to her mother's apartment. She dreaded their upcoming interaction.

Helen and Flora colored at the kitchen table and were surprised when the door opened.

Helen greeted her, "You're out."

Bedraggled and in no mood for pleasantries, Mita said, "You could have given me a ride."

Coolly, Helen responded, "You never called me. You're lucky I posted your bond."

"You knew I'd need a ride."

"You didn't call. And how was I supposed to know how long the process would take?"

Mita muttered, "You're unbelievable."

Pushing her chair back from the table, Helen exclaimed, "*I'm* unbelievable? You have the nerve to say that after what you've done?"

Building a head of steam, Mita yelled, "So you wanted me to grovel? Beg you to come get me?"

"That's one of your problems, Mita. You can't admit you need help."

Mita threw her purse across the room. "Screw you."

Flora jumped up and hid behind her grandmother, fearing what her mother might throw next.

Helen chastised her, "You can't go around throwing and destroying things when life doesn't go your way. Don't ever do that again."

Mita challenged, "Or what? You're going to send me to my room?"

"Mita, you are trying my patience."

Mita rolled her eyes. "I feel another lecture coming on."

Helen scolded her daughter, "You're right. I can't believe what you did to those people. What were you thinking?"

Hands on her hips, feeling a sense of entitlement, Mita answered, "I was thinking I would collect the child support that was rightfully mine. He owes me."

"That's not the way to go about it, Mita. You ruined everything for those poor people."

Enraged, Mita screamed, "Those poor people? Are you shitting me? *I'm* the injured party here. *Me! Not them! Me!* He ruined my life. I got stuck with that lousy kid."

Tears puddled in Flora's eyes. Her bottom lip quivered as she ran to her room.

Completely fed up, Helen declared, "That does it! No matter what happens now, I'm taking Flora away from you. You obviously don't care about her, let alone love her. She deserves better than you."

"No way in hell. I want that child support. He *owes* me."

"That's all Flora is to you, isn't she? A means to an end? A way to get money? You disgust me."

Making her way to the kitchen, Mita antagonized, "So what else is new?"

"Go after the money if that's what you want. I don't want a dime of that boy's money. But Flora is mine now."

"I will go after his money. You can count on that."

"You need to find someplace else to live."

Acquiring a hostile stance, Mita replied, "You're a piece of work. You dragged me all the way here, and now you're kicking me out on the street?"

Confronting her daughter honestly, she said, "I can't have you here. You're toxic, Mita."

Lashing back, she said, "Fine. I can't stand looking at you anyway."

"How you ended up this way, I'll never know."

Heavy on the sarcasm, Mita jabbed, "It was all of your wonderful parenting, Mother."

Helen suggested, "You can live at St. Peter's Mission until you get a job and find an apartment. You won't be out on the street."

Pacing, Mita erupted, "Wonderful! You've thought of everything! Everything except all of my things are in that room Flora's barricaded herself in."

Putting physical distance between them, Helen said, "I'll give you time to gather up your things. I need to go calm her down and repair the damage you've done. This was supposed to be a fresh start for you, and you blew it."

"Says you. My payday is coming."

Displeased with her daughter, Helen left the room to comfort Flora.

Helen knocked on the bedroom door. "Flora, honey, let me in."

The lock popped and the door opened slowly.

Flora's tear-stained face gazed up at Helen.

Helen knelt and squeezed her tightly. "I'm sorry you had to hear that. Your mother says things she doesn't mean sometimes."

Flora sniffled, "But she does mean it."

Helen rocked her. "Put those words out of your mind. You're going to live with me from now on. Your mother is going to find someplace else to live."

Flora blinked through the tears. With trembling lips, she asked, "Really, Nana?"

She confirmed, "Really, Flora. I'll be taking care of you from now on."

Flora wrapped her arms around her grandmother's neck. She whispered, "I love you, Nana."

Mita paced back and forth angrily. She was out of cigarettes, and there was no alcohol in the apartment. She contemplated calling a cab as the doorbell startled her.

As she squinted through the peephole, the unknown person knocked loudly.

Mita begrudgingly opened the door. "What?"

The courier droned, "Letter for Mita Scotto."

"That's me."

Holding out an electronic device and stylus, he said, "Sign here."

She signed for the letter and handed the device back to him.

He pressed the screen twice and handed her an envelope. "Have a good day."

"Yeah," Mita grunted. After kicking the door closed, she tore open the envelope.

Helen appeared. "Did I hear someone at the door?"

Mita unfolded the papers within. "Yeah."

"Who was it?"

She scanned the first sheet. "A delivery guy."

"And?"

Mita expected the documents to be from the courthouse. They were not. Absently, she answered, "Some papers for me."

Standing directly in front of Mita, Helen asked, "What kind of papers?"

Confused, Mita scanned the sheets.

Helen could see the logo was that of a medical laboratory. "Goodness! Those are the paternity results."

Outraged, Mita questioned, "What? You had no right!"

"We ran the paternity test while you were in jail. We all had to know for sure." Edging closer, she asked, "What does it say?"

Mita jerked the papers away from Helen's prying eyes. She turned her back on her mother as she read the results.

Impatient, Helen pressed, "Well? Tell me."

Mita spun around to face her mother. "It says, 'The alleged father, Joseph Lazaro, can not be excluded as the biological father of the child named Flora Scotto.' The percentage is 99.99%. Pay dirt!"

"Joe is the father then?"

Mita shoved the papers at Helen. "Read it for yourself, you old hag. Time for me to get what's rightfully mine."

Helen read the results. Mita had told the truth. The lab results confirmed Joe was Flora's biological father.

Mita packed her bags. She announced, "I'm leaving, just like you wanted."

Helen replied, "I never wanted it to be this way. I wanted you to start fresh and have a better life."

Almost giddy, Mita proclaimed, "Oh, don't worry. I am. It's going to be the perfect life."

Sternly, Helen stated, "I wasn't kidding about Flora. She's staying with me."

"You can have her. She'll just slow me down. But I *am* going to collect all that child support he owes me."

Helen shook her head.

Waving the test results, Mita announced, "These papers are my ticket to paradise!" After kissing the papers, she shoved them in her purse.

"All you think about is money. Don't you understand it doesn't buy happiness?"

"It sure helps though."

"Are you going to the mission like I suggested?"

Slinging a bag on her shoulder, Mita retorted, "Like you give a shit? You're kicking me out."

"It doesn't mean I don't care about you, Mita."

"Yeah, right."

The taxi driver dropped Mita off in front of St. Peter's Mission.

A cheerful woman greeted her, "Welcome to St. Peter's."

Direct and to the point, Mita asked, "Do you have any beds left?"

Smiling, the woman replied, "Yes, we do. Follow me. My name is Tory."

Mita looked around. Long rectangular tables and folding chairs filled the main hall. It was obviously used for meals and events. A large colorful mural covered one wall.

Tory explained, "We do have some rules here at St. Peter's Mission. No drugs or alcohol are allowed. And you must stay out of the men's dormitory."

"Okay." *No problem. These guys don't have any money. I'm not interested in giving it away for free.*

The woman continued, "We can help you find work and a more permanent living arrangement as well. We have several programs I can tell you about."

"Yeah. Maybe tomorrow."

Tory handed Mita a clipboard with a form on it. "I understand. I just need you to sign this. It says I've explained the rules, and you agree to abide by them."

Mita signed the papers without reading them and handed the clipboard back.

"Great. Now, let's get you settled."

They stopped in the supply room to get sheets and towels. Then the volunteer led her to the dormitory section upstairs. "This is the women's area. The bathroom is just down the hall."

"Thanks."

At lunch, Mita sat alone at one of the long tables. She assumed everyone would leave her alone. On the contrary, several women joined her.

"Hi! You're new. I'm Susan. And this is Joanie, and that's Barb."

She acknowledged them, "Mita." She looked them over warily.

Susan joked, "We don't bite here."

Mita smiled a fake smile. *But I might.*

Joanie asked, "Is this your first time?"

"Yeah."

Joanie followed up, "The people here are nice. They're very helpful. You'll like it here."

Mita snapped, "I won't be here long. As soon as I get the money I'm owed, I'm out of here." She got up and left the table.

In a critical tone, Barb said, "Talk about antisocial."

Susan replied, "Her loss."

The mission prohibited drugs and alcohol, but smoking was acceptable. However, Mita was out of cigarettes. She walked to the nearest convenience store and bought two packs of cigarettes. She asked the clerk where she could find the nearest liquor store. She unwrapped one pack and lit up a cigarette as she walked in the direction of the liquor store.

Once inside the liquor store, she purchased a bottle of vodka. She planned to get completely hammered before reentering St. Peter's Mission. Then she would sneak past the alcohol police and sleep it off.

As she strolled back, she saw cars pulling into the parking lot between the church and the mission. A limousine was parked just past the church. Two men in suits affixed a "Just Married" sign to the trunk.

Mita's pace quickened. *That's right! It's Saturday. The day of the big glorious wedding. This is going to be perfect! I couldn't have planned it better if I tried.*

She crossed the street and sat in the elementary school's playground area on a bench. She watched the church intently as she drank.

CHAPTER 35

ANNA helped Laura get ready in the bride's room in the back of church.

Laura slipped into her lace wedding gown.

Anna complimented her as she zipped her up, "You look beautiful, Laura."

"Thank you." She sighed. "It's so weird that Sara isn't here."

Anna agreed, "I know."

Laura realized she might have sounded ungrateful. "Not that I don't appreciate you being here and standing up for me, Anna."

Anna hooked the clasp at the top of the gown. "You don't need to explain. I understand."

Relieved, Laura replied, "Thanks."

Anna joked, "Now, let's get you married before you start showing!"

Sarcastically, Laura responded, "Thanks a lot!"

Anna winked. "No problem. One of my jobs is comic relief. Another is to make sure you have the something old, something new, something borrowed, something blue. Are you covered?"

"My mom gave me my grandmother's bracelet, so that takes care of old. My dress is new. And this entire day is borrowed from Sara."

"What about blue?"

Laura opened the shoe box in the corner. "Well, the white shoes I was going to wear didn't look right with the gown. So, I'm wearing my favorite sparkly blue sandals."

Pleased she did not have to search for something blue, Anna said, "Awesome. I guess you're all set."

There was a knock at the door.

Laura asked, "Who is it?"

The voice answered, "It's Dad."

Anna unlocked and opened the door. "Hi, Mr. Delaney."

"Hi, Anna."

His attention turned to his daughter. It was as if he saw her with fresh eyes. He had no words. Tears welled up in his eyes.

Getting choked up herself, Laura begged, "Dad, don't cry."

Squeezing her, he said, "You're beautiful, Laura. Your mother and I are so proud of you."

Her mind replied, *You wouldn't be so proud if you knew I was pregnant.* However, she responded, "Thank you."

Looking at his watch, he tapped it. "We better get out there. It's time. Are you ready?"

Smiling, Laura answered, "As ready as I'll ever be."

At the altar, John waited nervously for his bride. His father, Gene, stood by his side.

"Thanks again for agreeing to be my best man, Dad."

"Son, it's an honor."

CHAPTER 36

O**N** the corner of Third Avenue and Main Street, the four occupants of a black Chevy Suburban studied the pictures they removed from a large envelope. Their primary targets were Anthony Lazaro, a.k.a. Dominic Perno, and Delores Georgopoulos, a.k.a. Violet Perno. The envelope also contained the wedding announcement for Sara Taylor and Joe Lazaro.

When he had hired them, Al Fuentes' instructions had been clear. The primary targets must be eliminated. Collateral damage to Lazaro's immediate family was highly encouraged. Georgopoulos' family would be dealt with at a later time.

Once that job was complete, they were to move on to the pregnant girls and their families. Those deaths were to be made to appear as accidents.

There were approximately twenty guests in attendance. On short notice, Laura knew the church would not be full. She was satisfied that her parents and grandparents and John's parents and grandparents were able to attend.

Butterflies fluttered in Laura's stomach as the organist started playing. She squeezed her father's arm.

Tom Delaney smiled at his little girl as he led her down the long church aisle.

Laura knew Father Francis, Vinnie, and Anna were also standing up at the altar. But all she saw was John at the end of that aisle.

Laura floated on air as she walked toward her groom.

John was in complete awe of her beauty. To him, her presence illuminated the entire church.

John and Laura would later confess they barely heard the priest ask, "Who gives this woman to be married to this man?"

Tom Delaney replied, "Her mother and I do."

John whispered, "You're absolutely breathtaking."

Laura blushed. "Thank you. You're so handsome in your tux."

They could not take their eyes off each other throughout the ceremony. Vows were spoken. Rings were exchanged. All the while, they held hands and remained inseparable.

As John and Laura shared a church-appropriate kiss, the congregation clapped. The priest blessed their union and the congregation. Then on cue, the organist ushered them out.

Their excitement was palpable as they raced down the aisle.

John pulled Laura into a tiny alcove in the back of the church. They kissed passionately for the first time as husband and wife.

He held her tightly and professed, "I love you, Mrs. Lombardi."

Holding his face in her hands, she echoed his sentiment, "I love you, Mr. Lombardi."

The crowd gathered outside on the church steps as the photographer took pictures of the bridal party inside. Many fidgeted with their birdseed packets.

The doors finally opened. The well-wishers got ready to throw their birdseed.

Someone announced, "It's just the photographer."

The crowd groaned.

The photographer laughed. He was used to getting that reaction. He stood at the edge of the landing and waited.

Moments later, the doors opened again. The onlookers perked up.

Vinnie and Tony held the doors open as the couple emerged from the church.

Cheers went up from the crowd. Birdseed became airborne and pelted the happy couple.

The photographer and the newlyweds descended down the steps.

Dee's gut told her something was wrong. She scanned the street and noticed the black Chevy Suburban with tinted windows idling on the corner. She attempted to catch Tony's eye without attracting too much attention. He was not looking in her direction, so she sprinted up the steps.

He immediately noticed the expression on her face. "What?"

There was no ladylike way to retrieve her gun. She reached under her dress and freed her weapon from her thigh holster. She raised her chin in the direction of the vehicle. "Hostiles on the corner. Black Suburban."

He released the door. "Shit."

Vinnie's radar went off. He released his door as well and joined them. "What's going on?"

Tony cocked his head in the direction of the Suburban. "We've got company. Hostiles in the black SUV on the corner."

Dee asked, "Options?"

Before Tony could answer, the Suburban crept forward. Tony pulled his weapon.

With inopportune timing, Mita rushed up the steps, intercepting the bride and groom midway down. Waving the paternity test results, she yelled, "Here's the proof! I was right. You *are* Flora's father."

Anna fluffed Laura's train for the next picture. She looked up, not believing the audacity of this woman. She was glad Sara was not there.

John's and Laura's expressions turned sour.

The photographer stopped taking pictures. He turned to see who was causing the commotion.

Expecting to confront Joe, Mita asked John, "Who the hell are you?"

Laura recognized Mita from the shower. Infuriated, Laura shouted, "Get out of here, you crazy bitch!"

Tony swore, "Jesus H. Christ! Just what we need."

The Suburban crept closer.

Vinnie yelled, "I'll get her, you guys get out of here."

Vinnie nimbly rushed down the stairs, grabbed Mita by the arm, and jerked her around to march her back down the church stairs. He could smell the alcohol on her breath.

Mita struggled and stumbled. "Get your hands off of me!"

He tightened his grip. "Do you want to go back to jail?"

Belligerent, Mita kicked him in the shin. "No!"

Vinnie pulled her along against her will. "Don't make me tase you."

Mita squirmed and writhed. She yelled, "Police brutality!"

Frustrated with her histrionics, he pleaded, "Will you please stop already?"

Tony and Dee were not far behind, weapons at their sides.

The black vehicle crossed the length of the parking lot driveway. It was now positioned a few hundred feet from the church steps. The front and back passenger side windows came down. One gun muzzle appeared in each. A third shooter popped out of the backseat window on the driver's side.

Dee rushed forward, her gun aimed at the Suburban. She ended up next to Vinnie and Mita on the stairs, yelling, "Gun! Everybody down!"

There was no cover between them and the Suburban. The stairs trapped everyone. The only options were to retreat back up into the church or run toward the Suburban.

Vinnie released Mita's arm and pushed her aside.

The hostiles fired.

Tony and Dee returned fire and advanced, despite being outgunned and outmanned.

Vinnie kicked himself for not carrying his firearm to the wedding.

Drunk and oblivious to the dire situation, Mita ran back toward Vinnie and directly into the line of fire. Bullets peppered her body. She shrieked and crumpled on the stairs.

Confused wedding guests panicked and screamed. Chaos ensued.

Vinnie abandoned the notion of maintaining order. "Run!" he yelled, as he motioned to John, Laura, and Anna to run back into the church.

The guests heeded Vinnie's warning and stampeded back up the steps into the church.

Adrenaline pumping, John grabbed Laura and whisked her up the steps.

Anna followed but fell shy of the doors. She flopped down like a rag doll without uttering a sound.

Vinnie's heart sank as he watched it happen in slow motion.

Dee's first bullet sailed through the windshield and hit the shooter in the front passenger seat.

The shooter was wounded. However, he managed to get off several more rounds before Dee's second bullet mortally wounded him.

The photographer was taken out by a barrage of bullets. He screamed and dropped to the ground, writhing in pain. His camera cracked as it hit the steps.

Tony took out the vehicle's right front tire. At the slow speed, it didn't alter the SUV's course. But it would slow them down if they attempted to flee.

The driver picked up the dead man's gun. The SUV was now directly in front of the church. The driver shot through the passenger window, using the dead man's body as a shield.

Bullets continued to fly in both directions.

Dee and Tony advanced toward the Suburban.

Tony had a clear shot of the rear passenger closest to the curb. He aimed and fired until he emptied his clip.

Dee stepped off the curb into the street and fired at the driver through the windshield. He bailed out of the vehicle and ran into the playground. Without a driver, the SUV careened to the left and hit the opposite curb.

The fourth man jumped out of the backseat and disappeared into the playground as well.

John and Laura crouched behind the first church pew.

Out of breath, John asked Laura, "Are you okay?"

Dizzy, she replied, "I don't feel so well."

John saw a pool of red growing on the front and side of her wedding gown. "Oh shit! Lie down, baby. You're bleeding."

"I don't understand why they were shooting at us."

"I don't know either, honey. It was probably just a random drive-by shooting."

Tears trickled down her cheeks. "I'm sorry."

Wiping her tears away, he asked, "For what?"

"Forcing you to marry me today."

Kissing her forehead, he said, "Don't cry, honey. You didn't force me to do anything. I love you. We're married. That's all that matters."

John unzipped her gown and yanked it down to her waist. She had been shot in the side, under her arm. He guessed it happened as they turned to run. *I should have shielded her better.* He told her, "You're going to be all right, honey."

"What about the baby?"

Terrified his words were not the truth, he spoke them anyway, "The baby is going to be fine too. Don't worry."

John applied pressure to Laura's wound with his left hand. With his right hand, he pulled out his cell phone, called 911, and relayed all of the pertinent information. He stayed on the line as instructed. He held his bride's hand and promised, "Help is on the way."

Laura lost consciousness as gunfire continued to echo off the church's walls.

There were two paramedics on hand since John was a firefighter. They quickly assessed the crowd in the church. A few guests suffered minor injuries, such as scraped knees or twisted ankles, as they attempted to flee. They were told to sit quietly in the pews. Most of them prayed.

John monitored Laura's vital signs as they awaited help from the outside.

Torn between chasing the perpetrators without his firearm and tending to Anna, Vinnie sprinted up the stairs.

Reaching Anna, Vinnie brushed the blood-soaked hair out of her face. She had been shot once in the head. He knew she was gone. Overwhelmed with despair, he rested his head on her chest.

Tony had just finished reloading when Dee collapsed in the street.

Dee had been hit three times in the torso. She bled profusely.

Unaware of the extent of his own wounds, Tony tore off his suit jacket and used it to apply pressure to Dee's stomach wounds. His efforts did little to slow the bleeding.

"Hang in there, Georgie. Don't shut your eyes. Look at me. Stay with me, baby."

Quietly, she replied, "I'll try."

Police and ambulance sirens filled the air. Emergency personnel swarmed the area within minutes. The teams split up to treat the wounded.

In the main line of fire, Mita had been hit several times. She lacked a pulse and blood no longer flowed from her wounds. The paternity results rested in her lifeless hand. They were soaked in blood.

The EMTs threw a sheet over her and radioed for the coroner.

They quickly determined the photographer was deceased. They spread a sheet over him as well.

The second team had passed them on the stairs.

Vinnie held Anna's hand on the top landing.

The amount of blood was substantial. However, the medics were unsure if the blood was from one victim or more.

"Vinnie, are you hurt?"

Gazing up at them, he reported. "No. Anna's gone. Single GSW to the head."

When the church doors opened, those inside did not know if they would see friends or foes. They were greatly relieved to see the paramedics.

John yelled, "Guys, over here!"

They rushed over and attended to Laura immediately. John told them she was pregnant.

Family members and friends were startled by the news.

John stayed by her side as they carted her out. He insisted on riding in the ambulance with her.

Out of professional courtesy, the medics allowed it.

In the street, the EMTs forced Tony out of the way. Being weak from the loss of blood, he fell over.

Feeling lightheaded, Tony rolled on his side to face her. Pain seared across his chest and abdomen. As his adrenaline rush subsided, he struggled to remain conscious. He held Dee's hand. He encouraged her, "Hang in there, Georgie. You're going to be fine. These guys are the best. They're going to fix you right up."

Blood trickled from the corner of her mouth. Weakly, Dee gurgled, "I know it's bad. If I don't make it …"

He squeezed her hand. "You're going to make it. Don't think like that. You're tough. You've been in tougher jams than this."

She coughed up blood. "Shut up, damn it."

He followed her direction and listened.

She gasped for air. Wheezing, she whispered, "You'd make a great husband."

He kissed her forehead. "Oh, Georgie."

Her hand went limp in his. She lost consciousness.

Tony pleaded, "Somebody do something!"

The last words Tony heard before losing consciousness himself were, "We're losing her."

CHAPTER 37

EMERGENCY personnel busied themselves identifying all of the victims and notifying next of kin.

As soon as the 911 call went out, Lee contacted the team. "Shots fired at St. Peter's Church. Active shooters. Multiple casualties. Asset status unknown."

The team mobilized.

Lee monitored emergency frequencies and updated them, "Assets down. Two suspects on the run. TJ is en route to County General Hospital." He paused and sighed. "Georgie didn't make it."

Sully and Spaulding sped to the hospital. Ashby and White rushed to the Lazaro home.

Sal, Rose, and Joe were still reeling from the news that Joe was indeed Flora's biological father when the doorbell rang.

Throwing up her hands, Rose exclaimed, "Company is the last thing we need!"

Sal answered the door. "Yes?"

Ashby and White stood side by side on the porch. They flashed their badges.

Ashby asked, "Salvatore Lazaro?"

"Yes."

"I'm Agent Ashby. This is Agent White." Looking past Sal, he motioned and directed, "We need all of you to come with us now."

Sal questioned, "What's this about?"

White took over since Ashby's people skills were lacking. "Your son, Anthony, has been shot. We're taking you to the hospital to see him."

Rose shook her head. "No, you must be mistaken. He's at a wedding. He didn't get shot."

White calmly explained, "It's no mistake, ma'am. There was a shooting at St. Peter's Church. There were multiple victims. Your son was one of them. We need you to move as quickly as possible."

Rose sprang to action. "Holy Mary, Mother of God! What happened? How is he? Who did this?"

White replied, "We don't have all the details yet, ma'am. But we need to leave now."

"Let me get my purse."

Joe jumped to his feet. *Oh, God! I blew Tony's cover, and this was the result.* Under his breath, he muttered, "This is all my fault!"

Ashby put a hand on Joe's shoulder. He whispered, "Keep your mouth shut and remain calm. Don't make things worse."

Ashby's glare kept Joe's mouth shut.

Sal ensured his wallet was in his back pocket.

Purse in hand, Rose asked, "Well, what are we waiting for? Let's go!"

The scene at County General Hospital's Emergency Room was typical for a Saturday. The line was long. All chairs were occupied.

Rose outpaced the rest of the group. She reached the main desk first and walked directly to the head of the line.

The same redheaded nurse that attended the desk during Joe's recent hospitalization manned the desk today. When the nurse looked up and saw Rose, she groaned, "Oh hell, not *you* again."

Annoyed, Rose remarked, "I'm thrilled to see you too, sunshine. But I'm not going to take any lip from you today. There was a shooting at St. Peter's Church. Where is my son, Anthony Lazaro, and all of the other people who were shot?"

Desperate to get rid of Rose, the nurse replied, "I heard some of them are in surgery. There's a waiting room on the third floor. Go up the elevators, and turn right. You can't miss it."

Rose responded, "Thank you. Now why couldn't you have been that helpful that last time I was here?"

The nurse shook her head and held her tongue.

The third floor waiting room was not as full as Rose anticipated. Only John Lombardi and Laura's parents were there. Laura's parents, Tom and Terri, sat quietly.

John was hunched over with his head in his hands.

Rose rushed over. "We got here as quickly as we could."

John looked up. "Tony and Laura are in surgery now."

Patting John's back, Rose asked, "How badly are they hurt?"

John replied, "Both were unconscious when they were transported here. They won't tell us anything."

Rose gestured widely. "Where's everyone else?"

In shock, Terri Delaney responded, "Dead."

Stunned, Rose sat. "Dead? Who's dead?"

Terri Delaney answered, "Poor, sweet Anna."

"I just saw her a few days ago." Rose made a sign of the cross.

Terri continued, "And the girl with Tony. I overheard a policeman say the poor girl didn't have a chance."

She lamented, "Oh no! Poor Anthony! Did they catch the degenerate thugs who did this?"

Terri explained, "She and Tony shot the men in the SUV. They ran right out in the street. They killed two out of the four. They protected us the best they could."

Not comprehending what she heard, Rose said, "You're confused. My Anthony doesn't have a gun, let alone know how to shoot one. It must have been my nephew, Vinnie."

Quietly, Joe interjected, "Yes, he does."

Rose swiveled to face him. "Since when? And how do you know this, and I don't?"

On a roll, Terri fed more information to them, "The photographer and some other woman died too. I don't know who she was. I swear more would have died if it wasn't for their bravery."

Thrown for a loop, Rose stated, "I don't understand."

Joe offered, "I'll explain later, Ma."

Rose demanded, "No! You will explain this to me right this very minute. People are dead. Your brother is fighting for his life. I need to know now!"

Joe's explanation would have to wait as Laura's surgeon burst through the double doors. He called out, "Lombardi?"

John waved. "Here!"

He informed the family, "She came through surgery fine. The bullet nicked one of her lungs and lodged in one of her ribs. We were able to remove the bullet and repair the damage. She's in recovery now. The nurse will let you know when you can see her."

Afraid of the answer, John asked, "What about the baby?"

Rose shot Joe a look. She mouthed, "Baby?"

Joe nodded.

It was something else Rose did not know. However, at least this surprise was a good one as far as she was concerned. And now she understood why Sara had insisted that Laura get married on what would have been her wedding day.

The doctor assured John, "The baby came through fine. But to make sure, we're going to be monitoring them both carefully."

"Thank you, doctor."

Rose stopped the doctor from leaving. "What about my son?"

"And you are?"

"Rose Lazaro. My son is Anthony Lazaro."

"He's not my patient. I'll send a nurse to come talk to you."

Less than satisfied, Rose replied, "Thank you."

John and the Delaneys were thankful for good news.

Rose hugged John. "Congratulations on the baby."

"Thank you, Mrs. Lazaro."

Rose asked, "Why isn't Vinnie here? I'm sure he can straighten this mess out."

John said, "He wouldn't leave Anna. And I overheard the chief ask Vinnie to give a statement on what happened."

"I'm sure he'll come when he can. Poor boy."

Tony's surgeon came through the double doors.

"Lazaro family?"

Rose jumped up. "Over here!"

"Your son had multiple gunshot wounds to the torso. We were able to locate and remove the bullets. He had extensive internal damage."

Covering her mouth in shock, Rose interrupted, "Oh, my poor baby!"

The doctor continued, "We removed the damaged portion of the liver, the damaged kidney, and his spleen. We gave him several units of blood. He's in ICU. The nurses will let you know when you can see him."

Grateful for good news, Rose said, "Thank you, doctor."

Ashby discretely followed the surgeon back through the double doors. White remained with the family.

Sully and Spaulding had located Tony in the ICU and were standing guard.

A man in light blue scrubs entered Tony's room carrying a syringe. Seeing Sully and Spaulding, he said, "Time for some medicine."

Sully assessed the man in a split second. He wore no badge, and his shoes were too shiny. Within a blink of an eye, Sully disarmed the man and jabbed the syringe into the man's neck.

Ashby entered the room as the intruder collapsed. "Looks like I was late to the party."

Sully ordered, "Spaulding, get White and the family. Ashby, help me clean up. We've got to go. Now."

Spaulding immediately left the room and headed for the waiting area.

Sully dragged the assailant's body to the chair in the corner. He heaved and propped him up in the chair. He pulled two zip ties out of his back pocket and secured the man's hands together, then his feet, just in case.

Ashby disconnected everything except for the IV line. He transferred the bag to the hook on the bed. Alarms dinged and beeped loudly.

Sully asked, "Lee, how far out is air support?"

Spaulding crashed through the double doors and made eye contact with White. She stood immediately.

Rose was calling her sister on her cell phone.

Spaulding flashed a quick hand signal to White. She knew they were moving out.

Joe recognized Spaulding immediately. He realized things were going from bad to worse.

Spaulding spoke to the group, "You can see him now. No cell phones."

So overjoyed with the words, Rose did not question that the man telling her the news was not dressed in hospital scrubs. She disconnected the call. She would call her sister after seeing her son.

Sal, Rose, Joe, and White followed Spaulding through the double doors.

Joe whispered to Spaulding, "How bad is it?"

Scanning the surroundings, Spaulding replied, "If I tell you to do something, just do it."

Lee reported back to Sully, "Air transport in five."

Frantic nurses rushed in to find out why all of the alarms were sounding.

Sully flashed his badge. "FBI. We're moving the patient."

The head nurse protested, "FBI or no FBI, you can't take him anywhere. He's in recovery, and he's critical. Are you crazy?"

Sully argued, "Far from it. We have our own specialists. We'll take it from here."

Looking at the man in the chair, she asked, "What's the meaning of this?"

Tired of the nurse and her questions, he replied, "He tried to assassinate this patient. We subdued him. We need to move now."

Attempting to stall, she asserted, "I have to notify security and the doctor. You need transfer papers."

"Lady, I outrank everyone here. A chopper is landing in less than five minutes. How do we get to the roof?"

The nurse stood her ground. "This isn't standard protocol."

"FBI protocol outranks your hospital protocol. You want this man's death on your hands?"

She vehemently argued, "That's what I'm trying to prevent."

Detesting anyone who refused to follow his orders, he insisted, "No. You're doing the exact opposite. It's do or die. This is the last time I'm going to ask. What's the quickest way to the roof?"

With a sour expression on her face, she marched out. "Follow me."

Sully and Ashby steered Tony's hospital bed to the elevator.

The nurse directed, "Take the elevator to the top. Go through the blue doors on the left, then go through the next set of doors, and you'll have roof access there."

He nodded. "Got it. Thanks."

She informed him, "I'm still reporting this."

"It's your job. I'd expect no less."

The nurse scurried away as the elevator doors opened. Sully and Ashby wheeled in the gurney and closed the doors.

Spaulding led the entourage down the hall. White brought up the rear. In their ears, they heard, "Get them to the roof."

Curious by nature, Rose read all of the patients' whiteboards as she passed them. The next board had her son's name. Peering into the room, she saw a man bound in a chair. Her son was nowhere to be seen. Alarmed, Rose questioned, "What's going on?"

Spaulding flipped into critical mission mode. "There's no time. No questions. Keep moving."

Rose stopped in her tracks. "Of all the nerve! You must be joking! No questions? My son's missing from his room, and there's a man tied up in a chair. Who do you think you are telling me I can't ask questions?"

Spaulding grabbed her arm. "I'm one of the guys trying to keep you and your family alive, ma'am. I will drag or carry you if necessary. Just keep moving."

Frightened, she obeyed. "Joey, what's he talking about? I don't understand what's going on."

White remarked, "Way to keep them calm, Spaulding."

Without emotion, Spaulding said, "There's no time for pleasantries. We've got to get them to the roof."

They stopped in front of the elevator. The display indicated it was on the roof.

Sal, Rose, Joe, White, and Spaulding waited.

Two rapid bangs and loud commotion commanded their attention down the hall. They turned to look.

Nurses screamed.

An orderly hit the floor.

A determined tattooed man stepped over the sprawled orderly. Blood dripped from his right arm. In his left hand, he held a gun.

Looking at Joe, Spaulding pulled his gun and yelled, "The stairs! Take the stairs to the roof! Go! Go! Go!"

Pulling her gun, White reiterated, "Go! Go! Go!"

Terrified, Joe obeyed the order and shouldered the stairwell door open.

Spaulding and White engaged the shooter. Bullets flew in both directions.

Rose screamed.

Sal pushed his wife through the door.

Rose shrieked, "Oh my God! Oh my God! Holy Mary, Mother of God! What's going on?"

Before the door closed behind them, Joe heard Spaulding yell, "Get to the roof! Don't wait for us."

Sal, Rose, and Joe trotted up the stairs.

Rose yelled, "Why are people shooting at us?"

Joe shouted, "Just run, Ma! Run!"

"I don't understand!"

Out of shape and breathing hard, Sal yelled, "It doesn't matter, Rose! They're trying to kill us! What more do you need to know right now? Save your energy, shut your mouth, and run up these damn stairs!"

They reached the top floor, clutching their chests. Out of breath, they were relieved to see a helipad sign. They struggled through the blue doors and the next set of doors. Bright sunlight and a helicopter waited.

Sully motioned for them to crouch down and run. They did so. The turbulence from the blades was more forceful than anticipated.

Sully helped them board. As they buckled in, he asked them for their cell phones.

Joe and Rose held up theirs. Sal mouthed he left his at home.

Satisfied, Sully took their phones and removed the SIM cards. He pocketed the cards and threw the phones out of the copter.

Outraged, Rose's arms flailed as she yelled.

Sully was glad he could not hear her protests and grievances over the engine noise.

Once they were airborne, Lee reported to Sully, "Spaulding and White eliminated the immediate threat. They are headed back."

"Roger."

Rose wanted an explanation, but she realized the noise level was too high even for her to yell over it. She crossed her arms and thought about what she was going to say once they reached their destination.

When they finally landed, she asked, "Is someone going to explain to me what is going on here? Is it drugs? The Mob? What?"

Sully beseeched, "Ma'am, please get inside."

"Are you going to answer my questions?"

"Yes, please go inside."

Sully led Rose, Sal, and Joe into the safe house.

The helicopter took off with Tony on board.

Rose demanded an answer, "Where are they taking him?"

Sully explained, "He's going to a secure medical facility with the best care money can buy. Don't worry."

Testy and getting more agitated by the minute, Rose said, "I'm beyond worry at this point."

Sully proclaimed, "We're taking good care of him."

Tapping her foot, she asked, "Well? Are you going to answer my questions? Or do I need to talk to someone else who's in charge? I want answers. And I want them now! Do you understand me?"

Realizing Rose would not stop her interrogation, Sully said, "Your son was working undercover for our organization. His cover was compromised."

Joe swallowed hard.

"The targets of our investigation are after him and your family. Until we neutralize the threat, you all need to remain under guard in this safe house."

Gesturing as she spoke, Rose challenged, "What? This makes no sense. This one's a college professor. Anthony is some sort of entrepreneur. My boys are not in law enforcement."

Sully informed her, "Your son, Anthony, has been working under-cover for us for years. He's one of our best men."

In complete disbelief, she questioned, "Anthony? My Anthony?"

"Yes, ma'am."

"An undercover policeman?"

"Not exactly. We're more of an agency."

Probing, she asked, "Like a team on those crime shows on television?"

Resisting the urge to roll his eyes, he responded, "If that helps you to understand, yes, like that."

Jubilant, she exclaimed, "Oh my God! I can't wait to tell everyone! This is incredible! Wait until the family finds out! And the church ladies! Oh, Anthony will be the talk of the town!"

His patience wore thin. "You can't tell anyone."

Waving her hands in the air, she said, "My son is doing all of this important work, and I can't tell anyone?"

Appealing to her motherly instincts, he asked, "How much is your son's life worth to you?"

Astonished he would ask such a question, she proclaimed, "Everything, of course."

"Then you need to listen to what I tell you, and follow my orders."

Sal muttered, "Oh, this should be good."

"No phones, no e-mail, no contact at all with anyone while you are at this safe house. Period. Your very lives depend on it."

CHAPTER 38

VINNIE watched the coroner zip up Anna in a black body bag. He regretted that had he not been a better boyfriend to her. *She deserved much more than I ever gave her.*

Allowing him a few minutes to gather himself, the chief put his hand on Vinnie's shoulder. Sympathetically, he said, "Vinnie, I'm sorry for your loss. I truly am. And I hate to ask you, but we need you to give us an account of what happened."

Vinnie relayed all of the details he could remember without revealing what he knew about Tony and Dee.

When asked about a target or a motive, Vinnie shrugged. He did not know enough about the undercover operation to provide good intelligence anyway. Although he made sure his colleagues were aware that two unidentified assailants were still on the loose.

When the chief was done debriefing Vinnie, Vinnie hustled to the hospital. He made his way to the surgical waiting area.

John motioned him over. "Vinnie!"

Vinnie approached. "How is everybody?"

John replied, "Tony and Laura are out of surgery. They're going to be okay." He paused. "I'm so sorry about Anna."

"Thanks."

Noticing Vinnie was covered in blood, John asked, "Are you okay? Were you hit?"

Flatly, he stated, "It's not my blood."

Sadly, John nodded.

Vinnie inquired, "What room is Tony in?"

"I'm not sure. They just came back and got the family a few minutes ago. They went through those doors." John pointed.

Vinnie eyed the doors.

John continued, "Then there was a lot of swearing and what sounded like gunshots."

Vinnie questioned, "Gunshots? Here in the hospital?"

"It's what it sounded like to me."

Vinnie drew his weapon and headed for the double doors. He waved in front of the sensor.

The door opened, but a security guard stopped him from entering.

The security officer said, "You can't come through here."

Vinnie flashed his police badge. "I'm here to investigate."

The guard stepped aside.

Vinnie saw a doctor and three nurses working on the orderly that had been shot.

A large pool of blood was near the door. Then there was a trail of blood droplets that led to a separate pool of blood halfway down the hallway.

Vinnie inquired, "What happened?"

The guard replied, "Some lunatic shot an orderly and then continued down the hall. He was shooting at everyone."

Vinnie followed up, "Where did he go?"

The guard answered, "My guess is the morgue. He's dead. Two visitors had guns and killed him. A nurse said the guy was already bleeding before he was shot dead. And then there was another guy we found dead in one of the ICU rooms. He was dressed as an orderly, but he didn't work here. And the ICU patient that was supposed to be in that room was whisked away in a helicopter."

"A helicopter?"

"Yeah. The head nurse has been freaking out over it."

"Where? Which room?"

The guard pointed. "Four rooms down on the left."

CHAPTER 39

AFTER getting the Lazaros settled in the safe house, Sully flew back and met with the rest of the team in the war room.

Coming to terms with the loss, Sully said, "We've lost Georgie. She was one of the best agents I ever had the privilege of working with. We can't let her death be in vain. She fought the good fight. Sacrificed herself for others. We have to finish this mission as a tribute to her."

Spaulding concurred, "We won't stop until we take Fuentes down."

Sully resumed, "That's right. We won't. TJ is still fighting for his life. Fuentes hired thugs to attack in broad daylight. He's out of control. All four of his men are dead. We don't believe there are more. But, we need to remain vigilant. There could be a backup team. It's all-out war, people. You know what to do."

Ashby declared, "We won't rest until it's done."

Lee informed them, "I finally have intel on the lake house in the Thousand Islands. The lake house isn't owned by Fuentes or any of his family. It belonged to Sabrina's birth father. When he died, Sabrina inherited the house. But the title is under her birth name, Sabrina Clay."

Sully said, "Good work."

"Sending coordinates to your phones now."

When Al and Esmeralda arrived at the lake house, Sabrina was waiting.

Sabrina rose from the couch. Her handgun was aimed at them. "I was wondering how long it would take you to get here."

Al approached her.

She ordered, "Stop right there!"

Holding his hands out in a non-threatening position, Al said, "Okay, okay. Let's be reasonable. Put the gun down."

In disbelief, she answered, "Reasonable? The time for reasonable was over a long time ago."

"I'm sure we can work this out."

Speaking deliberately, Sabrina informed him, "I have it all worked out in my head. I'm going to make you suffer like you made me suffer."

"If you want money, I'll give you money." He tossed the duffel bag of cash toward her. "Here's a whole bag of money. It's yours."

Insulted, she questioned, "Money? You think I want money? Money can't bring back my virginity. Money can't erase my memory. Money can't bring back the months you had me chained to a bed."

"There has to be something you want."

"There is." Motioning with the gun, she ordered, "Both of you, into the master bedroom."

Reluctantly, they obeyed.

The room was stripped of everything except the bed.

Once in the room, Sabrina directed, "Esmeralda, get in the corner."

Esmeralda walked to the far end of the room. With a scowl on her face, she stood with her arms crossed.

"Al, get on the bed. Use the restraints you use on me to tie yourself down. I'll get the last one, don't worry."

Defiant, he refused, "No."

"If you don't, I'll kill her."

Calling her bluff, he said, "No, you won't."

Sabrina turned and fired the gun at Esmeralda. The bullet pierced her right bicep.

Esmeralda screamed in shock and pain. She swore in her native tongue.

Facetiously, Sabrina said, "Temper, temper, grandmother."

Esmeralda seethed as she held her arm. Blood trickled through her fingers.

Facing Al, Sabrina inquired, "Do I have your attention now?"

Angrily, he replied, "Yes."

"Tie yourself down or the next shot will be more accurate."

Al restrained his legs first. He left slack in them.

She ordered, "Try again. Make them good and tight."

He readjusted and tightened them. Then he restrained his left arm.

Sabrina approached him.

He attempted to grab her.

She hit him in the head with the butt of her gun.

"Jesus! You bitch!"

While she secured his right arm, she admonished him, "That was a bad idea, Al. Sorry, that's going to leave a mark."

Esmeralda gave her a disgusted look.

The look did not go unnoticed. Sabrina proclaimed, "Esmeralda, you are an evil person. You make the witches in fairytales look good. I really hate you. I hate you almost as much as I hate him. Do you have anything to say for yourself?"

Esmeralda held her head high. With a haughty air, she answered, "Are you expecting me to beg for my life, little girl? I am too proud to do that. I will not beg or grovel to the likes of you. If you are going to kill me, then kill me."

Disappointed she was not putting up a fight, Sabrina replied, "Okay. I will."

Esmeralda acknowledged the look in Sabrina's eyes and made the sign of the cross.

Sabrina aimed and pulled the trigger. The bullet cleanly pierced Esmeralda's heart. She gasped feebly and collapsed to the floor.

Al screamed, "You killed her!"

Nonchalantly, she replied, "Yup. I killed my own mother. Killing yours, a woman who meant nothing to me, was easy. And you, you son of a bitch, you're next."

He begged, "Now, hold on! I'm sorry. I'll make it up to you. Just tell me what I need to do."

She tucked her gun in her waistband at the small of her back. Then she approached him and unbuckled his belt.

Shocked, he asked, "What are you doing?"

Through gritted teeth, she responded, "You'll find out soon enough." She unbuttoned and unzipped his pants. Then she yanked his pants and underwear down to mid-thigh.

Al Fuentes enjoyed S&M thoroughly, although he always played the role of the dominant. To his surprise, he found being in the position of a submissive highly arousing.

Repulsed but not surprised at his reaction, Sabrina pulled some fishing line out of her front pocket. She straddled him and tied it very tightly at the base of his erect penis.

Sabrina demanded, "Tell me where my daughter is."

Breathing hard, he answered, "She died."

She drew a hunting knife out of her back pocket. She pressed it against his throat. "You're lying. Where is she?"

He reiterated, "She's dead. She was too premature. She didn't make it."

She increased pressure on the knife. Blood trickled down his neck.

In an effort to gain the upper hand in the situation, he commanded, "Untie me now!"

She laughed. "No."

Jerking against the restraints, he asked, "What more do you want?"

"Justice."

"Good luck. The court system will have a field day with you. You've killed your mother and grandmother. And you're holding me hostage. You're screwed."

Ignoring him, she insisted, "I'm going to get justice."

He argued, "You're going to get what's coming to you. You're going to untie me. Then, I'm going to tie you up and screw you until I decide you've had enough. Then, we're going to get on that boat and go where the cops can't find us. And the best part is that you can spend the rest of your life thanking me for saving you from jail."

She spat at him. "No way in hell, you sick bastard! You're insane! I am going to administer my own justice."

He challenged, "What are you going to do?"

Before Al knew what was happening, Sabrina firmly grabbed his penis and swiftly severed it with her father's hunting knife.

He shrieked in horror and pain. Blood spurted everywhere. He bucked and fought against the restraints. Expletives filled the air.

Holding the offending appendage in front of him, at the top of her lungs, Sabrina taunted, "This is my justice! Look at it! This is for what you did to me, to my friends, and to my baby!"

Bleeding profusely, he screamed, "You crazy fucking whore! I'm going to kill you!"

She laughed hysterically. "No, you're not, because I'm going to kill you first!"

Al continued to yell and scream, to no avail.

Sabrina tossed the penis on the floor and stomped on it. A wave of peace overcame her. "Much better."

Livid, Al thrashed around. "You're going to pay for this! You'll wish you'd never been born!"

Sabrina calmly removed the gun from her waistband. She aimed it at his scrotum and pulled the trigger.

Al Fuentes' world went pitch black.

The island was small and had only one house on it. Island dwellers coveted their privacy. So, the team did not want to use a low-flying drone, as it would attract attention. They rented a boat and cut the engine well before they reached the island. The element of surprise was critical.

The team surrounded the house. Lights were on, but they observed no movement.

On Sully's mark, they breached the doors.

The family room and kitchen were clear. An empty whiskey bottle rested on the floor next to the couch.

They proceeded down the hallway. In the master bedroom, they discovered Al and Esmeralda.

Sully entered the room first. He noted the discarded penis. "Don't step on the mangled penis."

Amused and disturbed at the same time, Ashby commented, "That's a new one."

Spaulding remarked, "Looks like she didn't need our help."

White assessed the scene, "I'd say Sabrina got her own brand of justice."

They moved down the hall and found Sabrina's body on the bed in the second bedroom. Another empty bottle of alcohol rested next to her body. She had succumbed to a self-inflicted gunshot wound to the head.

White lamented, "I just wish she hadn't ended her own life. May she rest in peace."

Chapter 40

WITH Esmeralda Fuentes, Al Fuentes, and their hired gunmen all dead, the Lazaros were free to go.

Sully travelled to the safe house by helicopter. He announced to the family, "Good news. The threat has been eliminated. You're free to go home."

Rose questioned, "Are you sure?"

"Yes, ma'am. I'm sure."

"Where's Anthony?"

"He's in a medical facility, not far from here. He's still critical. His wounds were serious. He's being treated by some of the best in the country."

Rose interrogated him, "Some of the best? Why not the very best? You should have gotten him the best doctors in the world after all he's done! I want to see him."

Sully sighed. "I'm sorry. That's not possible."

Rose warned, "I don't think you want to test me."

"Ma'am, none of you have the proper security clearance. It's not possible."

Rose argued, "I'm his mother. That's all the clearance I need."

"I'm sorry, ma'am. It's not possible."

She threatened, "If you say that one more time, I'm going to smack you into next week. You *will* take me to see my son, or else."

Challenging her, he asked, "Or else what?"

Getting into his personal space, she glared at him. "Do you really want to find out?"

Secretly admiring her gumption, Sully said, "Gather your things. We leave in five."

Rose, Sal, and Joe were escorted to Tony's room.

Tony appeared weak and pale. Monitors displayed his vital signs.

They were all within normal range.

The nurse moved out of the way for Rose.

Rose smiled at her. "Thank you. How's he doing?"

She replied, "All things considered, he's doing well."

"Thank you for taking good care of my son."

"You're welcome, ma'am."

Rose hovered over her son and held his hand. "Anthony, I'm so proud of you. I wish I had known. You're a hero. My son is a bonafide hero!"

Tony's eyes fluttered.

She caressed his head lovingly. "We love you, Anthony. You'll be home soon. I'll nurse you back to health in no time."

Groggy from the pain medicine, he nodded.

Motioning for Sal and Joe to come closer, she said, "Your father and brother are here too."

Sal said, "Good job, son. I'm proud of you."

Joe walked to the other side of the bed. "I'm sorry."

Tony shook his head negatively. He mouthed, "Not your fault."

CHAPTER 41

Aᴲᴛᴇʀ Anna Cristo's funeral service, Rose invited everyone back to her house.

As Joe assisted Tony to his car in the church parking lot, Vinnie accosted Tony, "I can't believe you had the nerve to show up here."

"Anna was my friend too."

Vinnie accused Tony, "Your secrets caused Anna's death."

Repressing his own feelings, Tony apologized, "I'm sorry, but there was no way we could have guessed that would happen."

Vinnie argued, "You should have known with all of your secret intelligence."

Incredulously, Tony questioned, "I should have known they were going to execute a drive-by shooting in broad daylight at a friend's wedding?"

Pounding his fist against the car, Vinnie ranted, "It doesn't matter now. The damage is done. If you would have told me what was going on, I could have done something."

Shaking his head, Tony said, "You know I couldn't tell you."

Putting his hands on the arms of Tony's wheelchair, Vinnie got in Tony's face. "Blood is supposed to be thicker than water. Anna is dead because of you. And you have to live with that."

"During any mission, there was always the possibility of collateral damage. Anna, Dee, and the rest of the victims were just in the wrong place at the wrong time. You know that from being a cop. It's no different."

Vinnie argued, "You should have read me in. They could have been alive today."

"I didn't have permission to read you in."

"That's bullshit. You could have done it if you wanted to."

Tony was used to pushing down feelings. However, the guilt of not being able to protect Dee weighed heavily upon him. He lashed out,

"You're not the only one hurting here. Look around, Vinnie. Everyone here is grieving."

"But I could have done something."

"It's survivor's guilt. We all deal with it. For Christ's sake, I lost my partner, but I loved her too. So, I get it. I understand your pain. You've got to work through it. Get some counseling or something."

Tony's admission of love for Dee stunned Joe.

Pushing off the chair, Vinnie threatened, "If you weren't in that wheelchair …"

Calling Vinnie's bluff, Tony goaded, "Go ahead! If you want to hit me, hit me! It doesn't change the fact that we survived, and they didn't."

Vinnie walked away from his cousins without another word.

Guests gathered in Rose's kitchen and backyard. Rose passed a cup of tea to Anna's mother, Geri.

Geri said, "Thank you for having us at your home."

Rose replied, "It's the least I could do. You live out of town, and Anna was part of our extended family."

Geri stated, "It was a beautiful service, wasn't it?"

Rose agreed, "Yes, it was."

Craning her neck, Geri commented, "Excuse me, but I seem to have misplaced my husband."

"He's outside with the rest of the men."

Making her way to the door, she said, "Okay. Thank you."

Rose turned to Carm. "How's Vinnie dealing with everything?"

Carm replied, "He's not doing very well. The chief gave him mandatory time off, with pay of course, and is making him go for counseling."

"Is it helping?"

"No, I think it's making it worse. He's going stir-crazy with nothing to do. He needs to keep his mind occupied. So, I've got him doing some projects for me around the house. I don't know what else to do with him."

"I'll say an extra rosary for him."

"Thank you. Although I'm sure God's tired of hearing from us by now."

John accompanied Laura into the kitchen.

Laura encouraged, "John, go outside with the other guys. I'll be fine in here."

Not wanting to leave her side, he asked, "Are you sure?"

"I'm positive. Mrs. Lazaro will keep an eye on me."

John knew that to be true. "Okay. But if you need me, let me know."

Laura kissed him. "I will."

Rose addressed him, "John, I'll look after her. Go outside."

"Okay. Thanks, Mrs. Lazaro."

Rose asked Laura, "Have you been able to reach Sara yet?"

"No. She's not answering her phone or replying to texts. And she hasn't been online at all. We just got that one message from her when she reached the Adirondacks days ago."

Rose assured her, "She's probably just out of cell range, that's all."

"I'm sure you're right. But she's going to be devastated when she finds out everything that happened while she was away."

Rose patted her. "You'll help her through it. You're both stronger than your realize."

"I know. But so much has happened. I'm trying to keep it together, but I'm a mess. It's just too much all at once."

Offering Laura a chair, Rose said, "You need to get off your feet. You're still recovering, and you're pregnant. Here, sit."

Laura sat. "Thank you."

Rose asked, "How are you and John getting along?"

"Good. I moved into his place. He's been wonderful through all of this craziness. I couldn't have asked for a better man in my life. He's my rock."

"He does seem to dote on you. I'm so happy for the two of you. How's the baby?"

Rubbing her stomach, she replied, "The doctor says I have to take it easy. But so far, everything's fine."

"That's wonderful news!"

Tearing up, Laura said, "And we decided that we're going to renew our vows on another day since our wedding day was marred by so much violence."

"I think that's for the best, once everything calms down. If you need any help, you let me know."

Laura acknowledged, "Thank you, Mrs. Lazaro."

Joe pushed Tony's wheelchair into the family room while the other guests chatted in the kitchen and backyard.

Joe remarked, "I'm sure once Vinnie cools down, things will go back to normal."

"I wouldn't count on that, Joe. I'm going to keep my distance. If I was in his shoes, I might feel the same way."

"I feel I need to apologize again, especially since I didn't know you had feelings for Dee. I thought it was part of your cover."

Tony struggled to hold back tears. "If I told you once, I've told you a thousand times, none of this was your fault. I knew it was a risk taking a job so close to home. So did she."

"But I'm the one who blew your guys' cover. I'm so sorry."

Tony choked up. "Thanks. She was one in a million, Joe."

Joe dropped to his knees and hugged his brother. "I don't know what else to say."

"I know. There's nothing else to say, Joe."

"I keep wondering if I could have done something different back at the hotel."

With his voice cracking, Tony said, "You had no way of knowing. You've got to stop beating yourself up."

"I just can't."

Attempting to minimize his brother's involvement, Tony claimed, "If it wasn't you, it could have easily been someone else. It's the nature of the beast, Joe. And you've had plenty of your own drama lately."

"Yeah, and all of that *was* my fault."

Trying to get his mind off Dee, Tony suggested, "Well, maybe now that Mita's out of the picture for good, Sara might change her mind."

"I doubt it. She's disappeared. Who knows if she'll ever come back."

"I'm sure she'll come back. And when she does, she's going to have to deal with Anna's death. You could be there to comfort her."

"I would love to, but I'm not holding my breath."

Attempting to lighten the mood, Tony commented, "I'm sure Ma will get involved sooner or later."

Joe argued, "She'll have her hands full being a grandmother. She's pressuring me to take custody of Flora."

"And you don't want to do that?"

"Honestly, no. I just want Sara. I want to build a life with her."

"But it's not the little girl's fault, Joe. She needs a father. I'm sure her grandmother is a nice lady, but it's not the same as a parent."

Uncomfortable, Joe changed the subject, "So, Ma says you'll be out of this wheelchair in no time."

Grasping the wheels of the chair, he replied, "Yeah. I need to build my strength up. Technically I don't need it. I can walk. But I don't feel well enough to walk for very long. Maybe you can help me with my exercises."

"Sure. It's the least I can do."

Rose appeared in the doorway. "There you two are! We've been wondering where you went. Everything okay in here?"

Tony replied, "Yeah, we're fine."

Rose responded, "Good. Then come back into the kitchen and join the rest of us."

After the guests left, Rose took Joe aside. "If this week's events have taught us anything, it's that life is short, and you can't take anything for granted. And that's on top of the horrible accident you had earlier this year. God's definitely trying to tell us something."

"I know."

Holding his face in her hands, she declared, "It's a wake-up call, Joey. Do you know how lucky you are?"

Joe shrugged her off. "Ma, I know you mean well, but I feel like the unluckiest person in the world right now."

"There are a lot of people who have it worse off than you. Take your brother for instance."

"I know things could be worse. I could be hurt really bad or be dead. I know I should be thankful that I'm alive, but I'm not. I don't want to live without Sara. I don't know what I'm going to do."

"For starters, you need to concentrate on family. And you know what that means."

"More family dinners?"

Rose threw up her hands. "Food? With you boys it's always about food."

Justifying his answer, Joe said, "Ma, you trained us that way. All the world's problems can be solved with food, particularly your lasagna, ziti, and chocolate cake."

Gesturing as she spoke, "Well, most of them can be. But, no, that's not what I meant. You need to see your daughter—my granddaughter—Flora."

Resigned, he agreed, "Yeah, eventually."

Stressing the importance of the situation, she said, "I know this sounds callous, but I'm happy that awful woman is dead. It's the best thing that could have happened. God, forgive me!" She gazed heavenward and made the sign of the cross.

Joe rolled his eyes.

"You're the only parent that child has now."

"And what kind of father am I going to be? I abandoned her."

She patted him. "You'll make up for it. I'll help you. We'll all help you."

The doorbell rang.

Exasperated, Joe said, "Please tell me you didn't."

Smugly, Rose replied, "I did."

Sal answered the door. He welcomed Helen and Flora into the house.

Flora asked, "Is there another party today?"

Helen answered, "It's a small party. Remember when I told you we had a lot of family here in New York?"

Flora answered, "Yes, Nana."

Helen extended her arm. "Well, I want you to meet your father and his family."

Flora walked up to Joe and looked into his eyes. "You're my daddy?"

In that moment, Joe realized that the gaping hole left in his heart by Sara's absence could be filled with the love for this child—his child.

He had not expected to feel this way. But the innocence of this beautiful child and her very presence warmed his heart in a way he could not explain.

Joe nodded. "Yes, I am."

Everyone in the room could tell Flora was processing the information by the changing expressions on her face. After thinking about it for a minute, she asked, "Can I give you a hug?"

Touched by the child's words, Rose teared up. She waved her hands in front of her eyes in an attempt to halt her tears, to no avail.

Joe's heart melted as he looked into his daughter's eyes. They were the same color as his. He knelt down and held out his arms. "Yes, I'd love a hug."

Flora flung her arms around his neck and hugged him tightly.

Joe squeezed her back. While embracing her, he said, "I'm so sorry about your mommy."

With a response that surpassed her years, Flora replied, "She didn't like me much. But Nana said that I have you now. So, I think it'll be okay."

Her innocent words hit Joe hard. He could not imagine anyone, let alone his daughter, growing up in a house without unconditional love.

Holding back tears, Joe said, "You have more than just me, Flora." He gestured to his family standing behind him. "You have another grandma, a grandpa, and an uncle too."

Dabbing her eyes with a tissue, Rose added, "And all of the people you met at the party are your family too. They're your aunts, uncles, and cousins."

Amazed, Flora exclaimed, "Wow! That's a lot of people. I can't wait to see them again. Can we have another party soon?"

Joe noticed she had his dimples too. "Yes, Flora. We're going to have a big party just for you."

Flora clapped and jumped up and down. "Yay! I love parties. Can it be a princess party? I love princesses! And can I get a new dress? Maybe I'll get a pink one this time. I love my blue dress, but I'd love a pink dress more. And can we have chocolate cake? It's my most favorite!"

Joe laughed. "Yes, Flora. You can have whatever you want. Your Grandma Rose makes the best chocolate cake in town. She makes me one every year for my birthday and special occasions. She can do the same for you. Right, Ma?"

Thrilled her son was warming to his daughter, she agreed, "Of course! Anything she wants."

Flora jumped up and down. "Oh wow! Thank you! We'll need balloons too. And pretty pink streamers."

As Flora prattled on, Rose smiled. Turning to Helen, she said, "Thank you."

Helen replied, "It was the right thing to do."

CHAPTER 42

THE next morning, Tommy appeared at Phil's door. "Hey, looks like you need your chainsaw back."

Thankful to see his brother, Phil replied, "I thought you'd never show up."

"Let's get going on that tree." Looking past him, Tommy saw Sara. "Oh, sorry, I didn't know you had company."

Phil introduced them, "Sara, this is my brother, Tommy. Tommy, this is Sara. Her car got stuck down the hill."

Sara smiled. "Nice to meet you."

Tommy nodded. "Same here. An Impala by any chance?"

Warily, she answered, "Yes."

Tommy reported, "We just towed it out. It's headed to Bob's Auto Repair."

Hoping for good news, Sara asked, "Is it badly damaged?"

Itching his nose, Tommy said, "Aside from the hail damage, it's hard to tell with all of the mud on it. Bob's a good guy. He'll hose it off and let you know if anything needs to be done or not."

"Okay. Good to know. By any chance did you see my phone?"

"There was one on the seat. But I left it there. Sorry. I didn't know I'd be running into its owner. But the good news is that cell service is back up. So, you can use my phone or Phil's to make a call."

Sara laughed. "The only number I know by heart is my parents' home phone number."

Phil rubbed it in. "That's what happens when you let the wonderful world of technology take over."

Tommy handed her his phone. "Here, it's charged."

"Thanks."

Tommy said to Phil, "Let's get going on that tree. It's a doozy."

Sara asked, "Can I help?"

Phil smiled and winked at her. "After you make your phone call, you can supervise."

The men went outside.

Sara dialed her parents' home number. No one answered. She left a message. "Hi, Anna! It's Sara. I'm assuming Laura is on some sort of honeymoon by now. I'm still in the Adirondacks. I had car trouble, but I found someplace to stay. So, I'm okay. Don't worry. I'll keep you posted. Bye!"

After a few hours of hard work, Phil and Tommy had successfully cut the tree into manageable sections and stacked them on the side of the house. When they entered the house to clean up, Tommy's phone rang.

Tommy answered and listened for a minute. "Sara, Bob says he needs to talk to you. There are a few things that need to be repaired."

She directed, "Tell him to fix whatever needs to be fixed."

"Don't you want to talk to him first?"

"No, just tell him to fix everything."

After relaying the message, Tommy said, "Okay. Bob says it'll take a week or so to get the parts in."

"Fine. What other choice do I have anyway?"

Tommy replied, "Okay. I'll tell him."

Phil offered, "You can stay here as long as you want. But I'm leaving tomorrow."

Curious, Sara asked, "Going out of town on business?"

"Sort of."

"I never asked you. What do you do?"

"I'm retired."

Skeptical, Sara noted, "You're awfully young to be retired."

Proudly, he stated, "I won the lottery."

Believing he was pulling her leg, she said, "Come on."

"Seriously. I won the lottery. So I quit my job in finance and bought this place."

"Must be nice. So what do you do every day?"

He shrugged. "A little of this and a little of that. I help some of the neighbors up here with remodeling or odd jobs. Gives me something to do and helps them out. It's a win-win."

"That's very nice of you."

"Yeah. But I need more of a challenge, which is why I'm going out of town. I heard about an interesting opportunity elsewhere. So I'm going to check it out."

She fished, "Are you going with anyone?"

He shook his head. "No. Couldn't find anyone to go with me. Tommy here is afraid to fly."

Sara pondered for a moment. "Take me with you."

Surprised, he replied, "I haven't even told you where I'm going."

Feeling daring, she declared, "I don't care. I'll go anywhere."

Testing her, Phil inquired, "Are you sure? I could be going to the South Pole to herd penguins."

Throwing caution to the wind, she said, "At this point, it doesn't really matter. I'll go wherever you're going, if you'll have me."

He smiled. "Well, you lucked out. I'm going to Hawaii."

Astonished, she exclaimed, "No!"

Amused by her excitement, he confirmed, "Yes! You can trade in those sweats and hiking boots for a bikini and flip-flops."

Giddy, she hugged him. "Oh my God! That can't happen soon enough. When do we leave?"

Early the following morning, Phil and Sara boarded Phil's private jet.

Sara settled comfortably into the leather seat. Phil handed her a mimosa before joining her.

She thought, *I could get used to this.*

Buckling up, he asked, "Are you ready?"

She gushed, "I'm more than ready. I'm so excited! I can't believe I'm going to Hawaii!"

Phil chuckled. "Believe it. It's happening."

In an instant, Sara's expression changed. She fretted, "Oh no."

"What?"

Placing her hand on top of her head, she said, "I forgot to call Anna to update her."

Handing her his phone, he said, "You can call her now before we take off. We'll get you a new cell phone once we land, so you'll have all of your contacts and stuff."

"Thank you."

Sara dialed the number. Again, there was no answer, so she left a message. "Hi, Anna! It's me. You won't believe this, but I'm on my way to Hawaii! I know, it's crazy! I'll call you again when we land. Talk to you soon. Bye!"

When the plane was cruising high over Colorado, Phil said, "After we get lei'd in Hawaii, we'll get you some clothes and a phone."

"Excuse me? How about if I don't want to get laid?"

"It's the custom. The islanders greet us with leis. It's disrespectful to refuse them."

"Oh."

"Wait. What were you thinking?"

"Nothing."

He laughed heartily. "If that's what I intended to do, I wouldn't wait until we landed. We'd be joining the mile high club right about now. And I think we're flying over the Rockies. So, it would be an unforgettable Rocky Mountain high." He winked.

She stuck out her tongue at him.

Phil laughed at her reaction. "You're something else. We're going on this trip as friends. Time will tell if it will lead to something more. Don't be in such a rush. Relax and enjoy yourself."

She reflected, "I'm always in a rush. And I don't know why."

"Aside from being a Type A personality kind of girl, maybe because in school, you were on a schedule. Same thing at work. You had meetings and deadlines. Everything in your life has always been on a timetable."

"Hmm, you're probably right."

Stretching, he stated, "Now that you're in between jobs, you don't have a schedule. You can do what you want, when you want, how you want."

"That's true."

Half-jokingly, he asked, "How does that make you feel?"

Answering honestly, she confided, "A little scared. I feel like my life is spinning out of control. I'm comfortable with structure. The lack of structure is unfamiliar and nerve-racking."

He urged, "You need to let go of everything. Learn to relax."

"I'm trying."

He laughed. "You need to try harder. I think going to Hawaii is perfect for you right now. Life moves at a much slower pace there. I guarantee you'll love it."

"I'll hold you to that."

Reclining his seat all the way back, he suggested, "You might want to take a nap. It's a long flight."

Not sleepy, Sara gazed out the window into the white puffy clouds. Those clouds insulated her from the world she wanted to leave behind.

The anxiety she felt about travelling on a private jet to Hawaii with a man she barely knew faded away. For some unexplained reason, she had a good feeling about the stranger who sat beside her.

She hoped the most impulsive decision she had ever made was not another colossal mistake. She prayed that when she descended from the clouds, it would be the beginning of an exciting chapter in her life—an adventure that would change her life forever.

ABOUT THE AUTHOR

Challenging Destiny is Suzanne's second romance novel. It is the sequel to her breakout romance novel, *Embracing Destiny.* Although, some life-altering events delayed the release of *Challenging Destiny,* Suzanne strongly believes it inevitably enhanced her creative process.

The third and final novel in the Destiny series, *Manifesting Destiny,* is due out in 2016.

Suzanne's blog, *Pursuing My Passion,* features her humorous online dating adventures and observations on life. Her dating series, "Mis-Matched to Miss Matched," has been so successful that she is planning on writing a book about her quest for "Mr. Right."

Her work has appeared in *The Polk Street Review* and *An Evening with the Writing Muse.*

For the past twenty-two years, she has resided in Noblesville, IN.

Suzanne loves hearing from her readers.
Email her at PurewalPublishing@gmail.com

Check out the latest news and events on her blog:
www.suzannepurewal.wordpress.com

Read more about her and purchase books from her website:
www.suzannepurewal.com